XURIA

THE ARCHIVES OF ANALICIA

BOOK ONE

ERICA EBANKS

Paperback ISBN: 979-8-9890641-2-0

Ebook ISBN: 979-8-9890641-0-6

Book Cover by Betty Martinez

First edition 2023

Content Warning: This book contains graphic situations, encompassing depictions of death, abuse (including sexual abuse), and drug use. Reader discretion is advised.

"This book is dedicated to my Sweet Gan and to my number one fan, my Hite"

ACKNOWLEDGMENTS

I want to take a moment to say thank you to everyone who played a role in making my first book a reality.
First, I want to give thanks to God for always having my back.
Thank you to my family and friends for believing in me. Your support, encouragement, and enthusiasm have kept me motivated throughout this incredible journey.
To my parents, thank you for instilling in me a love for reading.
A shout-out to the Boo Bears. Your feedback and our countless conversations have been nothing short of amazing.
Thank you to my awesome editor, Mike Waiz. Your skills and guidance have taken my manuscript to a whole new level and helped me grow as a writer.
A huge thank you to Stephanie for your valuable feedback and input.
A special thank you to Alese for inspiring the writer in me all those years ago.
Lastly, to John. You've been along for the whole ride and have been my rock.
To all of you, I am incredibly grateful.

My dear Lenala,

May Draygon speed the Murkes in finding you. Father found out about the Pitian prince and he went mad. He took a small group of the royal guards out of Xuria and into Piatees. He's captured both the prince and his sister.

The Dragons don't know. Yet.

He's burned and destroyed Piatees and has killed many of their people. He put me, the prince, and the princess in jail. I'm going to be tried in front of the high council on the next high moon. He'll either exile me or condemn me to death, and I fear the worst for the prince and princess. I can't let Father harm them.

We are making plans to escape before the trial, but I fear this letter won't make it to you in time. Meet me at Danix Point as soon as you can. If we're able to escape, we'll wait for you there. If not, go home and tell the Dragons everything.

More than a year has passed since you left, and much has changed. We desperately need your help.

May Draygon be with you,

Your sister,

Anala

Lenala, the princess of Xuria, is readying herself for the worst as she prepares to stand before her father, king of Xuria, and his high council. She's awaiting final judgment for revealing an alleged heinous crime. A crime that has been covered up for many years. A crime that threatens her people's very existence and is high treason to the Dragons. Her allegation is one she does not regret, nor will she ever forget. No matter the verdict, she will find a way to ensure justice is served.

Here is her story.

PROLOGUE

"Can you tell me the story again?" asked Princess Lenala.

Hivey's eyes softened. "It's time for bed, my love."

"Please, just this once," begged Lenala.

Hivey let out a sigh, but a smile soon crossed her weathered face. "All right, climb into bed and snuggle up."

Lenala giggled as she hopped into bed. Her big, amber eyes were filled with excitement.

"It all started long ago, with the lord of the dragons, your grandfather, King Hecktar. But long before he was given that title, our people struggled to survive. You see, our home planet had broken away from the pathways and as a result, it began to drift away from the heat of Haruelio. Do you remember what that word means?"

Lenala's eyes lit up. "It means *brilliance*."

"Exactly," said Hivey. "In the ancient tongue of the dragons, Haruelio means brilliance. It brings us daylight and warmth and the closer a planet is to Haruelio, the hotter it is."

"Are we really the closest?" asked Lenala.

"Yes, my dear, we are indeed the closest planet to Haruelio." Hivey chuckled as she replied.

"And what happened to our old planet?"

Hivey's expression turned solemn as she explained. "Our old planet broke away from the paths. It started getting colder and colder, and we knew we would freeze or starve to death if we were too far from Haruelio. So, we had to set out to find a new home.

For many years, we lived in the in-between lands, seeking refuge wherever we could. "

Lenala listened intently as Hivey explained the story of her ancestors.

"Do you know how our planets are connected?"

"Yes, they are connected by the paths," Lenala exclaimed.

Hivey laughed. "You've been paying attention in school, haven't you, Princess? You are right, there are two ways. The first is through a track that completely *surrounds* all of the planets at their edge. It has smaller trails leading from the main path that connect to each planet. This is called the..."

"The Outer Path!" exclaimed Lenala triumphantly.

Hivey clapped her hands. "Well done! And the second way is a path that goes directly *through* each planet. This is called the Inner Path, and it is much easier and quicker. Both of the paths are suspended in space and surrounded by the stars."

Lenala snuggled deeper into her covers. "Was it scary out there?"

Hivey's gaze drifted into the distance. "At times, yes. The lands could be harsh and we weren't welcome on any of the planets we passed by." She let out a sigh. "The people were afraid of us."

"Why were they afraid?"

"Because we had to live primitively and hunt wild animals in order to survive in the Outer Path. They thought of us as barbaric because of this. But that's just how we had to live to survive. They couldn't see who we truly were and who we still are.

"Our culture is rich with music and celebration. We love to gather to watch the fireworks at night, share stories and laughter. Our families are the center of our world, and we cherish them deeply."

Lenala listened as Hivey continued. "And our men, they are natural warriors. They are strong, tall, and fiercely loyal to our people. They have a deep sense of honor and duty, and they are willing to do whatever it takes to protect our way of life."

Hivey held out her arms, revealing the intricate tattoos that covered them. "These tattoos represent our family status, military skills, and special gifts. They are symbols of our identity and pride. They are passed down through generations, and they serve as a reminder of our ancestors' bravery and sacrifice."

Lenala's gaze was fixed on the tattoos. She was mesmerized by the designs and patterns. "I can't wait to have my own tattoos one day," she said, her voice filled with excitement.

Hivey smiled warmly. "Yes, my dear, it will be a great honor for you to receive the royal tattoos. But remember, you must always carry yourself with dignity and respect, and you must be willing to serve your people with all your heart."

Lenala nodded solemnly as Hivey continued to speak passionately. "As you know, Lenala, our people have a wide range of responsibilities, from gathering food and working the land to serving in the military," she said, her warm gaze fixed expectantly on the child.

Lenala's eyes sparkled with curiosity as Hivey asked her a question. "Can you tell me what the word 'Hite' means in the ancient Dragon tongue?" Hivey paused for a moment, waiting for Lenala's answer.

"It means *fierce one* and I want to be a Hite when I grow up," Lenala responded eagerly.

Hivey's expression darkened as she shook her head. "I'm sorry, my dear, but you know women are not allowed to serve in the military. It is forbidden by our traditions," she said sternly.

Lenala's face fell slightly, but she didn't give up that easily. "But I still think I would look good as a Hite," she said, a mischievous glint in her eye. "And I could get the warrior haircut and tattoos on my head and neck like them."

Hivey let out an exasperated sigh. "That look is not suited for a princess of Xuria. Only our men are required to learn the art of fighting. Your father would not approve of such talk."

Undeterred, Lenala continued to listen with rapt attention as Hivey spoke about the soldiers. "The Hite are sworn to protect our people and our way of life. We are thankful for their bravery and sacrifice," she said, her voice filled with reverence.

Hivey let out a heavy sigh. "Despite our many accomplishments and rich culture, we are still viewed as barbarians and tyrants by outsiders," she said, her voice tinged with frustration. "This is mainly because we do not allow visitors to our land. As a result, very little is known about us, and many are too afraid to cross the Dragons."

Lenala's eyes filled with compassion. "Oh, Hivey, it makes me sad to think of our people out there all alone for all those years, especially you," she said as she reached out to take Hivey's hand.

"There, there, my dear." She squeezed Lenala's small hand. "That was many years ago, and we've come a long way since then."

"I know, but it still makes me sad every time you tell the story." Lenala's tone was heavy with emotion.

Hivey's head nodded in agreement. "Yes, it was a challenging time for our people, but it made us stronger in the end. Eventually, we discovered Xuria. Unlike other lands where humans lived and kept us from entering, there were only the Dragons here. We were fortunate to find Xuria. Out of the seven largest planets in the Hamanan Galaxy, Xuria is the biggest," she explained.

Lenala's curiosity only grew from there. "What about the other planets? Are they inhabited like Xuria?" she asked, her eyes shining with wonder.

"Each planet is unique, with its own set of challenges and opportunities." Hivey's expression turned serious as she spoke. "Some of the smaller planets are uninhabitable due to harsh conditions or lack of resources. Others have been colonized, each with its own unique cultures and traditions.

"All of us in our galaxy share one thing in common—our language and our long lifespans. Each of us can live 150 years or more," Hivey explained to Lenala.

Lenala's eyes widened with wonder. "Wow. Grandfather was 175 years old, wasn't he?"

Hivey nodded. "Yes, he was. He lived a long and fulfilling life, and I hope to do the same. I will be 145 soon, but I feel just as young as you," she said with a smile.

Lenala burst out laughing. "Hivey, I am only eight years old!"

Hivey's eyes twinkled in the soft candlelight. "Is that so? Well then, I feel younger than you," she said playfully.

Hivey frowned in thought as she continued. "When our people first discovered Xuria, we knew we had been given a precious gift. The planet glows a beautiful crimson, thanks to its volcanoes, soil, and fire. I still remember the first time I saw the high mountains with their rocky cliffs and the majestic flames from the volcanoes burning constantly as far as the eye could see. And the eruptions at night, creating a sky full of fireworks and seas of hot, thick lava."

Hivey smiled warmly. "During that time, Xuria was a peaceful and harmonious place."

She paused for a moment, lost in thought before she continued, her voice tinged with a sense of nostalgia.

"To peacefully settle in Xuria, your grandfather had to seek approval from the Dragons, who had inhabited the planet for thousands of years. He set out on his own and managed to befriend the king of the Dragons," Hivey explained to Lenala.

"Lord Draygon!" Lenala interjected, remembering the stories she had heard about the Dragon king.

Hivey nodded. "Yes, King Hecktar promised that his

people would not disrupt the peace. He even offered to give the Dragons the sickly and the criminals to do with as they wished. Lord Draygon accepted his offer, and King Hecktar held true to his promise. Over time, he gained the trust and respect of the Dragons, and they allowed us to continue living in Xuria, making it our home."

Hivey's voice took on a reverent tone as she continued. "The Dragons protected our people, guarding the land from any intruders. King Hecktar ruled harmoniously among the Dragons for many years before his death. He was seen as a hero to our people for finding us a new home. That's why we gave him the name 'Lord of the Dragons.'"

"Hivey, was my grandfather a good king?"

Hivey smiled tenderly. "He was a wonderful king. He always cared for his people, including me. In fact, I have been with the royal family as a caretaker since before your father was born," she added with a playful wink. "Your grandfather was fair and honest, and treated all of his people with the respect they deserved, and in return, they were loyal to him."

Lenala let out a heavy sigh. "I miss him so much." Her eyes welled up with tears.

"I know, my dear," replied Hivey in a soft, gentle voice. "We all do. It's hard to believe that it has been almost two years since he left us. Your grandfather had a long, happy life. He loved you deeply and always wanted to make sure you were protected. That's why he gave you Farka." Hivey motioned toward the small sleeping Dragon in the corner of the room. "Taking care of a young Dragon was not something I ever expected to be doing at my age, but I can't help loving that adorable creature," Hivey chuckled.

"Tell me about my father," Lenala asked in a pensive voice. "Is he a good king, too?"

Hivey's expression faded as she delved into her memories of King Byreon.

The throne had been passed down to King Hecktar's only heir, Byreon. However, Byreon had a rebellious streak as a child and young man, causing disarray and problems. The Dragons, who had never liked nor respected him, were unhappy with the idea of him taking the throne. But because of their relationship with King Hecktar and out of respect for the people, Lord Draygon decided to present Byreon with an ultimatum. The Dragons would allow him to stay in Xuria if he agreed to a deal. They demanded a sacrifice of one female virgin every year as homage to Lord Draygon, and in return, they would continue to protect the people of Xuria.

Byreon knew that he could not rule Xuria without the Dragons' protection, and he also feared the prospect of finding a new land on his own. Fueled by greed and self-concern, he agreed to the deal, despite the inevitable disruption of peace and change in Xuria. The Dragons, not surprised by Byreon's lack of integrity, sealed the deal and secluded themselves in the mountains, leaving the people to rule themselves. They showed their faces only once a year to receive their payment.

"Hivey?" Lenala's voice snapped Hivey back into the present.

"Now, my dear," Hivey said, tucking her in. "Your father, King Byreon, loves you very much. It's time for you to get some rest. Sweet dreams, Princess."

CHAPTER
ONE

Princess Lenala's heart pounded in her chest as she slowly made her way up the side of the Great Red Mountain, the largest and most beautiful mountain on the entire planet. It was surrounded by hot, thick lava flowing freely from the stream of a nearby volcano.

The heat was oppressive, and the steep climb left her gasping for air. She paused to catch her breath and wipe the sweat from her brow, glancing back at Farka, who seemed hardly winded. Lenala took a moment to appreciate her companion, who could have flown up easily on her own.

As she continued her ascent, the world around her fell away, and she was left alone with her thoughts. This was one of her favorite ways to clear her mind.

Finally, she reached the highest peak on the mountain and found herself overlooking what was once her home. The castle, perched on the second-highest peak of the Great Red Mountain.

She closed her eyes for a moment, hoping to find some

peace within herself, but all she felt was darkness enveloping her. "Why can't he understand?" she cried out. Her fists were clenched so tight that her nails dug into her palms. She felt like she was going to explode. But just as she was about to lose control, Farka appeared by her side. The dragon's presence was calming, like a soothing balm on her troubled soul. She took a deep breath and put her arm around Farka's neck, finding solace in the creature's warmth and affection. Farka had been there for her through thick and thin, always by her side

Farka was a special breed of smaller Dragons. She loved to fly, soaring through the skies with grace and ease. What made her unique was her ability to expand her body size at will. She could grow many sizes, towering over her enemies. Her scales shimmered in the light, a bronze hue that gave her a regal appearance. Her piercing black eyes seemed to gaze right into your soul, while her sharp horns added to her majestic presence. As was common among Dragons, her horns grew in size as she aged, a testament to her strength and power. Her kind was known to be silent, unlike some of the other Dragons who were able to converse with humans and each other. But despite her lack of speech, she was very intuitive and was able to communicate with Lenala in a special way. They could feel and read each other's emotions.

They sat there for a long time, the silence filled with the weight of Lenala's thoughts and emotions. As Lenala gazed upon the castle, memories flooded her mind, memories of her grandfather, her childhood, and the countless adventures she and her siblings had had within its walls. They had been free to do as they pleased on the royal grounds, often spying on council meetings, playing pranks on the staff, and sneaking into the royal bakery at night. Those were simpler times, when the world seemed bright and full of possibility.

She couldn't help but feel a pang of sadness as she thought of her grandfather.

"If he were still alive, he would never have let things turn out like this," she muttered to Farka as she exhaled a deep breath.

Her grandfather always had a special love for the Dragons, and had negotiated in secret to give his grandchildren each their own Dragon before his death. She would be forever thankful for that, especially now in the midst of so much uncertainty.

The wind blew through Lenala's hair, and the sky above was a brilliant shade of blue. Despite the beautiful view, a shiver ran down her spine.

The sight of the castle that had once been her beloved home now cast a shadow over her heart. Her grandfather and the Dragons built the castle many years ago. It was elaborate and it had always been a source of pride for her people. Made of solid, black stone, it glistened and shimmered in the sunlight, giving it a sleek, smoky look. There were steeples and high arches accenting every corner. Each arch was detailed with ornate, intricate etching. The entrance had high doors with magnificent torches on either side of the walkway.

As she sat there with Farka, she knew that her world was changing.

Ignorance may have been bliss, but now her dreams were crushed and her eyes were wide open.

TWO

Princess Lenala had spent the first seventeen years of her life within the walls of the castle, but it was always understood that on her seventeenth birthday, she would be sent to the esteemed Castle of Nahkei. The word "Nahkei" was derived from the ancient tongue of the Dragons and meant "virgin." There, she would undergo training to become a high priestess, a great honor for the second heir to the royal throne.

In the Castle of Nahkei, Lenala would join the eligible girls who had been living there since the age of thirteen. It was a place where they were groomed for the ultimate sacrifice, a tradition that had been passed down for years.

The castle was originally built as a tribute to Lord Draygon, and had been known as the Temple of Draygon. However, after Lenala's father ascended to the throne, the name was changed to the Castle of Nahkei, in recognition of the pact he made with the Dragons.

Once a girl reached puberty, she became eligible to live in the Castle of Nahkei. The Day of the Dragons was the most important event in Xuria, celebrated every year. It was the day when a sacrifice was chosen, a revered tradition that honored the Dragons and ensured the safety of the kingdom.

On this same day, a new Nahkei was chosen to replace the girl who had been sacrificed. This was a great honor for the chosen girl and her family. Despite the gravity of the situation, the Day of the Dragons was a time of celebration and renewal. The people of Xuria eagerly anticipated this day, knowing that it would be a time for honoring the past, and celebrating their culture.

Lenala dreaded moving to the Castle of Nahkei and living a life of servitude and sacrifice. Instead, she dreamed of becoming the first female soldier in the Xurian military, a dream she had held since she was a child. Unlike other girls, Lenala preferred being outside and didn't mind getting dirty. She yearned for a greater purpose than just being a princess trapped within the castle walls.

As she grew older, Lenala began secretly training in fighting tactics and sword skills with some of the younger soldiers, risking punishment from her father if he found out. Most of her training was from a soldier named Semian, who was one of the best up-and-coming Hite. Lenala provided extra food and clothing for the families of the soldiers who helped her to train.

Her goal was to impress her father with her skills and earn his respect. However, she kept her dream a secret, knowing that fighting was not allowed for women in Xuria. She could never forget Hivey's words: "Your father would never approve. It's forbidden." But Lenala refused to let society's expectations hold her back. She found most of the women's skills and trades to be boring and knew she was meant for something more.

As her seventeenth birthday approached, Lenala meticulously crafted a speech to present to her father, hoping to convince him to let her pursue her dreams. She knew it wouldn't be easy, as her father was a stern and unyielding man, but she couldn't give up on her passion. The day finally arrived, and her nerves were frayed as she approached her father. Summoning all her courage, she cleared her throat and began her impassioned plea. "Father, I have spent years honing my skills in secret, and I believe I can make a difference. I want to fight alongside the Hites, to protect our people and uphold our honor."

Her father was quiet, his expression cold and unyielding. He listened to her words with a dismissive air, his eyes filled with disdain. "Lenala, you are a mere princess, a woman. Fighting is not meant for someone like you. It is forbidden."

Lenala's heart sank as her hopes were dashed. She felt foolish for daring to dream, for thinking that she could break free from the expectations he had for her. Her father's laughter echoed in her ears, mocking her aspirations.

With a smirk, he continued, "Your fate is sealed. You will become a high priestess. There is no room for your dreams of wielding a sword and leading warriors. End of story."

Anger surged within her, her frustration boiling over. "But Father!" she protested, her voice laced with defiance. "I have the skills and the determination. I can be an asset to our people. Why do you deny me the chance to prove myself?"

Her father's wrath was swift and terrible. His eyes blazed with fury as he unleashed his anger upon her. "How dare you question me?" he snarled. "You will obey my command, or suffer the consequences."

The memory of that confrontation haunted Lenala, threatening to crush her spirit. The wounds inflicted by her father's words were deep, and they lingered within her, a constant reminder of the limitations forced upon her.

Lenala would be sent to the Castle of Nahkei. What was supposed to be an honor felt like a prison sentence. She was trapped in a life that had been chosen for her, a victim of her father's thirst for power.

The dreaded day had finally arrived, and Lenala's heart was heavy with sorrow. Tears welled up in her eyes as she bid farewell to her loved ones, knowing that it might be a long time before she saw them again.

She tightly embraced her younger sister, Anala, their tears mingling. "I'll miss you, Anala," she said, her voice barely above a whisper. Lenala then turned to her older brother, Prince Tyralon. "Promise me you'll come visit me."

Prince Tyralon's voice was filled with emotion as he promised. Finally, Lenala faced her mother, Queen Nalana, who held her daughter's face in her hands. Their eyes locked, and Queen Nalana whispered words of love and encouragement. "Lenala, my brave daughter, never let go of your dreams. Your spirit is unbreakable. Remember that."

Lenala tried to stay strong, to show her family that she was prepared for the challenges ahead. But deep down, fear gnawed at her. She knew that once she entered the Castle of Nahkei, her life would be forever changed. The realization hit her hard, and she felt as if her world was turning upside-down.

The journey to the castle was a drawn-out and tortuous one. As she gazed out the window, the once vibrant landscape that she had admired so much now seemed dull and lifeless. The deep red-orange hue of the land, which had once filled her with a sense of pride and belonging, now only reminded her of the crushing weight of her new life. The mountains and cliffs in the distance, which had once been a symbol of Xurian strength and resilience, now seemed like barriers separating her from the life she had always dreamed of. The air was warm and dry, reminding her of the harsh realities of the world outside the castle walls. *A climate made for warriors*, she thought bitterly, burying her dreams of becoming one. Her heart felt heavy, and the darkness inside her seemed to grow with every passing moment. As the castle on the Great Red Mountain faded from her view, a pang of anger hit her. She took a deep breath and turned her gaze forward, determined not to let her emotions get the best of her. But every time she replayed the conversation with her father, the anger and frustration she felt only intensified. The glimmer of hope that one day he might change his mind would creep in, only to be replaced quickly by her logical side. It was a vicious cycle that she had been trapped in ever since that fateful conversation.

As Lenala approached the castle of Nahkei, she was struck by its beauty. The cream-colored stone walls were adorned with intricate black edging and ornate trimmings, giving it an air of elegance. The light of Haruelio was high in the sky, casting a warm glow over the castle and making it shine like a jewel. The balconies were adorned with traditional Dragon wing-like stonework, just like the royal castle. The yard was full of beautiful flowers and had perfectly landscaped gardens. It was a sight to behold, and many Xurians traveled to the castle just to witness the stunning beauty of the grounds. Flowers were a rarity on Xuria, and their presence here was a testament to the care that was lavished on the castle. But despite the beauty surrounding her, Lenala could not shake the feeling of being trapped and suffocated, longing for the freedom to follow her own path.

The Hite guarding the entrance were stoic and unyielding, their eyes scanning the grounds for any signs of trouble. Lenala took a deep breath and reminded herself to keep her head up and not let anyone see how she truly felt. With her head held high and her shoulders back, she stepped forward to begin her new life.

"Hello, my dear and welcome," said a woman with a bright, chirpy voice. "My name is Senleah. I am the house mother here at the castle. I know your father very well and we are so happy you are here," she gushed. "Please, if you need anything at all, just ask me. It is my duty to ensure that all of the girls are properly taken care of." Senleah was much older-looking than she sounded with thick, black braided hair and golden eyes that had a warm, soft glow. She had several, fine wrinkles around her eyes that showed when she smiled. There was a motherly presence about her. Her skin was aged but she was still beautiful. Striking, in fact. She had the tattooed symbols of the royal help along with several other symbols that covered her arms and shoulders. Her smile was worn but soft. She wore a typical garb of royal red. She had a lean, muscular shape. She seemed genuinely kind. "Come, my dear, let me show you around," she said, beckoning for her to follow. *The poor girl is so timid,* Senleah thought as she led her through the halls. *She seems like a confident young woman but it's obvious she does not want to be here. I wonder why,* she thought, feeling sorry for her. She was young and clearly unhappy. Most girls were ecstatic to come to live in the castle. It was an honor. But Lenala was the first girl to come from royalty and the first girl who wouldn't be a sacrifice.

Everyone was excited that she was coming. *She will warm up once she gets used to it here,* she reassured herself.

As Lenala stepped into the castle's grand entrance, the sound of her footsteps echoed through the halls. The sight was nothing short of breathtaking. The room was vast, with walls that soared. The back wall was lined with floor-to-ceiling windows, through which the warm light of Haruelio filtered into the room, bathing everything in a soft, golden glow. Two large chandeliers hung from the ceiling, their flickering candles casting dancing shadows on the walls. The room was filled with intricate details that spoke to the wealth and power of Xuria. In each corner stood a statue of a Dragon, expertly carved out of volcanic rock. Although they were smaller than the ones at the royal castle, the detail on each Dragon was exquisite, down to the last scale and claw. Elaborate, gigantic vases of fresh flowers sat in front of each window, their vibrant colors and sweet fragrances filling the room with an intoxicating scent.

It was as beautiful on the inside as it was on the

outside. Senleah could see Lenala's eyes light up. Just like everyone's first time inside the castle. Senleah felt a sense of pride as she watched Lenala take it all in. The castle was truly spectacular. After all, it was built to honor Lord Draygon. Senleah continued to chatter and tell Lenala about the castle but the more she spoke, the further away Lenala's expression became. Her steps had slowed down and she wasn't saying much. *Surely, she will like it here. We've got to snap her out of this.* Senleah suddenly stopped. "Girls," she said in a loud voice. "Come meet the newest members of the castle." She turned to Lenala and Farka. "We have been looking forward to this day," she gushed as the girls began to emerge farther down the hall. They lined the hallway as Senleah led Lenala closer. "Girls, welcome Lenala and Farka." The girls all murmured their hellos as Lenala nodded. Lenala was a vision of beauty. Her jet-black hair cascaded down her back in waves, framing her face. Her golden eyes, with their thick black lashes, held a fierce determination. Her skin was rich and tan, a testament to her Xurian heritage. The royal tattoos on her arms, which marked her as a member of the royal family, were complemented by intricate decorative details that she had chosen to personalize them. They snaked up her arms, a reminder of the traditions and history of her people. She was of medium height, with a muscular build that spoke to her years of secret training. She moved with a fluid grace, her every step showing her strength and determination. As she walked through the halls of the castle, all eyes were on her, drawn to the power and beauty that radiated from her. She looked like a warrior, with the grace and poise of true royalty. She was someone who was used to getting her way and had no problem speaking her mind.

"There will be plenty of time for you to get to know each other," Senleah said, cutting the silence as she ushered Lenala along. Let me show you to your quarters.'' As Lenala walked down the hall, the girls looked at her with a mixture of curiosity and fear. They were all dressed in beautiful robes, their hair pulled back in tight braids. Lenala could tell they were uncertain of her, and she couldn't blame them. She was not only a newcomer to their world but a royal princess, someone to be revered and feared in equal measure. Lenala was used to intimidating people, but she wished that she could be more approachable, more likeable. Her demeanor was similar to her father's, demanding attention just by walking into a room. Although she was always kind and gentle, that was not the first impression she gave. She felt a pang of anger as she thought of him again, but she kept her composure and continued down the hall. The girls continued to stare, giving faint smiles as she passed.

The feeling she had as she continued through the castle was one she did not like. She felt scared, angry, and vulnerable. She was unsure of what the future held for her, and she desperately hoped that somehow, she could find a way out. Lenala refused to let anyone see her vulnerability. She projected an image of confidence and resolve, even as turmoil raged within her. It was a mask that she wore with practiced ease.

All of a sudden, she felt a wave of cold air and darkness wash over her. Moments later, a man emerged from the shadows. As he approached, he extended his long arm and hand to her. He was tall and slender, with well-defined muscles and a shaved head that gleamed in the light. His dark eyes locked onto hers, smoldering with an intense emotion that she couldn't quite place. He wore an expensive robe that draped over his broad shoulders, leaving his toned arms exposed and revealing an array of Xurian tattoos, including military and royal insignias. He was a darkly handsome older man. She had always sensed something sinister about him from afar. However, being this close to him and seeing his aura was almost terrifying. His smile, in particular, sent chills down her spine. It was a smile that masked something truly evil.

THREE

Farka screeched and then emitted a low, threatening growl that echoed loudly through the halls. She jumped out, spreading her wings in front of the princess, and lowered her head. She took a few deep breaths and looked directly at the man. He quickly reacted and jumped back several steps in alarm. Senleah screamed as she jumped back as well. Lenala shushed her Dragon, while stifling a proud grin. Even though Farka appeared to be protective on the outside, Lenala knew her better and could see through her facade. She was thrown off by him and that was why she reacted like that.

Offering no apology, Lenala soothed her with her voice. She had never felt so grateful for Farka as she was at this moment. She thanked her grandfather under her breath. Farka's eyes were slanted and had turned red. She stared at the robed man menacingly. She was beautiful and powerful. Even the king could not interfere with the loyalty these Dragons had for the princesses and the prince.

Although every instinct she had was on high alert, she

smiled at the man and graciously introduced herself. He was classically Xurian by his skin, eyes and tattoos, but his hair had been shaved off, leaving behind a smooth, shiny head. He had an old scar right below his cheekbone that made him look as though he was always smirking. Clearly shaken by Farka, he gave a slight bow and returned the introduction. "My name is Brantog. I am the high priest of the Castle of Nahkei."

Lenala had a very strong feeling of unease around Brantog. Though he spoke in a composed tone and had a steady gaze, Lenala could see that he had a tiny bead of sweat forming on the side of his head. There was a slight shift in his weight and she felt a small tremor when he shook her hand. There was something about him that wasn't right. Farka, who was very sensitive, was also uneasy and nervous.

I hate this place, Lenala thought.

Brantog took the liberty of ushering her to her private quarters. To her surprise, it was an entire wing of the house solely for her. He didn't say much but led the way, walking leisurely and deliberately. His long robe made it look like he was floating. Aside from a small limp every few steps, he was very graceful, regal, and unnerving at the same time.

The wing he led her to was beautiful and quite large. All of the windows were from floor to ceiling like in the main entrance. This allowed an abundance of light to pour in. She had an unobstructed view of one of the gardens. The room was clearly suited for royalty and was large enough for Farka to feel comfortable. *Not bad. Maybe I can get used to this,* Lenala thought. It was certainly luxurious.

Senleah made quite a show of fussing around the

room. She was busy tying back the curtains and showing Lenala where everything was while Brantog stood in the doorway quietly observing. It was a whirlwind. Then, they finally left her alone. Lenala sat down on the edge of her bed, feeling extremely overwhelmed. Her "Gift" of feeling, sensing, and seeing emotions was sometimes too much to handle. Especially after what she had been through the past few days. This gift Lenala had since early childhood. She could see the auras that surrounded people, telling her their emotions. Her grandfather knew she had this gift, and he always told her it would develop more over the years. Eventually, she would be able to sense feelings, thoughts, and motives. For now, Lenala could read and feel emotions fairly well for her age, but she needed some fine tuning. She sighed as she sat on the bed and looked over at Farka. Farka was able to shield Lenala and absorb some of the emotions from her. Many times, Farka had been her grounding source when things felt too chaotic. Farka lay at her feet, looking equally overwhelmed. The past week had been a whir of disappointments and changes.

She'd been denied her lifelong dream, made to feel inferior, and then sent away from her home. Although she had always known she would be moving to the castle on her seventeenth birthday, she had hoped with everything in her that her father would see her skill and let her be free to do what she wanted.

She lay down, noting how the bed was soft, *one positive thing so far*. She sank into the yellow, plush linens and closed her eyes. *Just for a moment,* she told herself. Then she drifted off into a deep sleep. She dreamed of a dark, damp room where there were long, bony skeleton hands reaching out for her. They were pulling on her clothes and trying to grab her arms. *Dingggg.*

A deep ringing sound in the background seemed to perfectly time with the bony hands grasping at her. *Ding......*Suddenly, clarity came over her and she was awakened by a loud bell ringing. Unsure of how much time had passed, she jumped up, groggy and confused as she sat there trying to get her bearings. Then, she remembered Senleah mentioning something about a dinner bell and not to be late. Thankful to be pulled from that disturbing dream, she shook it off and headed out to find the dining hall. Farka was still asleep, so she left her behind. "Rest up, my girl," she whispered before she left.

The dining room was located downstairs through the grand entry of the castle and down one of the long halls. There were aromas of exotic spices and freshly baked bread drifting throughout the castle. It smelled wonderful, and she was drawn to it as she felt a craving for food. As she entered the dining room, she was greeted by an older gentleman who introduced himself as Henron, the keeper of the grounds. Henron was older and notably handsome. He was tall and muscular with especially bronzed skin from many long days in the sun. His tattoos were telling of his past and present. He had the same warm glow that Senleah had flickering in his eyes. He was kind and gentle. She could sense that he was a good man. Her gut rarely steered her wrong, and she was learning to trust it more and more. Lenala liked him. He led her to the table and showed her to her seat before taking his seat at another table filled with what appeared to be castle workers. Lenala assumed they were all Anae—the men and boys who were sworn to celibacy so they could work in the castle. They could be around the Nahkei without being tempted, therefore keeping the pact with the Dragons pure.

After a few minutes, the other girls began filing in, each one taking her seat at the table surrounding Lenala. There were fifteen girls in total. One new girl was added each year after the sacrifice. Once the girls reached the last day of their eighteenth year, if they had not been chosen for sacrifice, they were free to return to their homes and were replaced by a younger candidate.

The girls varied in age. Most of them were whispering and giggling amongst themselves.

"Ahem," a throat loudly cleared. "My name is Trayana," one of the girls said. "I am one of the oldest here and have been here the longest. We would like to welcome you, Princess. We are honored to have you in our presence." Lenala hated formalities, but she obliged and returned the greeting. The girls took turns introducing themselves. All of them were remarkably beautiful. Each one had the typical characteristics of a Xurian—silky black hair, golden eyes, tan skin, with tattoos marking their bodies. Lenala took a moment to study each girl. She took note of their auras. She could see that several of the older girls had dark, sad auras while the younger ones were bright and happy. After a few seconds, she realized she was staring at these girls and hadn't said anything. *Can you be any more awkward?* she said to herself.

So, she smiled and began making small talk...which was not her strongest quality, but this was going to be her home. She would have to befriend them eventually, or at least play the part.

As time went by, she started to relax and feel a bit more

comfortable. They did most of the talking, and that was a relief.

After what felt like hours, a large, bellowing man emerged from the kitchen, commanding everyone's attention. "Ladies and Gentlemen," he shouted in a dramatic voice, holding his hands up and smiling. The entrance elicited several giggles from around the table, causing him to smirk disapprovingly at the girls. His smirk only aroused more laughter, which he ignored as he continued to speak. "It is my honor to present to you dinner." He took a bow as he stepped aside, allowing the kitchen staff to pass by with trays of entrees. As the food was being placed in front of each person, the man hurried over and introduced himself as the head chef of the castle. He was a nice man, genuine and highly expressive. He used his hands to describe things and made faces to complement his words. He bragged about tonight's selection and how he had prepared it from the royal chef's menu, especially for her. He wanted her to taste the food right away and tell him if she liked it.

"Now, now, don't scare her," Senleah barked as she approached the table. "The last thing she needs is you watching her eat." Her tone was direct and her face was stern. He knew not to argue with her. Clearly perturbed at her, he muttered a few things under his breath and then smiled at the princess, bowing dramatically as he backed away. An eruption of laughter from the girls followed. Lenala also laughed. It was the first time she had laughed in days. It felt good. She let out a deep breath and took a bite, relishing the explosion of flavors in her mouth. The food was just as delicious as it smelled. She let her eyes wander around the room in search of the chef. To her surprise, she found his gaze fixed on her. Quickly, he averted his eyes. "Chef" she whispered loudly.

His eyes lit up as his head snapped back to her. She smiled warmly, giving him a nod and a thumbs-up. A broad smile spread across his face as he practically bounced back to the kitchen.

Moments later, the atmosphere changed abruptly, and a sudden silence fell over the room. All eyes turned downward toward their plates, as the room's occupants continued to eat in silence.

Brantog had just entered the room. He walked to his table, scanning over everyone with his dark eyes and scowling. He sat alone at his perfectly positioned table, where he could see over everyone. *He seems like the type of man who wants complete control,* Lenala thought as she noted the pleased expression that crossed his face as soon as the room fell quiet.

The chef came hurrying out with Brantog's entree; his funny demeanor was gone. He avoided eye contact with Brantog as he placed his food on the table. Everyone focused on their food, and spoke softly. Trayana leaned in close to Lenala and lowered her voice to a whisper. "You better keep that Dragon of yours with you at all times." She smiled casually and leaned away, giving the impression that her words were nothing more than a passing remark about the food.

Lenala felt a chill run through her body: That was a warning. A warning laced with fear and deep-seated hatred. She could sense that there was much more to it than what met the eye. The intensity of the warning left her with an unsettling feeling, as if there were malevolent forces at play.

That night, Lenala lay awake in bed, consumed by Trayana's words. The sheer intensity of the anger that seemed to ooze from Trayana filled her with an overwhelming sense of dread. Her thoughts drifted to Trayana's aura, which was dark and tinged with sadness. Despite her best efforts, Lenala couldn't shake the feeling of despair that Trayana's presence emitted. As she looked around her room, she couldn't help but shiver, sensing a deep ache that seemed to emanate from the walls of the castle. Someone within these walls was plagued with sorrow. The place felt cold and unfamiliar, a far cry from her home. She called Farka to her side. She immediately felt a sense of relief as Farka snuggled up next to her, providing a much-needed source of comfort. Eventually, Lenala drifted into a restless sleep, but her dreams were anything but peaceful. Once again. she was haunted by visions of long, bony hands trying to hold her down, the screams of little girls, and bloodied dragon wings.

FOUR

Haruelio was beginning to set. It was another beautiful evening on the planet of Xuria. The mountains were all made of clay and always turned a deep shade of red at sunset. Volcanoes littered the skyline. The sky was scattered with many different hues of pink and purple. There was a slight breeze in the air that was a welcome relief from the long, hot days. Every evening was beautiful like this. Off in the distance, fire spewed and lava erupted from the volcanoes. The people of Xuria loved to watch them ignite. It was a magnificent sight.

The lava rolled from the top of the mountains into the molten hot rivers below. It sizzled and popped as it poured down rhythmically. The sound of crackles from the fire echoed through the mountains and the smell of the burning embers lingered in the air for hours. This all made for a perfect night. Everyone looked forward to this time of day. Everyone except for him.

He hated seeing all of the people enjoying themselves and being happy. He detested the way they curled their faces into smiles. In reality, they were just hiding behind their masks. They would all parade around their yards in their finest garments laughing and carrying on. It was sickening. His own family had been the worst of them all. Night after night, they put on a show. Their yard was the biggest in Xuria aside from the royal grounds. It had been perfectly manicured and was a stunning visual. The flowers were vibrant and the grass was beautiful and green. He hated the flowers. They represented the fake happiness his parents tried to portray. Having any grass at all was a sign of wealth in Xuria. The land was so arid that grass was hard to come by, let alone maintain.

His parents held esteemed positions as diplomats and had served on the king's high council for many years before their deaths. Despite being well-respected Xurians, their public image was carefully crafted to show only what they wanted the people to see. He had been forced to play a role in this charade since he was a child, with the responsibility of always making his parents look good and avoiding their wrath. Each night, he stood alone on the royal grounds, watching the fireworks. Memories of his traumatic past flooded his mind, leaving him filled with an intense hatred toward his parents that never faded. Even now, he couldn't forget the day they died.

Though it was short-lived, that day marked the first time he ever felt a sense of freedom.

They had always been consumed with keeping up the appearance of being well-to-do. So obsessed with it that they had neglected him as a child and growing up. They chose to prioritize their royal status over him, and they expected him to conform to their rigid standards. Sometimes, he still wondered why they even had him in the first place. They never loved him.

He was their only child, and he grew up alone with hardly any friends. Most of the other children were scared of him or they shied away from him because of his parents. They were not welcoming or kind. They thought he was too good to be friends with the commoners. That was how they wanted it. They wanted him to be alone. The few times he tried to make friends, his parents quickly ridiculed him for associating with peasants. They would call the children names to their faces. If the children got upset, his mother and father would threaten to hurt their parents. Pure wickedness. They thought it was funny when the children got upset. He was mortified. His only friend was Prince Byreon, the son of King Hecktar. His parents even limited his time with him because the prince was reckless and liked to cause trouble as a child.

They ingrained in him that he was to be groomed to be the high priest and could not waste his time with childish things. They forced him to believe this was a high honor for him. That he should be strong enough to withstand childish pleasures. There had been many times over the years when he tried to rebel and fight against the plan they had for him. This always resulted in a beating from his father while his mother watched. She approved every single beating and every punishment. Any childlike actions he exhibited earned him a beating. Any behavior at all that swayed away from what they expected of him resulted in a beating.

He did all of his academics at home under the teachings of the royal educators. He lived what many considered to be a privileged life, but to him, it felt like a prison.

Still to this day, he felt like he was a prisoner in his own life. Although he had risen in power and was one of the most respected and powerful men in Xuria, he still had become the man his parents pushed for him to be. He had all of the power and the finest things, but he still felt empty inside.

As memories flooded back, he shuddered and closed his eyes, pressing his hand to his temples. The trip down memory lane was never something he could get used to; it was a daily haunting. He let out a heavy sigh as the sight of the fireworks only served to disturb him. He despised having to put on a show, just like his wretched parents.

"Beautiful night, Your Grace," a voice interrupted. It was Senleah, the keeper of the house of the Castle of Nahkei.

"Indeed," he replied as she passed him. He grimaced inside. She had sneaked up on him out of nowhere. She was a smart woman who always seemed to know too much by the way she looked at him. He shook it off. She was a beautiful, warm woman who was loved by everyone in the castle. However, she served as a constant reminder of what he could never allow himself to have in life— love. Over the years, a deep resentment had taken root within him. Love was a foreign concept, something he had never received nor given. He had become hardened and jaded, disillusioned by life's harsh realities. He was powerful, yet alone. He possessed everything, but it felt like he had nothing. As she walked away, he laced his fingers and gazed up at the sky, taking a deep breath before painting on a mask of his own.

He was a part of what he hated the most. He smiled a hollow smile and began his nightly walk around the castle grounds. As he passed by some of the others, he gave a nod and a slight grin. There were staff, other royalty, and the girls outside enjoying the evening. The girls ranged from ages fourteen to eighteen and they were all Nahkei. Each one had been specially chosen and was eligible to be sacrificed at the yearly ceremony. Children were not his favorite and the younger girls were too childlike at times with their irritating habits. They knew not to act childish when he was around. They were afraid of him, and he liked that. He certainly would not be babysitting any children. There was no time for that. He couldn't be bothered. Any time he saw or heard one of them acting childish, he would have them punished. They learned quickly to not cross him and to behave in front of him.

It was up to Senleah, the house mother, and the maids to groom them and get them ready to be sacrificed. He had nothing to do with their daily care. He only intervened if someone was out of line. Most of them were in the castle for four years and if they missed the sacrifice date, they would get to return to society once they turned eighteen. Their service to the Castle of Nahkei was considered to be complete. He tried to avoid the little pests as much as possible. After all, he was raised to be antisocial and preferred to keep to himself.

His parents had made sure of that. He lived a life of solitude for the most part. He had the same routine every day. There were no surprises and no changes. Every day ended with the masquerade, as he referred to it. Night after night, he sat through the charade reliving memories that he wished could be forgotten. He attempted to numb the pain with his vices, but oftentimes the memories would become too much to bear, forcing him to act on the impulses that arose from them. He was a man of many secrets. Many dark secrets.

FIVE

The next several months in the castle passed by quickly. It had now been nearly a year since she moved in. Lenala had been very busy learning the ways of the castle and integrating.

The Day of the Dragons was fast approaching and a sacrifice would soon be chosen. There was excitement in the air as everyone was getting ready and making plans for the upcoming ceremony.

The underlying darkness that she had been feeling had been somewhat smothered during the busy months of preparing for the ceremony. Still, not a single night passed that she didn't dream of deep sorrow and shame. She felt it clouding over her every night. Her sleep was restless and she dreaded going to bed. If it weren't for Farka protecting her, she felt as if she would have been engulfed in whatever this spellbinding darkness was. *Maybe one day, I will get used to it,* she kept telling herself.

Her only release was when she was alone. Any chance she got, she would practice her footwork, a military art that she had learned. It was part of swordsmanship. It was a rhythmic movement of her feet and arms. She couldn't use her sword unless she was alone in her room, but she could practice her movements anywhere when she was alone. Her mind was open and free. She was focused on that exact moment and didn't think about anything else. It was therapeutic. She always felt centered when she was done.

The girls were all busy being groomed as the choosing day rapidly approached. They had their hair and skin treated with the finest oils. They were fed the richest and most indulgent foods. The spices and herbs used in the foods were ones the Dragons liked. It was assumed that the Dragons would eat the girls but in reality, no one knew how they killed them.

It was out of sight and out of mind. It was such an honor to be chosen that no one even considered what the girl may go through once the Dragons had her. Choosing day was one of excitement and nervousness for most of the girls. Lenala did not have to worry about being chosen since she was a princess. She was thankful that she was exempt. However, she had grown fond of the girls and hated the idea of choosing one to be sacrificed. She would be the one who drew the name; this was a high honor in the eyes of the people—an honor that further reminded her of her father's dark greed, and one that only deepened her anger toward him. How could he agree to kill his own people? Especially innocent girls. Why couldn't he have thought of a better way to make peace? Surely if his father, King Hecktar could maintain peace, Byreon could, too. It sickened Lenala every time she thought of this. How could the Xurians be so simple-minded? How could killing an innocent young girl be an honor? She didn't understand her people. There must be a better way. The only person who could change it was the king, and he would never take a chance of ruining what he had built. This was just an ugly truth behind the peace in Xuria.

The fact was, he was greedy. He wanted complete power and he did not want to sacrifice anything of his own to get it. So, he chose to sacrifice others instead. She'd had plenty of time to think about this while she was in the castle, and had come to the conclusion that it was greed. Plain and simple.

The day had finally come. It was time. All of the girls were lined up in their gorgeous red gowns. Red was the color chosen many years ago for anyone who lived in the Castle of Nahkei. It represented loyalty, peace, and purity. It also represented the natural elements of the planet. Each gown was unique and slightly different from the others. The girls all had gold earrings, bracelets, and necklaces. Their hair was adorned with pendants of flowers or Dragons, all gold, of course. The gold was a tribute to Haruelio, the brightest star in the sky. The dresses were vibrant and beautiful. They were all sewn by the best seamstresses in Xuria, and made of the finest material they had. Even the Anae and the other castle hands had on their fanciest red garments. Everything about each girl was prepared to a T. Their hair, nails, faces, skin, and clothing were all the result of fine grooming and preparation. They looked stunning. These girls were the most beautiful in the whole land.

Each year, after the sacrifice, there was a huge ceremony, and all of the families with eligible girls were invited. The next Nahkei was chosen based on her beauty. In the past, she would be chosen by Brantog and some of his assistants. However, this year, Lenala would have the honor of helping choose.

Excitement and fear gripped the room.

The sacrificial ceremony was held in an outdoor arena large enough for everyone to see. It was a tradition that had been carried on Lenala's entire life and many years before she was born. The whole city would be in attendance. This was the biggest day of the year for the Xurians. After the girl had been selected, they had to wait five more days before presenting her to Lord Draygon. During this time, the girl would have the chance to bid farewell to her loved ones and make further preparations for her journey with the Dragons. Then the Dragons would swoop down from the mountains and whisk the girl away, and the next girl would be chosen to take her place. This was almost as significant as the day of the initial selection, with another grand celebration following.

Lenala's family—the king, queen, prince, and princess—were positioned with the best view in the royal seating area. They were a striking family. Lenala studied them closely as she sat in the section reserved specifically for her and the girls. A mixture of anger and sorrow arose in her as she looked at her parents. She had not seen them since she moved away almost one year ago. She had been so busy and was only supposed to see them at the ceremony. This was a rule that had been long kept for fear that the girls would be distracted if they could see and visit their families. Some of these girls had not seen their families in years. Had she not been so angry with her father, she probably would have tried to bend that rule. She hated the deal her father had made with the Dragons. It was dark, dirty, and selfish. The worst part was that the people were brainwashed into thinking the Day of the Dragons was a good thing. Being in the Castle of Nahkei made her see the darkness even more. She even began to resent her mother for supporting him. How could they have sent her away knowing they would hardly see her? She turned her gaze to her mother and sister. They were very beautiful. They looked like twins, and they were both tall and slender, unlike Lenala, who was shorter with a lean, muscular build. They had golden eyes and tan skin. Her mother had soft lines on her face, showing her age only slightly. She was a strong yet soft woman loved by her people. Oftentimes, she was the only one who could reason with the king.

Another flash of anger and sadness struck Lenala when she saw her sister. Anala's fate was to be the same as hers. Anala was so smart. Nothing got past her. She was strong and able to control her emotions and was one of the few people who could help balance Lenala. She understood Lenala's gift and was a rock for her when things got too intense. Although she was the younger sister, sometimes it felt like she was the elder. Lenala's heart ached. She longed to hug her. She would be of age soon, one more year. *At least I won't be alone.* Anala would be joining the Castle of Nahkei as soon as she was seventeen. She would also be groomed to be a high priestess as third in line to the throne. They had to serve as high priestesses in the Castle of Nahkei until they were at least twenty-one years old, the marrying age in Xuria. Or until their father found them suitable mates of his choosing. She shuddered at the thought of marrying someone he picked for her.

Her gaze drifted back to her father. He was a tall, well-muscled man. His hair was silver with remnants of black streaks from his younger years. His face was etched perfectly, outlining his sharp, strong features. His skin was tan and thick. He had royal tattoos as well as warrior tattoos. He was a strong man with a commanding presence. He could be a tyrant ruler with no compromise, yet at the same time, he could be charming and very persuasive. He was able to sway the people to do exactly as he wanted, while making them think it was their choice. He was feared and respected by his people.

Then there was the prince, Tyralon, who was the oldest. He was already nineteen years old. Lenala loved her brother very much. She felt a sense of admiration as she looked at him. He was always on her side, encouraging her to learn the ways of the Hite. He had kept her secret for years. He even tried to persuade their father to listen and consider her case when she spoke with him about joining the army. He supported and comforted her when her father ridiculed her and shut down her dreams. Tyralon had always confided in her.

He was even more handsome than his father. Slightly taller than the king, with big roped muscles. His eyes were amber with flecks of gold that flickered when he smiled. His long hair was tied back with a thick piece of leather, in the style of a Hite haircut, with the sides of his head shaved and the rest of his hair left long.

The women loved him—he was a charmer like his father but he was boyish and kind. He was lighthearted, yet a powerful Hite in the elite forces. Lenala had always envied his lightheartedness. She wished she were able to see things in a different light. Her gift, or as she often referred to it, her curse, always showed the ugly side of things. She seemed to be able to see right through people, and it was a rare occasion when she was not sickened with other people's emotional baggage. She could see it and even worse, feel it. This created a dark picture of happiness for her. Only in the presence of her siblings, Farka, and when she was training did she feel at peace. They were her balance. They were both happy and carefree and she loved that, needed that. There was a sense of emptiness in her chest as she looked at her siblings. Maybe that was why she had been so off while she was at the Castle of Nahkei. She didn't have her usual people to balance her. Only Farka, but things had been so intense. Maybe she needed them, too.

Lenala continued to scan the crowd. The people were all seated and the sound of voices echoed throughout the arena. She kept looking, hoping to see Semian. She hadn't seen him in almost a year. He was nowhere to be seen. She had heard rumors that he had been promoted to the Elite guard. This was a huge honor for him and his family. She wanted to congratulate him. He was becoming one of the top soldiers in her father's army, and she was proud of him. She knew how lucky she had been to have had training from him. Sadness filled her once again as she glanced back at her father. Maybe one day, he would change his mind. She would be eighteen in a few days. She closed her eyes and took a deep breath. *I can stick this out until I'm twenty-one.*

Her thoughts were interrupted by trumpets blaring. Brantog had emerged and was standing in the front of the room holding the small vessel of names. He was looking at Lenala. He smiled his slow, wicked smile as he motioned for her to come forward and draw the name. Nerves jumped through her as she stood gracefully and walked to him. She returned the smile as she approached him and turned to face the crowd. There was a hush in the room. The anticipation was bouncing off the walls. Brantog continued to smile and nodded at Lenala, giving her his approval to draw the card. With a shudder and a silent sigh, she reached into the basin. The drums began to roll as she reached forward. They played a deep, slow rhythm as she pulled the card out. She waited for the drums to stop before she read the name out loud.

"Trayana," she said triumphantly with a forced smile as she glanced over at Brantog. She watched as an expression briefly appeared on his face, causing time to seemingly stand still. It was unclear whether he was shocked or horrified, and the expression disappeared and was quickly replaced with a smile.

Lenala looked away before he could realize that she had seen him. She continued to grin at the crowd, but she had the image of his smile in her head. A smile that to the others looked genuine, but Lenala saw through it. He was good, and fast. Clearly, he was experienced in shielding himself from others. She was the only one who could see beyond his facade, thanks to her gift. She caught a glimpse of something he thought was well-hidden, and he was struggling to keep it concealed. Despite appearing calm, his emotions were seething just beneath the surface, like a turbulent whirlpool. It felt as if he was slapping her in the face with them. Her skin began to turn clammy and a wave of nausea arose. The room began to spin, and she had to take a few steps back to steady herself. It was clear that he was trying to hide something monstrous and sick. The room around her erupted in applause as the girls congratulated Trayana. She was so happy that she was beaming, laughing, and smiling from ear to ear. Brantog graciously presented Trayana to the crowd as the chosen sacrifice. As she stepped forward, she turned to smile at Brantog. Lenala felt another wave of nausea wash over her. She could see that Trayana's smile was not genuine, but rather a sly, victorious grin. A smile that said *I beat you, you bastard.*

CHAPTER
SIX

His chambers were always cold and dark. He liked them that way. Every night after the sunset and the lava charade, he would return to his room and sit in front of the fire.

He had a large stone fireplace that he kept stocked with wood. The maids always had the fire lit for him. To anyone else, his room was fit for a king. To him, it was a reminder of how miserable he was. He would sit alone deep in his thoughts and just stare into the fire. He would drink enough wine to escape the dark memories. There were many nights when the wine was not enough to make the thoughts go away. Those were the nights when he needed something more. Something stronger.

In his drawer, he kept a small bottle hidden away. A bottle of something he had to exercise heavy caution with. He was a man of discipline and could control everything and everyone he encountered. He held fast to the fact that he wouldn't be controlled by anyone or anything. Especially a substance. However, some nights, it was the only thing that allowed him to forget and let him sleep. Just one drop of Dragon's Blood was usually all he needed. One drop took him to a magical place where he didn't care about a thing. Those were the only nights he slept deeply. Long ago, when he was a child, Dragon's Blood—DB—was used as medicine. It had amazing benefits if used properly. It was great for numbing wounds and helped alleviate pain. It was commonly used until one too many of the citizens began abusing the drug. They were using it to get high. The misuse of DB caused the crime rate in the city to rise rapidly. The addicts were breaking into homes and stealing from anyone who was prescribed the blood. Then, they began stealing it directly from the healers, one of whom was assaulted and almost killed by a user who was desperate for DB. The Dragons had become angry with the people for misusing their gift, and stopped supplying it to them. They forbade anyone to use it. The crime was punishable by death. Nowadays, Dragon's Blood was extremely taboo and forbidden in Xuria. Despite that, there were still addicts. If they were caught, the king dealt with them. He would punish them or turn them directly over to the Dragons, who would feast on them or cast them out of Xuria to their certain death.

The drug was hard to come across and very risky, but if the addicts were careful, they could get away with it.

Tonight was turning out to be one of those nights. A night when he felt like he needed just one drop to feel free and normal, to forget. He hated when he started feeling this way. It reminded him that he was still weak, and that made him angry. Even after all these years, he still struggled with the lasting effects of the wickedness from his childhood. When he got this way, it felt like a darkness was growing inside him, and he had an uncontrollable desire to hurt someone or something.

As he held the tiny bottle in his hand and looked at the fire, he began to flash back to when he was a younger man. The only time he remembered feeling freedom was when he was a Hite. He served his mandatory two years and during that time, he had complete freedom from his parents. He wanted to stay in and serve longer, but he was soon to be the high priest of the Castle of Nahkei. A choice that was not given to him, but rather decided for him. He snarled at the thought of that and took another gulp of wine. *They should have just let me be.* He'd lost count of how many times he'd told himself that. During his time serving, one of his favorite pastimes was to sneak women into his quarters. Many of the young men in the service would do this, but he had to be especially careful. He was not supposed to act on his personal desires. Not with the position he was going to be in. He had to sneak to fulfill his needs, which made it all the more fun.

He would be allowed to marry eventually, but it would have to be someone of high bloodlines and of his parents' choosing. Not for love and certainly not his choice. Love had been nonexistent in his life. He had never experienced it from his parents, so he had no idea what it was supposed to feel like. There was one time, many years ago, when he thought he might be capable of loving someone. He had just finished his service in the military and was in training to become a high priest. It was then that he found himself smitten with a girl.

"Ugh," he grumbled to himself as he had another swig of wine. *Why do I have to think of her tonight? It was so many years ago.* Mina was her name. She was a gorgeous girl and she had the most beautiful smile. She was everything in a woman that he could imagine he wanted. She was funny, pretty, smart, and passionate. She would come to his chambers almost every night, and gradually, he began to feel himself softening toward her. He found himself thinking about her more and more, until she became all he could think about.

But he battled with his thoughts toward her, knowing that she was only a peasant—and a call girl at that. He was painfully aware that it was her job to make him feel this way, and that she made other men feel the same way. She was good at her job, just like he paid her to be.

He wished he could ignore the thoughts and feelings he was having. It enraged him to imagine her smiling at another man or laughing with someone else. He tried his best to keep his emotions in check, but when she was with him, he would forget all of his reasoning.

He wanted her, and he wanted to make her his. He dreamed of running away with her, of starting a new life together, far away from the expectations of Xuria. He knew that if anyone found out about her, it would be a disgrace to his parents' name, so he kept her a secret.

As time passed, he continued to sneak around with her. He didn't understand what love was, but he liked the way she made him feel. Being with her was all he wanted.

"I was so soft," he chuckled in a deep voice, shaking his head at the memory. But even as he laughed, he couldn't shake the feeling of repulsion that came with it. He took another sip of his drink, trying to push the memories away as he eyed the tiny bottle on the table.

One night, in a moment of passion, he asked her to run away with him. He wanted to leave everything behind and start fresh. He could never forget the look on her face—first surprised, then solemn, as if she was contemplating whether to take this bold step. Eventually, she agreed, eager for a chance to start over.

They began planning their escape, but first, they had to sort out their personal affairs. They decided to meet secretly in a few nights before leaving Xuria for good. Over the next few days, he experienced a spectrum of emotions—doubt, fear, excitement, and hope. This was his chance to escape the life he detested so much.

Finally, the night arrived. He had meticulously packed his belongings and loaded them onto his horse. But upon reaching their agreed meeting point, he discovered that she was nowhere to be found.

He waited for a while, hiding in the shadows, hoping that she would appear. However, as time passed, it became clear that she wasn't coming. The longer he waited, the more his anger and frustration mounted.

Where is she? Is she standing me up?

Angrily, he headed to the brothel where she worked and lived.

He stormed in. He had been there a hundred times and could find his way to her room with his eyes shut. Music was playing loudly and the people were laughing, but he didn't care. He had tunnel vision. Nobody seemed to even notice him as he went up to her room.

He remembered trying to open the door but it was locked. He knocked hard and fast. The door cracked open. "Brantog? Mina looked surprised. "What are you..."

Before she could finish her question, he snapped, "Are you standing me up?"

"No," she said, seeming genuinely surprised. "I

thought we agreed on tomorrow night, I'm not ready, but, but I can be," she stammered. "Give me a little while and I'll meet you downstairs," she responded hastily. She bit her lip and let out a small sigh. Brantog's eyes narrowed as the door creaked open a little further, revealing a man in her bed.

Brantog's face grew hot. He was already angry but now he was fuming. He slammed the door open, pushing past her as she let out a scream.

He grabbed the man from the bed by the neck and threw him on the floor. He had been out of the service for a while but remained sharp with his skills and training. "No, please," she said, "he's just a customer."

"I'm waiting for you and you are here pleasing some-one, on my time? For more money?"

With a swift and forceful kick, he struck the man in the ribs, causing him to let out a pained groan and a crunch. Despite his anger, he couldn't deny the sense of satisfaction that came from seeing the man in agony.

"Please," she said again, "don't do this, let me pack my things and we will go." She started bustling around the room, gathering the rest of her belongings. Tears streamed down her face as she begged him to leave the man alone. "It's my fault," she pleaded.

He continued to feel rage surging through him and couldn't hold back. He didn't want to hold back. He wanted to hurt this man. He continued to beat him with skilled hits and kicks. The man was a whimpering pathetic heap and Brantog loved seeing him suffer. This man had obviously forgotten his training and was too drunk to react. "Swine," Brantog spat out at him.

He looked up at Mina, and saw her eyes were wide and

she was trembling. He could see the fear etched in her face, and it angered him even more. He blamed her for the situation. He wanted nothing more than to slap that look off her face. She looked ugly when she was scared. To him, everyone looked ugly when they were scared. That was the only thing his mother ever told him that he agreed with.

"Get your things now," he growled at her. He knew he should have left her behind, but he had a weakness for her. He wanted happiness and he wanted it with her.

He stood there with his arms crossed while she finished getting her things. The man lay on the floor groaning. He was hurt but he would live.

Brantog had his horse waiting downstairs. The plan was for them to ride to the edge of Xuria and sneak past the guards. He hoped he wouldn't have to fight them but if he did, he had his sword and was ready. After that, it would be a long trek on horseback to Analicia. But they would be free. That was the only thing keeping him calm at the moment. The taste of freedom.

As they rode into the night, he carefully checked their surroundings to be sure no one had seen them leave. He was ready to escape this planet and never look back. Even though he was furious with Mina, he was taking her with him.

He was pacing in his chambers. He still remembered the feeling of freedom that he had been craving all those years ago. It was a feeling he still tried to suppress to this very day. He shook his head and closed his eyes as the memories continued.

They rode fast toward the gates. After a few miles, the thunder of horse hooves began to pound in his ears. His horse neighed and jumped hard to the side, almost throwing them off. "Whoa," he said as he pulled on the reins. He quickly reached for his sword, placing his hand on the hilt. "Who is it?" Mina asked. Her voice was shaking.

"We've been followed," he whispered. Moments later, his reality changed. They found themselves surrounded by horses and armed men. He drew his sword and spun his horse in a circle. It was dark, so he couldn't tell how many there were. They weren't royal guards. They looked like thugs. Were they robbing him or did someone send them after him? He hadn't said a word to anyone. Anger and adrenaline flared through him. "Mina, did you tell anyone about this?"

She began to cry. "No," she sputtered out.

"Liar," he hissed through clenched teeth. "Don't you lie to me," he said. He could feel immediately that she was lying and that she was too afraid to tell him the truth. Now they were in danger and it was her fault. He never should have brought her. She didn't care about anything except her own freedom and was willing to jeopardize him to get it. *How could I be so stupid?* he scolded himself. There were three of them. He knew he could take them. He carefully dismounted his horse, leaving Mina on. He crouched, entering his fighting stance. One by one, they got off their horses and began advancing on him. He lunged into the first man, his sword sharp and fast. The man jumped aside, barely avoiding the hit. Another man approached from behind and Brantog spun, ducking to avoid a blow. He extended his sword as he turned and sliced the man right at the ankles. The man screamed and fell forward. In one strike, Brantog severed his head. The first man jumped on Brantog's back, trying to pull him to the ground. Brantog stepped to the side and planted his foot behind the man's leg, sending him to the ground. He landed on his back with a thud as Brantog drove his sword into him. He turned to find that the third man had Mina with a knife to her neck. "Drop your sword," he said to Brantog calmly. "Or I will kill her." Brantog took a step forward and the man pressed his sword into her neck, drawing blood. She screamed. Brantog came to a halt. "Drop it, '' the man warned again. Brantog stood there for a minute. No way was he going to surrender to this man. No way was he going back. He wanted to have Mina with him. As he stood there, his thoughts were racing. The fact that this was her fault was all he could think of. He had already sacrificed so much to bring her and he would not sacrifice his freedom any further, not even for her.

The man with the knife decided to take this opportunity to speak. "Your little girlfriend has a big mouth," he said, provoking Brantog. "It doesn't take long for news to travel amongst the right people.'' He snarled. "Let's just say we didn't have to wait long for you to make your move. Didn't think it would be tonight," he spat before he continued. "But I'm glad we aren't dragging this out. We are getting a pretty good ransom for bringing you and your little lady in—your parents think you are worth a healthy sum."

Heat filled Brantog. He started to lunge, but then, he saw Mina's face. Tears were pouring down her cheeks. "I'm so sorry, Brantog,'' she said. "I never meant for this to happen. I just wanted her to know where I was going." Her fingers were digging into the man's arms. The knife was pressing on her neck. She was taking fast and short breaths. A moment of pity passed over him. She was so beautiful. Her voice sounded innocent and sweet. Just one look at her and his anger dissolved. He would have been better off leaving her behind, but there was a reason he wanted her. Companionship, hope of a future, hope of love. Hope of one day having a normal life.

Did I really sacrifice so much just to let her die? He lowered his sword and took a step back. The man lowered the knife and shoved Mina toward Brantog. He pushed her behind him and lifted his sword. He wasn't giving up. Suddenly, Mina screamed behind him and as he started to turn, things went black.

SEVEN

The city was buzzing with an electric, unbridled excitement, and everyone was celebrating. Lenala needed to process everything from earlier, so she decided to take some time to herself and gather her thoughts. The only way she could clear her mind in the castle was to practice her footwork. This was one of the ways she had learned early in life. She grabbed her sword and stood still with her eyes closed as she took several deep breaths. Then, steadily, she started to work her hands and feet in rhythm as she began to replay Trayana and Brantog's expressions in her mind. She couldn't figure it out, but she knew there was something there. Something she shouldn't have seen and something they were trying to hide. Whatever it was, it was dirty. She continued to breathe and step in a rhythm. The more she focused, the clearer what she had to do became. She knew without a doubt that the only way to figure this out would be to pay Trayana a visit. She took a few deep breaths and tried to calm her fluttering stomach. Even though something inside her said to leave it alone, she knew she needed to talk to Trayana. There was a sense of urgency pulling at her and she couldn't drop it. Something wasn't right. The more she maneuvered around, the more certain she became. This could be the key to resolving what she had been trying to ignore ever since she got here. She thought of the countless restless nights, the vivid dreams, and the wrenching sadness she had been experiencing. Sweat dripped down her forehead as she continued her movements. Her eyes remained closed the whole time. Her mind was becoming clearer. She would not be able to rest until she knew what was behind that exchange between Trayana and Brantog. She stopped her dance. Her feet were firmly planted, her eyes opened, and her gaze was fixed straight ahead. She knew what she needed to do. Her plan was simple: As soon as she was sure everyone was gone, she would go looking for her. All she needed to do was wait.

She sat in the middle of her room until her heart rate calmed back down. Farka was watching her intently. She knew Lenala was focused on something very important. She understood everything before Lenala even explained a word. She walked over to her and put her head on Lenala's. Lenala immediately felt another rush of relief. Farka was absorbing some of her emotions. As soon as Farka touched her, she was able to feel exactly what Lenala was feeling.

Lenala always confided in Farka, even though Farka didn't speak. She could understand. She was highly intelligent and very in tune with Lenala at all times. Her physical nudges were how she helped alleviate emotional burdens from Lenala. They were also able to tap into each other's emotions without touching. It had only happened a few times, but it was becoming more powerful.

Night had fallen on the castle and everything was quiet.

Lenala was ready to take her chance and go looking for Trayana.

She wandered around the castle for a while. Once she realized Trayana was not inside, she headed outside. Eventually, she found her sitting alone in one of the gardens. Lenala approached her cautiously. She started by casually congratulating her, all the while trying to get a better feel for what she may be feeling. She sat down next to her and quickly sensed a mix of happiness, relief, and sorrow. As they continued to chat, she began to see her aura more clearly. It was dark and showed a very deep sadness. Red flags were shooting up in Lenala's head. *This girl is supposed to be happy that she was chosen. Enough small talk,* she thought.

"Trayana." She made up her mind to be blunt. She would know if Trayana was lying and did not want to waste any more time playing games. "When I called your name today, I saw something in your eyes when you smiled at Brantog." Trayana's eyes widened. "I know something terrible is happening here and I want to help." Trayana looked at Lenala for a long moment. Her cheeks were turning red and her breathing subtly became more rapid. Her eyes glazed over. She was looking at Lenala, but her expression was distant. Lenala waited for her to reply. Trayana's fists were clenched tightly in her lap then suddenly she blinked, focusing on Lenala.

"Do you think that because you are the princess, you can just waltz in and save the day?" Lenala was taken aback by her coldness and anger. Trayana had chill bumps forming on her arms and her breathing was increasingly rapid as she spat the words out. "Screw it," she said. "I'm out of here in five days anyway. Be careful; he will be looking for another one soon, now that I am leaving."

"Another one?" Lenala echoed.

Trayana took a deep breath and continued. "You see, I beat him at his own game, in a way he never would have expected." Her gaze shifted and she almost laughed as she spoke. "I am leaving before he is ready." Suddenly, she grabbed Lenala's hand. Her eyes were turning red and tears began to stream down her face. Her sudden change from a hardened cold girl to a crying, broken one threw Lenala off-guard. The wind began to blow, causing her hair to stick to her wet face. She looked so innocent and afraid.

"Maybe you can actually stop him. Don't let him near the others." She rushed the words out desperately. "He is monstrous and he will stop at nothing. I wish I could have, I mean, I should have just killed him. I was too afraid." She hardly took a breath between words. "Nobody ever breathes a word of this. Everyone is too scared of him."

Lenala couldn't move. She felt like she was in a daze. "What are you saying, Trayana? What is he doing?"

Trayana shuddered and looked around. "No, no, no," she stammered as she wiped the sticky hair off of her face. "Never mind. I've said too much. He can't be stopped and if he finds out I said anything..." She trailed off. She was shaking as she held back more tears.

"He won't find out," Lenala barked. "You are leaving us

soon and you must tell me what is going on. How can I help if I don't know?"

Trayana gave Lenala another long stare. "Exposing Brantog will mean that treason has been committed on our planet, but..." She stared off into the distance again, silent for a moment. "Maybe with you...you are the princess..." She sat up taller. "Maybe you can find a way to stop him." Lenala braced herself for what she was about to hear. Trayana took a deep breath. She wiped her face and with a reluctant sigh, she began her story. "For the past four years, Brantog has been using Kineah and me as his personal sex slaves." She paused for a second as she looked at Lenala. Her expression became cloudy and her shoulders slumped back down. Anger began welling up inside Lenala. This girl had been robbed of the life she deserved, and not only her but Kineah, too. Trayana's eyes were bloodshot from crying and her hair was matted to her cheeks from the tears. She was so beautiful and yet so broken. Lenala felt the relief and guilt spill out of Trayana as she continued to speak. "He threatened us. He said that if we ever told anyone, we would be killed for blasphemy." She scoffed at the thought of that. "He had us so scared, just how he wanted us. It started as an occasional thing, and we were so young—I was fourteen but unfortunately for me, I looked older. Kineah came along a couple of months later."

Trayana took another moment before she continued. It was a lot to absorb and Lenala felt heavy as she sat there and listened. How could this be happening? These girls were supposed to be protected. They were supposed to be safe and sacred. Even if the pact with the Dragons was atrocious, they were never supposed to be subjected to abuse. They were the chosen ones. Everyone envied them. They were supposed to be the purest in all the land. Yet here they were suffering at the hands of the high priest. Lenala felt a nudge from Farka, who was sitting nearby watching intently. She knew Lenala was enraged. Lenala closed her eyes and took a deep breath as Trayana continued.

"We didn't know what to do. As time went by, it got worse and more often. He got darker and more sinister. He would rape us, beat us, and make us do whatever he wanted. Many times, he even drugged us so we wouldn't scream. It's been going on for years but no one else knows." She turned to look at Lenala. "I believe there are others and I know he's done this before. He always compares us to the 'other' girls and uses stories about them to scare us. I remember when he told us that he only liked to have two girls at a time, but I never believed it. I was sure that he was involved with some of the other girls as well. He told us that we were gifts from Lord Draygon. It wasn't until we finally figured out his twisted scheme that we realized the truth. When the girls were old enough to be released from the castle, he would tamper with the selection cards to ensure that his chosen ones would be the ones selected. He has undoubtedly been doing it for the past few years, skipping over my name and Kineah's so that he could keep us around for as long as possible. Who knows how many were before us?" Her gaze drifted away as she let out a deep sigh. The reality of the fact that Brantog had been doing this for so long hit hard. He had a sick regimen that had worked perfectly. "Well," Trayana continued, "this time I beat him. The joke is on him. I tampered with the drawing so my name would be drawn.

I'd rather die than stay any longer under his cruel thumb," she said with a shudder. "I should have had the guts to do this sooner. Much to that bastard's surprise, he thought he had me a while longer." She laughed a hollow, emotionless laugh again and a smile spread across her tear-stained face. "Now he will be looking for a replacement for me and he will be angry." She paused for a moment and looked at Lenala. She sat up tall again as her voice got louder. "You have to stop him. Expose him. You are the only one who can. Try to get Kineah to talk to you. Gather evidence. Go to the king. Maybe he can fix this. You are his daughter; he will listen to you and protect you."

That statement stabbed Lenala in the gut. She wondered if her father would even do anything. Then it dawned on her—years ago, there was a similar case in the high court. One of the Anae had accused someone in power of this very thing. At the time, she didn't know who. Lenala only knew of the case because she and her siblings over-heard it once while spying on a council meeting.

Her father had several people killed in secret for blas-phemy and treason. If this had really happened, the Dragons would revoke their deal and be terribly angry that the sacrifices were not all Nahkei. The Dragons were powerful creatures and her father feared them greatly. They didn't know who they were talking about and figured that they were accusing an Anae—the word in the Dragon tongue for "less than."

Anae were men chosen at birth to serve in the Castle of Nahkei. Although this was an honorable position, they were chosen because they were smaller or weaker than the other boys. They would not be strong enough to serve in the army. Many of the other men looked down on them, but the Anae had a sense of pride in their work. They were sworn to celibacy and felt that their work was honoring Draygon.

The Anae who was killed was a boy named Larsen, a young groundskeeper at the Castle of Nahkei. The girls of the castle loved and trusted him. Lenala had even heard stories of him. The information she knew from his meeting with the high council was not public knowledge. Not even the people at the Castle of Nahkei knew what happened to him, and if they did, they did not speak of it, for fear of repercussions. Larsen accused a man in power of rape, abuse, and treason. He had two other Anae with him and two of the girls as witnesses. Now she realized that it must have been Brantog they were accusing of the crimes. Lenala and her siblings had never spoken of it again. They believed the king and his reasoning.

"Lenala, whatever you do, keep your Dragon with you. He will not touch you as long as you are with her. He is very afraid of Dragons."

Lenala felt a wave of nausea rush over her and her insides felt like they were on fire. It was as if she swallowed hot lava and it was moving inch by inch through her body, ripping her apart. Her gift had grown over the past year, and she was having trouble dealing with the intensity of the emotions that came with it. Farka stepped in and placed the tip of her wing on Lenala's back. She knew Lenala was struggling to cope. Eventually, she started to feel a little relief. She needed to think. This information was heavy and dangerous. If this was true, Brantog would be looking for a replacement soon and he would be very angry.

Trayana's last five days passed by quickly, and soon, she was gone.

She looked glorious on that final day and for the first time since Lenala had known her, she looked happy. She walked down the heavily decorated, floral path that led to the mountain where the Dragons would come to take her away. She didn't look back once. She was finally free from her secret prison. Lenala felt a lingering pang of sadness as she watched her go. She had hugged Trayana before she started her final walk, and Lenala felt the sweet serenity Trayana was feeling. She felt like she had won. She got out. But despite knowing she was happy and free, Lenala was deeply troubled by everything she had learned. Over the next few days, she could not give rest to the internal battle she was having. She needed to get to Kineah soon and get as much information as she could. She had been brainstorming ideas for the best way to do this. Kineah was a very guarded person in general. Lenala knew this the moment she met her. Getting information out of her would be nearly impossible. She would have to wait for the right opportunity to present itself. Weeks went by with no sign of her. It wasn't uncommon for time to pass without some of the girls seeing each other. The castle was huge and each girl had her own private wing with everything she needed. Most of the time, they would see each other at dinner, but it was never any question if some girls skipped on occasion.

This was different—Kineah had not been to any of the common activities in the past two weeks. At night, she could barely drown out the sobbing. Although it was something she had gotten used to, this was more intense. It had gotten worse. *It must be from Kineah.* Lenala knew something was very wrong and she needed to get to her. Finally, she decided to take matters into her own hands and go looking for her. If she could find her room, maybe she could get her to talk. Lenala sneaked out of her wing late one night with Farka. She wasn't exactly sure where Kineah's room was, but she was being drawn toward the sobbing. *Surely, it's her.* They tiptoed across the cold floors and made their way toward the west wing.As she approached the entrance, she heard a little shuffle. It was very faint, but it was there. Farka heard it, too. Her ears perked up as she and Farka paused in their tracks. Fear shot through Lenala as they listened. The castle was eerily silent and dark as they waited. There it was again, louder this time. It was footsteps and they were getting closer. She and Farka quickly hid beside the doorway to the wing. There wasn't any place to conceal themselves except behind a large vase of flowers by the door. They tucked themselves beside the vase. They weren't totally hidden, but if the person coming didn't turn their way, they would be safe. The doorknob turned. Lenala pressed herself against the wall as she held her breath. She was afraid to even exhale. Her heart was pounding. Then, a shadow emerged through the doorway. A tall, lanky, devious shadow.

CHAPTER

EIGHT

The shadow quickly passed. She already knew who it was way before the light revealed him. She waited, stricken with fear of being seen or heard. Farka's eyes were narrow and fixed on him. She sent vibes to Farka to stay calm and quiet.

He continued to walk away. He didn't look around, only forward. She waited until he was all the way down the stairs and heading toward his own wing before she made any moves. Then she waited a little longer. She knew she needed to remain still until he was far enough away and couldn't hear her. Moments stretched long as the two of them waited. Finally, her heartbeat began to slow. Once she was sure he was far enough away, she let out a big sigh. "Ok, girl, let's go," she whispered as she and Farka crept out of hiding. They sneaked through the door and into the wing.

This wing was very large, but not as big as hers. As soon as the door closed behind her, she felt it. There was immense sadness and pain in the air. *This is it.* It was very dark and hard for her to see where the bedroom door was. She took a moment and closed her eyes, trying to press into her senses and feel where the pain was coming from. Farka nudged her and rushed past her, leading the way. Her senses were more advanced than Lenala's, but her reactions were harder to contain. Her natural Dragon tendencies caused her to be extreme and unbridled at times. Lenala had to calm her down on many occasions. Farka found the door. Lenala felt the full burden of what she had been feeling every night since she had been in the castle, now coming from behind that door. It was heavy. She took a deep breath and looked at Farka, bracing herself. *Tap tap tap*. She tapped on the door, and it creaked open. She was greeted with a shaky, husky voice. "Haven't you had enough?" Kineah was exhausted emotionally and physically. He had been less than generous with the blood lately. Her body hurt all over from her head to her toes. It was almost unbearable, but nothing compared to how badly she hurt inside. Trayana had always been stronger than her. She was the tough one and wasn't afraid. She was always able to stand strong. Kineah depended on her and drew that energy and strength from her. She was able to be strong when Trayana was around, but not anymore. She was left to absorb everything on her own and had no one to turn to. Now, she was all alone. She sat up a little and winced in pain. "What more do you want from me?"

She thinks I'm him, Lenala realized in horror.

"It's me, Kineah, it's Lenala," she said in a whisper.

"Lenala? What are you doing here? You can't be here—he will hear you," she said in a loud, panicked voice.

"Shh," she warned as she closed the door and rushed over to her. The room was dark, with only the faint, flickering light of a candle. Kineah, who was usually a strong, beautiful young woman, was tattered and helpless. She had nothing but a sheet wrapped around her and was curled up in the corner of the room, looking extremely vulnerable. Even in the faint light, Lenala could see her eyes were puffy and bloodshot. She was covered in bruises. Lenala hadn't seen her in weeks, so she knew these bruises must have been bad when they were fresh. It was deeply disturbing to see her this way. She quickly sat beside her and reached out to comfort her. As soon as she placed her hand on Kineah's shoulder, the Nahkei began to sob. She sobbed a racking sob, hollow and sad, from deep within her soul. Lenala quickly pulled her into her arms and hugged her tightly. Something about Lenala's touch gave Kineah comfort. Her touch seemed to draw out every emotion she was holding inside. It pulled them from her, even though she didn't mean to release them. She couldn't help it.

Lenala was not prepared for what happened next. The impact of her hug sent a shockwave through her body and all of a sudden, thousands of memories began flashing through her head. These were not her own recollections — they were Kineah's. From when she was a little girl running through the streets of Xuria, happy and laughing, memories of her parents and her siblings. Her childhood became so vividly stamped into Lenala's brain. It felt like they were her own experiences playing before her eyes. Then came the wave of memories from the day she was chosen to move to the castle. Her family had celebrated. This was a huge excitement for her. She couldn't wait to go and she was so happy that she had been chosen over all the other girls. She had just turned fourteen. Soon, after her birthday, she moved into the castle. It wasn't long before her joyful memories took a turn for the worse. Shadows and darkness began to swarm into her mind. Brantog's face loomed and his voice was the only sound she could hear. He initially told Kineah that he wanted to give her a special welcoming gift. He said that she would usually have to wait until she was older, but she was lucky because she looked old enough. Her appearance meant that she was ready. He explained to her that she was going to be his from now on. That he would train her for the afterlife so that she would be pleasing to the Dragon gods. He assured her that this was an honor. He also threatened that if she ever told, she would be considered tarnished and unable to be a sacrifice. At first, she was excited and felt important because she had been chosen by him for this special training. That excitement didn't last long. Soon, she started to feel used and dirty inside. When she started to question him, he began getting violent. In the beginning, she tried to fight back and stand up for herself. She even threatened to turn him in. Every time she tried to stand up for herself, he would make detailed threats on how he would harm her family. He promised that he would kill her and her loved ones if she ever told on him. She believed him. He was so horrific that she knew he wasn't issuing empty threats. He was capable of carrying out everything he said he would do. He had her so afraid of him that she would never tell. She was too scared of what he would do to her family. She had two sisters who were younger than her. The thought of him hurting them was unbearable.

Eventually, she started to give up and lose hope. His face haunted her. She loathed him. Lenala could feel the hate radiating through her. It was raw and angry. Her mind was dark and clouded with thoughts of him. The abuse went on for years and it became more frequent as she got older. He would visit her just about every night. He was a smart man and he was very careful not to leave visible bruises. Still, there were many occasions when he got carried away and it showed physically. When that happened, he would lock her in her room until she healed. Many times, he would drug her to help with the pain he had caused. Other nights, he brought Trayana in and would make them do unspeakable things. He tampered with the drawings every year to keep the two of them alive. He always justified himself by telling them that they were his gifts, promised from Draygon, for him. He convinced them that they should be grateful they were chosen. He told them that he was only allowed to have two girls at a time. He had them brainwashed into believing that he would kill their families and that they would be betraying the Dragons if they opposed him. He gave them just enough DB to keep them wanting more. That shut them up and numbed their minds. This all continued until Trayana outsmarted him. Lenala felt like she was watching everything unfold right in front of her. Kineah's thoughts and feelings were so vivid. When Trayana purposely had her name drawn in order to escape him, Kineah knew he would take his anger out on her, but how could she ask Trayana not to do it? How could she be mad at her for wanting to leave this prison? She deserved freedom, even if it meant Kineah would bear the consequences of her actions. Trayana didn't want to leave Kineah alone. She had even suggested that they take all of his DB and let him find them dead. Visions of Trayana pleading with her flooded Lenala's mind. Trayana had begged her to take the

DB with her, but Kineah was too afraid. She wanted to find her own way out. She held onto the small glimmer of hope that one day she could be free and with her sisters again. Trayana was so broken and wanted to escape him so badly that she gave up on protecting anyone else. She wanted out, and this was the only way she saw fit. She wanted to make him mad and she didn't care about the consequences for anyone else. No one else mattered anymore. All she wanted was to be rid of him.

After Trayana was sacrificed, Brantog was very angry. Kineah had expected that, but he had never been this angry. It was far worse than she imagined. He locked her away, beat her, and abused her. She knew she had made a huge mistake by not listening to Trayana. Guilt and regret hung heavily on her. The little bit of hope she had was smashed into pieces.

It was a long time before either of the girls could speak again.

After all of these years, no one in the castle suspected a thing. He had a perfect scandal going on. The girls were too afraid and addicted to DB to tell on him. The people either respected him too much or feared questioning his integrity. When the castle workers had blamed him years ago for questionable behavior, they were put to death and no one spoke of it since. The king was too afraid that the Dragons would hear of this and kill them all for treason. So, he chose to ignore it and kill anyone who knew about it. The king wanted to protect his little planet, and would do anything to keep himself in the Dragons' good graces, including turning a blind eye to the heinous accusations. Brantog was never accused again and the matter disappeared. Brantog came from a prominent family and was well-to-do. He was chosen to be the high priest and head of maintaining the pact with Draygon. He was sworn in and trusted with one of the most sacred jobs in Xuria. There was no getting rid of him in the king's eyes. If the king got rid of Brantog, it would raise too many questions. So, he decided to downplay it and leave it alone. Brantog played a wonderful part.

Lenala was overwhelmed by the knowledge she had just received. It left her weak and speechless. Farka's shield was not helping, because the grief was too much for her to bear. Finally, Lenala came to her senses. She knew now more than ever that he had to be stopped. She needed to act fast before he found his second replacement. She had to stop him before he continued taking out more of his anger on Kineah. Lenala needed time to think. She had to weigh out her options. But the longer she waited, the worse it would get.

What would she do with Kineah? She looked at her and felt a deep sense of responsibility for her. She barely knew her, but after seeing and feeling her most hidden thoughts, she felt like she was a part of her. She didn't want to leave her.

She stood and started pacing. "Kineah," she said gently. "Let me help get you cleaned up and into your bed. I am going to find a way to stop him and fix this. I have a lot to think about." Her mind was spinning as she spoke, and the words were just flying out of her mouth. Kineah was unsteady on her feet and taking slow steps. Lenala tried to help her but Kineah was too weak. Farka jumped up and lifted Kineah with her wing. She scooped her up, and helped her get into a hot bath. As Lenala carefully cleaned Kineah's bruises, her heart ached. Anger, hurt, and compassion were flooding through her. Kineah was in so much pain inside and out.

"Lenala, please, I need you to get my medicine from my top drawer," she said, wincing with each word.

Lenala quickly went to her drawers and found a small bottle of red liquid. She turned to Kineah, who was staring at her. "This? How did you get it?" she asked. Her eyes widened. She had never seen Dragon's Blood.

"Yes, Lenala, it's his fault. He got me hooked on it. He left it here by accident one of the nights. I only use it when he hurts me."

She groaned in pain.

Lenala ran over to her. "Kineah, please, is there anything else I can give you instead of this? I'm sure there are herbs or some other type of medicine I can find for you."

"Nothing else helps. Please, just give it to me. I just want to sleep and forget it all," she sobbed. Her eyes were weak and pleading.

Lenala's heart ripped open for Kineah as she handed her the bottle. Before she left, she made sure she was settled. She gave her one more hug and promised her she would do everything in her power to stop him. She carefully sneaked back through the castle to her room.

She needed to think. So much had happened in the past few days. She drew a hot bath and sank in, completely submerging herself.

She began to run ideas through her head. The options were pretty bleak. She could tell the king, but this posed a risk she was uncertain of. Would he believe her or would he have her killed like he did Larsen? Or she could tell the castle workers and rally a group with hopes of overthrowing Brantog and forcing him to step down. As she began to play with these ideas, she was quickly reminded that the fear of the king's wrath would prevent any of the castle workers from telling. The people were afraid of the king. They knew what happened to people who crossed him.

The reality of this situation was sinking in. She was in a very difficult scenario.

She thought back over the year, of all the strange dreams, the crying in the night, the dark auras and the unsettling feeling she couldn't shake. It all made sense now. Her heightened senses allowed her to pick up the feelings and the secrets, and to see the truth in the auras. She was beginning to understand her cursed gift more and more.

After much deliberation, Lenala decided. She would request a meeting with her father and the council. She would go alone, and surely her father would listen to her. Surely, the council whom she had known her whole life would believe her.

CHAPTER
NINE

He strained to focus as he opened his eyes. The pounding in his head was so severe, he could hardly move. He tried to move his hands and feet but they were bound tightly to a chair. The earthy, damp scent of old wood filled his senses and he immediately recognized where he was. He was in his parents' house, deep down in the wine cellar. His vision became clearer as he looked around.

Mina was tied to a wall in front of him, and she wasn't moving. He could see that she was bleeding.

His father and mother were standing nearby waiting for him to wake up. "What is going on?" Brantog demanded. "Let her down immediately," he barked.

"That is exactly what we have been asking ourselves," his mother said in a condescending voice. "Why don't you tell us what is going on? *She* certainly didn't want to talk," she said as she slapped him across the face and then pointed at Mina.

Her slap had lost power as she was a much older

woman now, but the anger was as strong as ever. His eyes blazed with fury as a boiling heat burned within him.

"You were trying to run away?" she continued. "With a whore?" Her lips curled into a snarl as she spoke, and with each word, a small spray of saliva escaped her mouth.

Her temper was something Brantog despised.

"What does it matter?" His eyes narrowed into slits. "I hate this place."

"Shut your mouth," his father jumped in, knocking his chair over and kicking him. "After all we have done for you? The life we have set up for you? You ungrateful swine." His father's kick had also lost power. Their age was showing, but Brantog acted like he didn't notice it and winced in pain.

He continued to pace around his room as he recounted the events of that night. These were the most painful memories and they came far too often. "Why can't I bury these?" he growled as he took another big sip.

"So, this little whore is worth throwing your entire life away for?" his mother asked, a sly smirk playing at the corners of her mouth.

"You are willing to disgrace yourself and your parents by risking people knowing that our son is a traitor?" His mother continued spewing words at him.

"After all of the training you have had and everything we have given you. You choose to commit treason by running away?" This time, his father was yelling at him. "Coward! We could have you hanged, and she will certainly hang for this," he said as he motioned toward Mina.

Those words pierced Brantog. He didn't want her to be blamed. Even though it was her mouth that got them in trouble, this was his plan and idea. She was just going along with it.

He looked at her slumped body against the wall. Flashes of anger shot through him. She was just a whore. How could he have let himself fall for her? Now they were both going to suffer the consequences of his weakness. *I am so stupid!*

"Do you love her?" His mother leaned in close to his face, her tone dripping with sarcasm as she asked the question.

Brantog scoffed at the question. "Of course not, Mother," he said, oozing disgust. "She is a companion and nothing more." Deep down, he believed what he was saying. He cared for Mina, yes, but he was quickly able to shove those feelings down. Regardless of what he did or did not feel, he didn't want her to get hurt.

"Well," she continued, dragging out her words, "we will see about that and we will teach you to never disrespect us again."

He was all too familiar with those words, the same ones that always preceded a beating. It didn't matter whether he had done anything wrong; his parents would find any excuse to vent their anger and frustration on him. There were times when they would return home from parties, drunk and high, and lash out at him without any reason.

He was a man now, living on his own and hadn't been

beaten in many years. But he was tied to a chair and defenseless.

His father slapped him. It was another weak slap.

His mother walked over to Mina and grabbed her by the face. "What are we going to do with you?" she said as she squeezed hard. "Such a pretty face," she said. "For trash." She laughed as she pushed her head away. Mina groaned and began to open her eyes. Her mouth was taped shut, but her eyes shot wide open as soon as she realized where she was. She immediately tried kicking her legs at Brantog's mother. She couldn't reach and this only made his mother laugh harder. "Oh, she is quite spirited. What to do, what to do," she said as she paced deliberately in front of Mina.

"Well, we can't have her running free and risk the people of Xuria finding out that she tried to sneak away. After all, we know she can't keep secrets." Her eyes fixed on Mina with a cold, hard stare.

"The only way to leave Xuria is if you are exiled, but you will not be exiled. No, you would like that too much." She stopped pacing and stood in front of her.

"Perhaps we could keep you as our slave," his father chimed in as he moved closer to Mina. "But then you would find a way to tempt my son to commit treason again, wouldn't you?"

As they looked back at Brantog, their eyes seemed to glow with a yellow tint in the dimly lit room. Their faces were twisted into menacing masks. They gave off such an overwhelming aura of wickedness that all he could see when he looked at them was ugliness.

His father picked up a piece of wood from the ground and slammed it into Mina's head. She screamed a muffled cry. Brantog tried to jump up and scoot back to his feet. The other leg of his chair broke off, making a loud bang. His father quickly came running over to him and whacked him on the head with the chair leg. The hit sent Brantog flying back to the ground. Had his father been younger, the hit would have knocked him out. He was dazed and unable to get up for a few minutes.

His parents took turns beating the girl. Blow by blow. Blood poured from her body and she had begun taking ragged breaths.

"You see what you made us do," his mother taunted. Brantog had tried to rise to his feet several times, only to be set back by more blows to the head from his father. This time, it was his mother who came to deliver the blow, but before she could swing, he countered and tripped her with his foot. She hit the ground hard, groaning loudly.

His father turned and came running to her aid. "What have you done?" he yelled. Brantog used every ounce of strength he had to hurl himself forward to tackle him. The chair broke off his body as he made contact and the ropes slid off. He stood quickly and hovered over them. They were both on the ground and for a moment, they looked helpless and pitiful. Their masks had faded and he saw their age showing through. A surge of anger ran through him, causing a flicker of fear to appear in their eyes as they looked up at him. Then, the sound of Mina's groaning filled the air, and he immediately rushed to her side. With a swift motion, he cut the ties that bound her arms and gently helped her down from the wall, laying her on the ground. He care-fully removed the tape from her mouth. She was bleeding badly all over and taking slow, shallow breaths. She was dying, he could feel it. He held her face in his hands. "Mina, stay with me."

He could hear their grunts as they struggled up off of the ground. It sounded like thunder as they ran toward him. Their voices were loud, but he ignored them. All he could do was look at Mina. His father reached him first and slammed a chair leg across his back. With a sudden burst of adrenaline, Brantog launched himself at his father, shoving him backward and causing his mother to fall again as well. As his father stumbled backward, he lashed out with the chair leg, catching Brantog across the cheek and leaving a deep gash. Brantog was thrown off balance, and he stumbled backward, crashing to the ground right in front of Mina, his face coming to rest just inches from hers. Despite the growing pool of blood around them, Mina's eyes still held a faint light. "I'm sorry," she managed to sputter out, her words barely audible.

Brantog gently brought her face closer to his, urging her not to speak in his desperation. Her mouth trembled slightly as he spoke. "I wish things could have turned out different for us, Mina," he whispered to her, his voice thick with emotion. As he spoke, her eyes softened. "May you find peace and the freedom you were looking for." Mina stopped breathing, and her face became still and lifeless.

Grief filled him as he lay there looking at her. His parents had recomposed and were still delivering blows, but he hardly felt it. He was in another dimension. She was gone and there was no more hope of happiness. He thought about giving up and letting his parents end his life, too. For a moment, he almost envied her. She was now truly liberated. Maybe this was the freedom he really wanted. Freedom in death. Suddenly, his thoughts were interrupted by his mother's laughing. "Look at him, lying next to her. He did love that whore."

Then it hit him—if he died, they would win. Those monsters he called parents would win. Anger began to rise in him. Heat burned in his chest and rage began taking over. The next blow he intercepted one-handed, and he sat up with it, shoving his mother back. She hit the ground, smacking her head on the hard floor. Once again, his father yelled and started to go to her aid, but Brantog jumped up and pushed his father down hard. He fell face-first then rolled over on his back. Both of them lay there breathing heavily. His father was struggling to get up again. He pushed him back down and put a foot on his chest. Glaring down at them, he said, "You did this. You could have let me go. You could have let her go. You don't need me. You never have. You never even wanted a son," he spat at his mother, his voice shaking with rage.

His mother looked up at him and let out a cold, heartless laugh. "My life would have been perfect if I had never had you." Her words stung like a thousand cuts, as he was consumed by a wave of darkness. The next thing he remembered was running off into the night.

He found himself deep in the foothills, hiding in a crevice and covered in blood.

He sat there for hours in complete darkness. He was confused and disoriented. His mind was racing as he tried to recall the events of the night. He knew he had killed them and he knew Mina was dead. All of their bodies were still there.

He had to make a plan to get out of this mess. He thought about running away but if he did, they'd hunt him down and charge him with murder. The king was too powerful. He could never be free. He could never leave. He lay in the crevice, under the night sky, and thought long and hard about what he was going to do. The look on Mina's lifeless face was ingrained in his brain. The pain was unbearable. How could he let this happen? He had let her die.

How had he been so weak to think that he could ever escape this place? The illusion of happiness had been a trap, and now he had to pay for falling into it. He let out a blood-curdling scream and buried his face in his hands. He sobbed until his breaths were ragged. He sobbed until he fell into a deep sleep.

Hours later, he awoke and crawled out from the crevice. The night sky was still upon him. As he stood there under the stars, a sense of heaviness settled over him. He faced a grim reality. He now had three people's blood on his hands. He vowed to never let himself be weak again. He would never let anyone control him like his parents did. He would never let his emotions control him again. He made his way to a stream nearby and submerged himself. The water was cold and stung his skin, but he didn't care. He stayed in the water until all of the blood washed off of him. He carefully considered his options. His only choice was to return home and lie that someone murdered his family and escaped. He was beaten up enough for them to believe that he was attacked. Then, he was going to find that friend of Mina's and make sure she never ran her mouth again. Period.

So, that was exactly what he did. The royal council believed him and in turn, he inherited all of his parents' riches, making him one of the wealthiest men in Xuria. He went on to finish his schooling and continued with the plan to be the high priest of the Castle of Nahkei. No one would ever know his secret. He buried it deep down and hoped it would go away. This was the life he was given. The life he never wanted. The life they chose for him. The life he tried to leave but it chose him anyway.

"Damn those memories," he growled, slamming the bottle of wine down on the table. He had never regretted killing his parents. They deserved to die after what they did to Mina and the way they raised him. His only regret was pulling Mina into his mess. He took a deep breath and looked at himself in the mirror. His face was dripping in sweat. He wiped his brow with one hand and looked down at the tiny bottle. He carefully opened the lid and placed his pinky inside. One drop was all he needed to drown the darkness out.

TEN

It had been only four days since she met with Kineah, but it felt like months. Her eighteenth birthday had passed, but she could not enjoy it. All she could think about were her recent discoveries. Her mind was consumed with thoughts of Kineah and Brantog. She felt like she was in a dark hole. Sadness and despair were taking over. She was on the brink of breaking down. She had taken on the full weight of the situation. She knew she was handling this wrongly. She knew she needed to do a better job of dealing with the emotional impact the brutal truths of life brought on her. She just couldn't yet. She had contacted her father two days ago, but just confirmed the meeting with the council today. Now she had to wait.

She sat in her room that night, trying to convince herself to get a grip. She knew the right things to say to herself. She knew all of the positive affirmations to encourage herself. These were the things that had worked before. It was just that she wasn't able to snap out of it. The emotional weight was too much. As she lay on her bed, she sensed a pull of energy from across the room. She turned her head and there was her sword glowing bright orange. Her eyes locked on it. She jumped up and ran over to it with a sense of urgency. As soon as her hand touched the hilt, energy began to transfer. She closed her eyes and relished the feel of the grip. The handle was warm and her hand wrapped around it perfectly. "Why didn't I get you out sooner?" She could have used it A LOT lately amidst all the stress. This was always one of the best ways to soothe her. Anytime she felt worried, she would practice with it, but today it was different. Instead of her going to the blade, it was summoning her. It was as if the sword knew she needed it more than anything else. She immediately felt the darkness pouring out of her and into the weapon. Almost automatically, she whipped it into a fighting stance and began to do one of her favorite drills. The more she moved, the brighter it glowed.

This drill was rhythmic and skilled. The movements were deliberate and powerful. Her feet moved with grace as she closed her eyes. She swept her sword through the air, stepping lightly from side to side. Gradually, she started increasing her pace and moving more quickly. She repeated the same drill over and over, faster and faster. Sweat began to form as she became lost in the movements. She soon forgot the troubles at hand as she focused on her sword. A long time passed before she stopped suddenly. Her head was now bowed and her sword lowered. It was glowing white. It felt as if the sword was reflecting her emotions. She'd kept it hidden for years, just as her grandfather instructed. She had only used it in the privacy of her own room. She opened her eyes. As she looked down at it, she felt centered and calm. She felt clarity and determination moving through her like the lava flowed from the volcanos. Slow and steady. *Escitalo*. The name came to her. It almost sounded like a whisper. The hair on her neck stood up as she repeated the name out loud. "Escitalo." It came from the ancient Dragon tongue and it meant *serenity*. That was her sword. It was her Escitalo.

The moment she had touched it, the calmness had begun working its way in. After days of turmoil, she felt rational and had peace of mind. After all of the thought and deliberation, she was finally ready. Her meeting was the next day.

She lay down and for the first time in over a year, she slept peacefully. No nightmares, no wailing or sadness. Just silence.

The next morning, she woke up knowing she was ready. Lenala left the castle of Nahkei before anyone else was awake and flew with Farka to her home on the Great Red Mountain.

The castle was a sight to be seen and the inside was even more spectacular. There were beautiful white marble floors as far as one could see. Such a stark contrast to the black exterior. The stairs were made with the same white marble with black stone rails and trimming. Two large statues of Dragons stood at the bottom—one on each side of the double stairs. The elaborate staircases led up to the living area of the royal family. The entire downstairs was divided into multiple areas for council meetings, dining, parties, and any royal to-dos.

She hadn't been home in over a year. It felt strange to her. The castle felt cold and hollow. A feeling of unease rushed through her as she entered what used to be her comfort zone. Now it felt foreign.It was unnerving. She didn't like feeling this way. Especially with what she was about to do.

Lenala was escorted to the great hall. This was where the council met. It all felt so formal. When she lived there, she roamed as she pleased. Now she was being ushered around like a stranger. "I wish you could come in with me," she said as she put her arms around Farka's neck, "but the council will frown upon it; business matters are all they are interested in." Farka snorted in reply. She didn't like being left behind, but she understood how things were.

Lenala waited alone in the room at first, and soon they began to trickle in. Before she knew it, she was seated in front of her father and his entire council. The room was very big and decorated with the finest furniture and tables. The furniture was dark and hand-carved by some of the best carvers in the land, and the floors were all white marble. Despite the beauty of it all, it felt cold and empty. It was just as she remembered from her childhood. She used to love hiding with her siblings behind the drapes and listening to the council debate.Now, at the age of eighteen, she was about to have the biggest meeting of her life in this same room.

The council members all stared at her, some with fondness and others with dark, cold eyes. Even the ones who looked at her kindly were hiding behind their masks. Their auras gave them away. They all had a yellow, hazy film that hung heavily in the air around them. There was evil lurking in their expressions. Although Lenala portrayed the perfect picture of calmness and confidence, she was trembling inside. She longed for Farka as she would help keep her calm. She placed her hand inside her coat. Escitalo was concealed. Just one hand on his grip would be enough to help. She sighed internally, her gaze fixed ahead and determined.

Her father sat at the head of the table perfectly poised. He was stiff, expressionless, and ready to hear what she had to say. "Lenala, why have you requested this meeting today?" Typical of the king to cut right to the point "This better not be another plea for joining the army." He smirked, obtaining a few snickers from around the table.

She had half expected something condescending from him and was not surprised. Rather, she was irritated. Remaining calm on the outside, she began. She had a full speech prepared and had hardly slept the last few days preparing it. "Father, mighty ruler of Xuria, wise council," she said, nodding and giving a proper slight bow. "As you know, I have been living in the Castle of Nahkei for the past year." Her voice was loud and her words were concise. "I have recently come upon some very disturbing information that is critical for you to hear." The king's expression darkened. "Well, get to it," he said, crossing his arms. He didn't have time to waste. He knew his daughter and knew she had a nose for trouble. "I have thought long and hard of the consequences of bringing this to light," she continued. "This information tarnishes the promise between the Dragons and the humans, and will be detrimental to our society if it is not dealt with now." A sudden shift in energy happened, almost throwing her off track with her speech. She looked closer at her father. He nervously glanced at the council and started slightly tapping his foot under the table. "If this information is not addressed, many lives are at risk," she continued. "I bring it to you and the council so that you may decide how to best deal with this situation."

Her opening speech caused a few eyebrows to rise.

"Lenala," he interrupted. "Choose your next words careful-ly," he said, dragging out his words. He sent her a push to let her know there was more to what he was saying.

She felt the push but it wasn't clear what he wanted. Was he trying to warn her? *He is not acting like himself. Why is he so nervous?* He was calm on the outside but she could see right through his tyrant demeanor. Then, she felt it. Fear. He feared what she was going to say. He was trying to stop her from continuing. She waited for a minute as her mind spun trying to figure out what he was trying to convey to her. *He must be afraid of the Dragons, but they will understand. It's not his fault that Brantog is doing this. If he deals with it properly, they may never even know,* she concluded before she continued. *He needs to know. The council needs to know. Even though they are evil, they will do the right thing if it means keeping peace with the Dragons.* She was certain of her conclusion. After all, this was her father and the council that had known her for her entire life. She took a deep breath.

"You all need to hear this: Our people are at risk. Bran-tog, the high priest," she continued, "has been abusing some of the Nahkei in the castle." She paused as her eyes moved across their faces. She could hear sighs and slight gasps. Some of the members began to shift in their chairs. She proceeded to explain all that she knew. "He chooses two girls around the age of fourteen. He keeps them until they are almost too old to be drawn, before they can be released. He has been tampering with the drawings to ensure certain girls don't get selected, so he can continue to use them for his own devious purpose." Every eye was on her. Her father sat there listening, but his eyes told her he was not happy. Another round of emotions hit her, relief. *Relief?* She was thrown off a little by that. But she didn't miss a beat. "Once they reach eighteen, he tampers with the drawing and has them selected. This way, they don't go back into the public. This information is true and I have witnessed it with my own eyes." She inhaled sharply, and as she did, she felt a huge burden lift from her shoulders. She knew she had done the right thing. Now, it was in the proper hands and she had hope that her father would believe her.

Just as soon as the burden lifted, she felt an intense rush of anger and disappointment coming from the king. Before he even changed expressions, she felt his emotions. He looked at her for a long moment, thinking about what to say next. Disappointment spread across his face. His words came out deliberately.

"This information will not leave this room," he started. "I cannot have childish fantasies being spread about my kingdom." He could never admit the truth. He almost laughed as he said it. "The accusations you make are blasphemous," he lied. "Brantog is a high priest. He is highly trusted and was chosen to fulfill the sacred duties."

Lenala felt as though she had been punched in the chest by his reaction. "I do not see how these claims you make are true."

"Father," Lenala interrupted, "I can bring you proof, one of the girls."

"You think I'd believe just one girl?" he quickly interjected. "For all I know, she could be lying just to get out of being a sacrifice." His eyes locked on Lenala's for a moment. "If you can produce *five* witnesses, then maybe I will listen." He already knew the answer. Of course, she couldn't find five witnesses.

"Can you do that? Do you have five?"

Lenala's stomach began to churn. She knew no one would admit to anything, for fear for their life. Rumors of Larsen's death were enough to scare anyone.

Her only witnesses were Kineah and Trayana. They had never told anyone except Lenala. "Father, I have only one witness, and myself."

"Then you have no case here," he laughed. "You will go back to the Castle of Nahkei and never speak another word of this. It's settled."

"Pardon my interruption, your highness." A tall beady-eyed woman stood up.

The king dug his fingers into his chair under the table as his heart rate increased.

"But do you remember what happened when Larsen the Anae made a similar accusation years ago?" Her voice was high-pitched and whiny. "Do you remember what had to be done in order to keep the peace and ensure the Dragons never got wind of this?"

"Of course I do," the king scoffed. "But you're talking about my daughter and I will not have her executed." His voice was low and threatening. "She will go back to the castle and this will never be mentioned again."

"But sire..." This time, a man stood. "We cannot take the risk. If she goes back to the castle and takes this any further, whether it be true or not, she could cause problems later. We cannot send her back to the castle. This is treason any way we look at it, whether she is your daughter or not." His eyes moved around the table as other members nodded in agreement. Lenala listened as her worst nightmares were playing out before her. "I make a motion to vote that she be executed," he continued. "For high treason against the Dragons and against the Castle of Nahkei."

A shuffle went throughout the room, with whispers and gasps, then a hush fell. Lenala's head began to spin. She certainly had not imagined it going this way. She felt a stabbing pain as she focused her gaze on her father. The pain was from him—he was torn and in turmoil. She felt a moment of remorse. *What have I done? Why did I even get involved?* If she was executed, she wouldn't be doing anything to help. If she went back to the castle, maybe then she could figure out a way to fix this. This may be her only hope. But there was a problem. They knew she would do just that. They could not risk letting her continue to dig around. Her father knew this as well, He knew the council would never agree to let her go back. She felt him stuff his emotions away. He was the king. He would not let his emotions rule him. Lenala's heart sank as he began to speak.

"We will vote," he said, breaking the silence. His fingers were still digging into the chair. "Those in favor of sending Princess Lenala of Xuria back to the castle, with firm instructions of never speaking of this again, raise your hand."

CHAPTER
ELEVEN

Many years had passed since he had been named high priest. He had become renowned and trusted by the king and the Dragons. Although nobody noticed, his dark past loomed heavily in the shadows. To everyone else, he was just a quiet and mysterious man, and he preferred it that way. He managed to keep his personal life to himself and stay in the background. His role in society had become somewhat of a silent one. He maintained the Castle of Nahkei but didn't have to do much. The castle was a well-oiled machine at this point. All he had to do was keep up his presence and make sure nothing got out of line. This life made for a lonely one, and a very private one. His heart had become hardened and filled with hatred. Hatred of his parents and hatred of himself. He loathed the fact that he let that situation happen. He could have gotten away if he hadn't been weak and let his guard down for Mina. He had never fallen for another woman after her. Falling for someone meant giving control to them. He never gave control away, just as he vowed the night she died. He kept his skills sharp but never had to use them. He practiced his footwork and weaponry nightly. He wanted to be ready for any situation at all times. His memories never let him rest. He sat in front of the fireplace, looking down at the glass in his hand. The liquid was a dark red and it moved gently as he swirled the cup. The rim of the glass felt cold in his lips as he savored the taste of the wine. He let out a deep sigh. Life had changed drastically over the past year. His mind drifted back to when it all started, at the most recent day of the Dragon.

It was morning, and the castle was buzzing with excitement. It was the day of the Dragon. The most sacred day of the year, when one of the little brats would be sacrificed. Also, the day when a new brat would join the palace. *Another one to tolerate.*

He referred to them as brats because he couldn't stand their childish ways. They all knew how to behave when he was around. If they misbehaved, his punishment was harsh. He would make them go without food in their rooms for days at a time. Or send them to the basement to be alone in the dark.

They quickly learned not to mess around with him, and that was just how he wanted it.

He splashed water on his face and looked in the mirror. He had aged. He was no longer a young man. He still had many years ahead of him, but he could see the lines forming on his face. His eyes were dark and hard. His long, black hair had begun to thin, so he cut it all off. His head was now shaved and slick. His limbs were long, lean, and muscular. His facial features were sharp. The scar on his cheek had faded over the years, but it was still there and prominent. The scar curved upward, giving him what looked like a permanent smirk. His arms, neck, and chest were tattooed with various symbolic markings telling his status. He was a good-looking man.

He was dressed in his finest robe. It was deep red with black trim. The length went all the way to the floor. He wore black gloves and black boots.

He must admit, he liked the way he looked. He felt in control. He hoped one of the younger brats would be chosen for sacrifice since they were so naive, and annoying. They were of no use to him at that age. He liked them a little older. Old enough to act like a woman when he needed one and old enough to keep their mouths shut when he was done with them.

Over the years, he had chosen girls he liked to call "his own" and had begun tampering with the drawings to ensure they were not chosen for sacrifice.

He would secretly visit them as often as he liked and do whatever it was that he felt like doing. He had developed a system that worked. Many nights when the drink and blood weren't enough to numb his pain, he would take it out on the girls. If he felt pain, he wanted them to feel it, too. When they felt pain, he felt better. He liked to make them hurt. He didn't care if they cried or screamed. Pain was all he knew and all he knew how to inflict. They were nothing but tools for him to release what was boiling up inside him. They were his until he tampered with the drawing so their names would be drawn. No questions asked. No secrets told. The Dragons would never know because the girls were too afraid of his consequences to ever tell. It was a flawless plan and had worked for years.

On the Day of the Dragons, the whole city came together to celebrate. It was quite a production. A production of ridiculousness, if you asked him.

The sound of musicians playing echoed all over town. The smell of different foods floated through the air. There were people lined along the roadways selling handmade trinkets, specialty food items, clothing and knick-knacks. The celebrations lasted from choosing day to sacrifice day. A five-day span that Brantog loathed every year. The smiles, the laughs, and the way people looked dancing around to the music was all buffoonery. They looked like fools parading about in their finest garments. All of the families of the girls were special guests at the castle on choosing day. Brantog knew neither of his girls would be chosen. He had already removed their names again this year as he had been doing since he chose them. Trayana had one more year with him and Kineah had two.

He had them both well-trained and would definitely be keeping them until they were eighteen.

He liked to keep them about a year apart in age. That way when one was gone, the other one could help train her replacement.

There they all stood, perfectly lined up. They were dressed in their finest red gowns. The people in the crowd smiled and whispered, in awe of how beautiful they looked. The girls were the stars of the show. All of this was a waste of time to Brantog. His mind was foggy and his head was pounding. While everyone else was having fun, he was miserable. He wanted to escape to his room. *It's just one day.* He told himself this every year. He hated his people. They were all fake. Just like his parents were. As he scanned the line of girls, his eyes landed on Princess Lenala. She had joined the Castle of Nahkei this past year. She was undeniably the most beautiful of them all. He had strongly considered bringing her into his private circle. She was just the right age, but there was something incredibly unnerving about her. Perhaps it was her Dragon, or the obvious fact that she was the king's daughter. He had decided she was not someone he wanted to get too close to. In fact, he tried to avoid her at all costs. He didn't like the way she looked at him. It was as if she was peering into him. He knew that look when he saw it. She was trying to read him. He was trying to read her as well, and it became a mutual subconscious standoff. He was a master at keeping up an impenetrable wall. He could see that she was pretty good at keeping up a wall herself. He was cordial with her but that was it. Something about her just didn't sit well with him. He couldn't put his finger on it but he didn't trust her. Despite his unease with her, if he played it right, the benefit of having the Dragon may be worthwhile. Her Dragon could become useful to him. Getting DB could be very difficult and risky. He had decided to give it more time. He needed to feel her out a little more. He continued to watch her for a moment. She was looking at her family. He could see a mix of emotions crossing her face as she looked at them. She was trying to hide those emotions, but he was too good and he saw right through it. *Hmm, interesting*, he thought. *She is angry with them.* His gaze trailed over to the royal family. He respected King Byreon. He had always been one of the only people he semi-trusted. Mainly because the king let him run the castle however he wanted and never bothered him. Even when the Anae named Larsen was suspicious of Brantog. He had caught wind of what was happening and had gone to the king. *That bastard*, he thought. He tightened his fists for a moment at the memory of Larsen. To Brantog's luck, neither the council nor the king believed that he would put the country at risk. Instead, they believed that perhaps the Anae had developed feelings for one of the girls and was trying to set her free by accusing Brantog of raping her. He was executed for treason.

If only they knew, Larsen didn't even like girls. A small smirk crossed Brantog's face.

When the accusations from Larsen came, the king sided with Brantog. He didn't really seem to care what was happening or if it was even true. He just didn't want it to be exposed. He was ruthless and would kill anyone who compromised Xuria's relationship with the Dragons. The king was terrified of the Dragons and never wanted to cross them. He would do anything to maintain his rapport with them. The thrill of pulling off what Brantog was pulling off made it all the more satisfying. The situation with Larsen had been a close one. He learned that he needed to be more careful and over the years, he had become very careful. He developed a system and it worked. He never visited them during daylight and most of the nights, he gave them DB. It helped to numb the pain so they wouldn't scream as loudly. It would also help them forget.

Trumpets sounded and drums thundered in the room, snapping his attention back to the present. His head ached and felt swollen. All of these people were draining every ounce of patience out of him.

It was time to draw the name. There was a large basin

full of small, folded papers. Each piece of paper had one of the girls' names written on it. Lenala was going to be drawing the name this year. It was a high honor to draw the name. After the royal song of Xuria was played, he would give her the signal. She would reach in, draw it out, and read the name aloud.

Why does the music sound off? Why is it taking longer than usual today? he thought. *Perhaps there is a new musician who is playing the wrong note. Or maybe it's all of the wine I drank last night.* Whatever it was, it was fueling his headache and making him more irritable. He took a deep breath and let it out. The drum roll finally ended and it was time to move into action. Brantog raised his hand, signaling Lenala that it was time. She stepped forward. She was graceful and elegant. The way she walked was confident and mesmerizing. She looked at him briefly before she reached into the basin. Her eyes were piercing as she nodded and turned toward the crowd. As soon as she turned her gaze away, he laced his fingers and squeezed them as hard as he could. Every muscle in his body tensed up. He covered it well but had to take several deep breaths before he could relax. *Maybe I need to back off of my dose,* he thought, remembering the generous portion of DB he had taken the night before.

Lenala began digging around dramatically, putting on a little show for the crowd. They loved it. He wanted to slap her for it. She pulled out the name and looked to Brantog for the nod of approval to announce the name. He nodded. She turned the card over and read the name aloud. For a brief moment, time stopped. Had he misheard? How could this be? His heart skipped a beat as adrenaline spiked through his veins. The families were all clapping and cheering. It felt like he was trapped in a room of mad people screaming. The girls and the staff were all congratulating her and laughing.

The drums playing seemed to match his heartbeat and made his head throb even worse. Sweat began pouring under his robe as he tried to make sense of what was happening. Then, it dawned on him, and he squeezed his fingers together again behind his robe. *They must have tampered with the drawing themselves. Those little devils.*

The pause only lasted a split second. He was so good at hiding his emotions that no one saw it. Now he had to present her to the crowd. He smiled charmingly, using a well-rehearsed mask, and motioned for her to step forward. "People Of Xuria," he started—the same words he said every year. "May I present to you our chosen sacrifice, Trayana."

As Trayana stepped forward, her gaze landed on him. She was smiling and looked happy. Their eyes locked for a moment. Then hers narrowed, and her chin lifted slightly. She had played him at his own game and won. Her eyes told him *I beat you.*

Everything inside him was screaming. He wanted more than anything to grab her by the neck and make her pay for what she had done.

How could she have pulled this off?

After Lenala moved away from the basin, he took that moment to nonchalantly dig around in the bowl. He began flipping the cards over one by one. They all had Trayana's name on them. *"That little whore,"* he whispered to himself as he stepped away from the cards.

A chill suddenly enveloped him, and he darted his eyes up. Lenala was looking right at him. She quickly averted her eyes. *What did she see? Did she notice me looking at the cards? Does she know? Has she been helping Kineah and Trayana? She better not have had anything to do with this or she will be sorry.* The pounding in his head was relentless. He shook it off. *That damn DB.*

He knew he was being paranoid. *There's no way she knows.*

Lenala casually moved away, talking and laughing with the girls. *I will keep a better eye on her. Just in case her nosey eyes have seen too much.*

CHAPTER

TWELVE

One by one, their hands rose, including the king's. *Only four?*

"Those in favor of alternative measures," he said, stressing the word *alternative*, "raise your hand." Seven hands rose quickly.

It felt like a kick directly to the gut as her mind ran wild. This couldn't be real. The majority of the council was voting against her. *Their own princess? Snakes!*

She felt a wave of guilt washing over her. Then there was sadness followed by immediate anger.

The king's emotions and hers were combining. She could feel what he was feeling, and she knew that he did not want this. She watched in horror as his face twisted into realization. He was outnumbered, frustrated and angry. He was quiet for a moment as he looked at Lenala. His expression softened for a split second before he turned his gaze back to the council. His face became tense and hardened again.

"I will confer with the queen," he said in a deep, rough

voice. He already knew exactly what she would say, but he needed her to back him up so he could override the council smoothly. Queen Nalana was in another engagement with some of the locals, and that was why she did not attend this meeting. "Someone fetch her immediately," King Byreon barked.

The snake-like man quickly obliged and hurried out of the room.

Minutes passed but it felt like days. There was a hush in the room. Every now and then, a whisper or a shuffle would echo through the room. Lenala wondered if this was even worth it. One side of her was saying that she should have kept quiet. The other side was contrasting and saying that she needed to do the right thing. *Damn being moral and damn this place*, she thought. Why had she risked her life for this? She should have stayed out of it. Her saving grace would be her mother, who would never allow an execution to happen. Lenala knew that if the queen didn't want something to happen, it wouldn't. She was strong-willed and had always known exactly how to get her way.

The thunder of footsteps approaching came to ear. They were quickly getting louder. Lenala could feel the presence in the room shift. The king went from masking his anxiousness to relief. The queen came in. She was poised and dignified. Her face was stern and her jaw was tight. She stood in front of the king with her arms folded tightly. "My King," she said, as she turned to address the council, "what is so important that could not wait until after my meeting?" She trailed off as soon as her gaze met Lenala's. There was an immediate change in her demeanor. Her eyes softened. She went from a dignified queen to a compassionate mother. This was something the queen had always been—a wonderful mother.

She ran to Lenala and embraced her tightly. Worry and concern swept over her face as she began to feel the tension in the room.

"My Queen," Byreon cautiously started. She released Lenala and turned to him, her eyes narrowed as she placed her hands on her hips. He proceeded to tell the queen of the contents of the meeting and the vote that was cast. He was careful with his words because he knew the queen could be temperamental, especially when it came to her children.

As the queen listened, her expression became dark. She deliberately folded her arms across her body. Her hands were starting to shake as she balled them up. She almost couldn't wait until he finished talking. *How could you even let it go to a vote?* she whispered through clenched teeth.

Just as the king expected, she exploded; "No one will lay a hand on my daughter and she certainly will not be executed," she said with a menacing expression. "I don't care what vote was cast. I will personally kill each and every one of you who opposes me. Along with your families," she said, pointing her finger in the faces of the council. The council members looked embarrassed and afraid. "Byreon, have you no spine?" she hissed at him. Her deep amber eyes were blazing.

Lenala was not shocked at the emotions her mother was feeling. She could feel her anger and hurt, but there was something else. She could feel the emotion as if it were her own. Her chest felt tight, sweat began to form on her back, and her heart rate was rising. It was Fear. *Why is she afraid? What does she know that she is afraid of?* She was the queen and her say was more powerful than the vote of the council. The fear became Lenala's as she continued to try to analyze her mother's emotions. "My Queen," the king said. His voice was low and his tone was sharp. "This is more than just a family matter. She has brought to us what would be considered treason for our whole country, and she has no witnesses. Rest assured, I will not execute my own blood," he continued. "I am overriding the vote and we will come up with a reasonable solution today." The queen's expression cleared as she unfolded her arms, but she gave him a look that said *you better figure something else out*. She was the only person who could change his mind or even reason with him.

He turned to the council. "Sit," he barked.

They sat, no questions asked. Everyone knew when the king was angry, you didn't push him. Lenala was sent to another room while they deliberated. She waited patiently and replayed the events of the day in her head. She had no idea of what to expect from them. All she could do was wonder what they were talking about.

She replayed the conversation with her father and the back and forth he had with the council. She thought of Kineah and Trayana as she sat there. They deserved justice. Brantog needed to be taken down. Reassurance began to help ease her mind. She knew she had done the right thing. She prayed a silent prayer that they would feel the same and bring Brantog the punishment he deserved. Time felt like it was dragging along. As soon as she started to get impatient, the sound of footsteps approaching jolted her out of her seat. She was ready to hear what they had to say.

All eyes were on her as she entered the room. She tried

to read their faces to get a feel for what she was about to hear, but she was quickly interrupted by her father. "Lenala, sit down. We have come to a conclusion," he said. His eyes were fixed and his brow was lowered. She sat, her heart thudding in her chest.

"You will leave the Castle of Nahkei and you will come back home. The only condition is that you must stay within the confines of the Great Red Mountain and you will never mention this again," he said, emphasizing the word *never*. "This will take effect immediately, and if you ever mention one word of this, you will be executed." His words were quick and emotionless, throwing her off-guard. "Or if this is something you do not agree with, you will be exiled immediately."

She was taken aback. There was a certainty in the air, a certainty that she would agree to these terms. They continued with the plans of how to remove her from the castle and what the story would be. Several ideas were being tossed around. The council chimed in with their thoughts. She had a sudden illness; she needed to help care for her family. Ideas were going back and forth; it was a whirlwind. They were so sure she would take the option to stay. Why wouldn't she? *Why wouldn't I?* she thought as she sat there listening. If she chose to be exiled, she could try to find a way to bring Brantog to justice, but she would risk not being able to save Kineah in time. *How can I leave her there knowing what he has done? I can't just leave her behind.* The consequences of honoring her convictions meant Kineah would continue to suffer at his hands. It made perfect sense to stay, to just be quiet and continue the life she had always known. She carefully weighed what was being said. If she stayed in the castle, she could still sneak around and try to get the evidence she needed. She would just have to be careful. *Yes, that may work.* On second thought, she knew her father would have her watched closely. She'd be a prisoner in her own home. She'd never be able to bring any type of justice to Kineah and Trayana like this. *There has to be another way.*

"No," she said suddenly, interrupting everyone in the room. Silence fell upon the king and council as they looked at her. She was convinced that she had done the right thing and that she would find a way to shut down Brantog somehow. Even if it had to be by herself.

She hadn't planned on saying anything; the words just came out. "I cannot live in hiding and secrecy." She stood up as she spoke. Everyone looked shocked. "I know what I know and if you give me time, I can prove it without causing any problems. We can work together to make sure this remains a secret. You have my word," she said, carefully observing their reactions. "Please, give me a chance to get the witnesses. I just need time." She was pleading and she hated to beg. But she knew she needed to; it was her only chance. "If we ignore this, he will continue to hurt the innocent and put our entire planet at risk." The room was still silent. "You can't keep killing the ones who are exposing Brantog," she said. Her father's eyes darkened and his brow lowered even further, but she didn't care. "Maybe you made a mistake with Larsen, but it's not too late to fix it now," she pleaded.

"This, Your Highness, is what we cannot have," the snake man said, emphasizing each word as he stood up. The others mumbled in agreement.

"She cannot prove this. It is too dangerous."

The queen interjected, cutting her eyes at the man. "So,

what do you propose?" she asked. "Do we just let it go? We continue letting innocent girls get hurt?" Her voice was strong and steady. "We allow him to betray the Dragons' treaty while we sit in silence?"

"My queen," Byreon said, "I will investigate this on my own, and find out the truth." *A lie.* Lenala felt the deceit in his words.

"But until then, Lenala, you will be confined to the castle grounds." Lenala knew she would never be able to prove this if she were confined to the castle. He was lying. She knew it without a doubt.

"No, Father," she said defiantly, "I will not sit back and let this continue. We must work on this now, together."

"She leaves us no choice, Your Highness," the snake man hissed.

"My King, we must exile her. She is a danger to the safety of our planet," several of the council agreed in unison.

"Lenala, please." Her mother's voice had changed from stern to high-pitched as her eyes darted back and forth between Lenala and the council. Her strong, beautiful features looked so soft and vulnerable.

"You know what a grave danger this has presented to our people. If the Dragons knew of this, they would destroy us and everything we have worked for."

"Mother, how can you ask me to sit back and be in silence? You and father both taught me to stand up for what I know is true, and now you are asking me to do the opposite. I understand the risk. But the risk of being caught by the Dragons is not worse than what he is doing. What he is doing is horrible. He is diabolical. If only you could see what I saw."

Suddenly, she felt a resolve, a strange calm passing over her as she realized what she needed to do.

She scanned their faces as she began to speak.

"I choose to be exiled," she said calmly. *I will find justice for the Castle of Nahkei one way or another,* she thought.

"So be it," said the snake. "She has made her choice."

Byreon slammed his fists into the table, his eyes narrowed as he looked at the man, who quickly looked down. "Lenala," the king said quietly. There was no sparkle in his eyes. "You are my daughter and I do not want to send you away. Please reconsider my offer." Lenala studied him for a moment before she answered.

"I have made up my mind."

"Sometimes you are too much my daughter," he said, barely holding eye contact with her. "You have one chance, stay and be silent or go."

As she looked around the room, all she saw were corrupt and wicked faces. She knew who she was dealing with. The same faces who executed Larsen and the others.

She would leave. She would find a way to expose Brantog and get rid of him altogether.

THIRTEEN

The conditions of Lenala's exile were discussed. The exile would be that very night, done in secrecy. She would be allowed to take personal belongings and of course, Farka. She would have to sneak out of Xuria without being seen by any guards or other Xurian citizens. It was imperative that the people did not know the truth. They had decided that they would tell them a story of how she was sent away to another planet to get medical attention. They would say she had an illness that the Xurian herbalists could not cure. Lenala was skeptical that the people would buy this. The king never let people leave Xuria. She could only think of a couple of cases when he approved someone leaving Xuria, and that was years ago. But she was the princess, and who was really going to question the king?

She was not to return to the Castle of Nahkei. She was taken back to the Great Red Mountain, to her old room to gather some things. She changed out of the gown she was wearing and put on the clothes she used for outside activities. Dark pants and a tank top. She wasn't taking much—Escitalo, some clothes, a few supplies, and a bag of food her mother brought her. She wiped the tears from her eyes as she looked around the room. She hadn't even been in this room for over a year, and she would likely not see it for a long time, if ever again. Lenala only got to say a real goodbye to her mother. The queen was strong but could not hold back the tears. She begged her to stay but deep down, she knew she would not. "You are your father's daughter," she said as she wrapped her arms around Lenala, squeezing her tightly. "But I know you will do the right thing and if this is what you feel you need to do, then so be it. Where will you go?"

"I don't know, Mother."

"Please find a way to send word to me once you find a place to go. There are many planets you can settle on. Just follow the roads toward their glow. Farka will protect you and lead you to safety." Lenala knew she said those words to reassure herself more than anything. Sadness, anger, and pity filled Lenala as she hugged her mother for the last time. She could not blame her. After all, she had tried to convince her father and the council. Nightfall was upon them. It was time for her to go. She was taken out to a covered carriage. She would be smuggled out by one of the king's most trusted men. Much to her surprise, it was Semian. She hadn't seen him in over a year. Of course, he didn't know the real details of why she was leaving—he had been fed the lie. She and Farka got into the carriage and lay down.

The journey to the border was a long ride. They had to make haste because they wanted her to be gone before sunrise.

As she lay in the back of the small carriage, she began to recount everything that had happened that day. She still could not believe how it all took an unexpected turn for the worse. Although she was frightened and concerned about abandoning Kineah and leaving her to further suffering, she knew she had no choice. Even if it meant not being able to save her. The only way to bring Brantog down and stop him from abusing any more girls was for her to leave Xuria.

Now here she was alone and being exiled. She let out a big sigh as she rubbed Farka's head. "It's you and me, girl. We will find justice."

Time was passing slowly when the carriage came to a sudden halt. "Don't say a word," Semian said in a low voice. The sound of footsteps crunching in the dirt was getting louder. They were guards. *They must be the guards of the border.*

"What business do you have here?" a gruff voice demanded.

"I am on private matters of the king, and I have his permission to pass through," Semian replied calmly.

"Do you have papers?" he retorted.

"Of course I do; I am with the royal guard," Semian said.

"Well, hand them over," the gruff man demanded with a snarl.

Semian obliged. The man took his time reading them. Then he eyed Semian. "You have a sick person in the back, eh?"

"Yes, I do. I am on strict orders from the king. Now please move so I can be back in a timely manner." He sharply gestured for the man to move as he repeatedly tapped his foot on the carriage.

Farka began to get fidgety, as she always did when she sensed danger. Lenala calmed her. "Easy, we are almost through."

"We have been dealing with an increase of citizens trying to sneak out, and in order for you to continue, I will need to search your carriage," the guard stated with a tone that said this was not a question.

Lenala squinted to see through the cracks of the carriage as she sent soothing energy to keep Farka still. Farka was too big to move around without them being noticed. The second man spoke up. He sounded younger than the gruff man. "Sir, we need to search your carriage or you cannot pass through. What do you care anyway? It's just a sick one. What, are you dumping them off at the edge to die?"

"You have no right to search my carriage," Semian retorted.

"Ok then, we can do this the easy way, or the hard way," the guard said flatly, narrowing his eyes at Semian. Semian raised an eyebrow and a small smirk formed on his face. These were new Hite, guarding the border. He remembered his time as a border guard. He'd advanced quickly and now was one of the most elite Hite. Neither of the men said anything. "So be it," he said, no longer hiding the fact that he was losing his patience. He stood up, showing his size and stature. He was a large man, in his mid-twenties. He had the typical bronzed skin and thick, black braided hair of the Xurian men. His tattoos quickly showed his ranking in the army and the two men cowered back. With a thud, he landed in front of them. Lenala held her breath as she watched. Her heart was pounding. He was standing in a warrior's stance, hand on his sword and ready to draw. It was dark out, and the light from the guards' torches made their faces look like twisted monsters. Flashes of fear and excitement lit their faces. They were both part of the king's army and skilled Hite, but she could tell they were not as experienced and certainly not as decorated as Semian. They were strong and looked like typical warriors. The king's army was large and these men were not familiar to Lenala. Although he was outnumbered, she knew his style and knew he could easily handle them. She let out a sigh of relief. Just as soon as she assured herself he would be fine, another Hite approached from the shadows. He stood behind Semian, and now he was surrounded. Lenala's body tensed up as she watched. Their swords were drawn. The swords of the Hite were lightweight and swift. They were made of steel and forged in volcanic lava. They were long and slender, which made them easy to whip around in a fight. The handles were thick enough to get a good grip. They were the strongest swords in Xuria. Each soldier was granted one upon graduation from training. Every sword was handcrafted and carefully made. Each sword was rumored to carry a part of the soldier's soul, and to keep a part of any soul it took. Semian lurched forward, quickly taking out the younger man. *That was easy*, she thought as she watched him withdraw his sword and regain his stance. The gruff man and the other guard circled Semian. They began to fight, and it looked like a dance, forward and backward. Side to side. Semian was in the middle, methodically swinging his sword and calculatedly blocking hits. Slices and stabs coming from Semian, grunts and groans coming from all three of them as they continued to fight. His footwork was flawless. They were gaining on him in one minute then retreating the next. Semian was a force to be reckoned with when it came to fighting, and Lenala knew this firsthand. She had seen him fight many times. He had been a huge part of her many lessons in secret. Suddenly, the gruff man swooped and swung his sword at Semian's feet, causing him to jump back, right into the other guard's grasp. Letting out a sinister laugh, the guard pinned him on the ground. The gruff guard stepped in, raising his sword high. The sword was glowing red and shining on the man's crazed face. Lenala's mind was racing. She needed to act quickly.

"Stay here, Farka, wait until I call you," she whispered. Farka snorted and stirred anxiously. She wanted to fight but Lenala didn't want her to get involved unless it was absolutely necessary.

She quickly grabbed Escitalo. As she wrapped her fingers around the grip, a surge of energy shot through her. This was a sword she knew so well but a sword she had never used in public. She had only used this sword in the privacy of her room. Nobody even knew she had it. She closed her eyes and saw her grandfather's face, and she smiled at the memory of him. He had given her this sword on his deathbed. She could still remember his words. He told her to hide the sword from everyone and learn to use it. He told her that one day, she would use it for the good of Xuria. He told her that she was the chosen one to have this special sword. He said she was gifted and would bring about great change. He told her the sword was a gift from the Dragons. It was made with Dragon's Blood, making it invincible and giving it special powers. Powers that she had not yet unlocked. She never fully understood what he meant but she knew it was important, and as she held the sword, she knew she was ready for this moment.

She carefully got up and sneaked around to the side of the carriage, deciding the element of surprise would be best. Farka was shuffling around. "Shh, I'll let you know if I need you." Raising her sword high, she felt elated. The moonlight radiated off it, giving off a beautiful light blue aura. She jumped out and began swinging quickly at the gruff man. Just as soon as she swung the sword, a vision flashed before her eyes. It startled her because although it wasn't her memory, it felt real. She could see her sword and everything that was happening at that moment, but it was very distant, like she was in a daydream. She could see the men lying on the ground dead, in pools of blood. The heat of the blade shot up her arms. The intensity smacked her in the face. She snapped back into the present.

Startled at the sound of her approach, the man spun, but as soon as he saw her, he began to smile. "What do we have here?'' he asked. "Isn't she a pretty thing?" He dragged his words out. "Well, won't this be fun? Perhaps we should have some fun with her before we kill her, eh?" he said as he nodded at the other man, who was still wrestling with Semian. "A young beauty like you should not go to waste" His eyes moved up and down her body. Semian continued struggling with the man who had him pinned. He was on Semian's back with his legs wrapped tightly around him. Semian's sword was out of reach and the man was trying to suffocate him with his arms, squeezing them around his neck. He watched Lenala helplessly. His body was drenched in sweat. He wanted to protect her, but he couldn't.

"You've probably never had the pleasure of a man

before, have you?" the guard continued taunting Lenala. "Well…" He paused for a moment. "I can't say it will be a pleasure, at least not for you." He smirked as he stood there.

"A man of many words," Lenala stated coldly. She felt rage overtaking her and flowing down into her sword. She lunged, clashing with him. Escitalo was now glowing bright red, matching her anger. Suddenly, there was a shaking and vibrating in the ground. It felt as if a wave of thunder passed beneath their feet. Lenala felt rage. It was coming from Farka. "Farka, stay," Lenala commanded. Just at that moment, Semian used the momentum from the ground moving, and managed to break the grip around his neck to free himself from the guard. They both scrambled to their feet. He grabbed his sword and they began fighting again. Lenala was strong and well-versed with a sword. She was much smaller than the man and was able to work her way in close to him. She had never killed a man before. She had never even been in a real fight but somehow, her mind was clear. She had tunnel vision as she gained ground on him. She lunged one more time just as another vision popped into her mind. The blade was buried in the enemy's stomach, leaving him dead. She blinked fast and didn't even think twice as she drove her weapon into his stomach. She drove it inward and upward, feeling the rage leaving her body and transferring through Escitalo into him. There he was just like in the vision. She looked him in the eyes. She flung him down to the ground and stood over him.

His eyes were wide. As he gasped for his last breaths, "Princess?" he asked, realization spreading across his face.

Lenala looked down at him. "You got one thing wrong,"

she said. "It *was* a pleasure, at least for me." She would never forget the look on his face as he drew his last breath. The look of defeat. She withdrew blood-covered Escitalo as the adrenaline rushed out of her. Chills tingled up and down her spine as she saw the same picture before her that she had seen in the vision. She closed her eyes and whispered, "May Draygon guide your soul." The metallic sound of the blade sliding into its sheath echoed in the silence, amplifying the weight of what she had just done.

Her heart was pounding in her chest, and her hands were shaking as she tried to process the situation. She couldn't believe that she had taken a life, even if it had been in self-defense and to save Semian. The thought of wiping out someone's existence, of taking away their hopes and dreams, filled her with an overwhelming sense of guilt. Tears welled up in her eyes. She knew that for the rest of her life, she would have to live with the memory of what had just happened.

She took two steps back and collided with Farka, who was standing behind her. Her wings were completely expanded. She had been waiting for the right moment to step in. She turned and embraced Farka, who wrapped her wings around her to comfort her. "Are you okay?" Semian asked, placing a hand on her shoulder.

She looked up at him. "I don't know." Her voice trembled slightly. "I killed that man."

Semian nodded. "I know this is hard for you, especially since it's the first time you've taken a life," he said. "It's normal to feel guilt and sadness."

She nodded. "I just can't help feeling that there might have been another way," she said, her voice filled with uncertainty. "Maybe I could have done something differently, avoided the situation altogether." Her voice trailed off.

Semian's gaze never left hers. "You have to remember that you acted in self-defense." His words gave her comfort. "Thank you," she said quietly.

"You did what you had to do to protect yourself. There's nothing wrong with that, and you saved my life," he said. "Quite impressively," he added.

"Well, you taught me," Lenala said. "What was I going to do, let them kill you?" She laughed a little, feeling the weight lifting from her shoulders.

"I thought you were sick," he said.

"Something like that," she sighed. "It's nothing you can catch from me and it won't kill me anytime soon." She hated that she elaborated on the lie, but it was better this way. If he knew the truth, he'd be in danger.

"Where did you get that sword?" he stuttered.

She looked down; it was pulsing and still glowing white within the sheath. "It's something my grandfather gave me," she mumbled. She had felt that same feeling of being drawn to it that she felt the other night. She knew she was connected to it in a strange way. "Now you have a piece of a soul," he said. "That's nothing to take lightly. It means you are a Hite. And Farka, she was incredible. You should have seen how she stood behind you with her wings spread out and her head down, just waiting for you to show one sign of need." Lenala looked at Farka, forever thankful for such a gift. Farka knew her better than anyone else in this world did and was fiercely protective of her. Semian looked at Escitalo again. "You will become one with your sword more and more over time," he said as he sheathed his own sword. "I owe you a debt, Lenala," he said in a low voice. He walked over to her. His expression was blank as he leaned in and put his forehead on hers. His smell flooded her senses. Despite the fact that he had just battled for his life, it was intoxicating. She was frozen for a split second. *What is he doing?* Then he pulled her close and kissed her deeply. As soon as he touched her, a rush of emotions flooded over her. She felt fear, confusion, and compassion rushing out of him and into her. "Thank you," he said, sighing heavily as he pulled his head back, looking into her eyes.

For a moment, she was paralyzed—he was mesmerizing, a whirlwind continued to sweep over her as she tried to recompose herself. She had just killed a man and now, she was flooded with feelings that she didn't even know she had. Let alone for a man she had known her whole life. She had never seen this passionate, softer side of him. She pulled back farther. "You're welcome," she stuttered.

He turned away and began to look over the bodies. All business again. "We need to take care of the evidence."

They decided they would dump them outside the border, where it was likely no one would find them.

Semian would make up a lie about there being no guards around and leave it at that.

After another hour of them hiding the bodies, Haruelio was starting to rise in the distance. Semian needed to leave.

"Lenala," he said as he put his hands on her shoulders and leaned in close. His dark eyes took her breath away and gave her a sharp wave of butterflies. "If you ever need to get word home or if you need help, do your best to find a way to get a message to the Murkes. They know how to get in and out of planets without being detected and they can contact me directly."

She nodded. "How will I find one?"

"You will have to be careful but if you search, you can find them. Remember, I owe you," he said, looking at her somberly. "Please be careful and may Draygon watch over you."

Lenala stood there as he rode away. Reality hit her. She would be in the Hamanan Galaxy for the first time ever, alone. She had never been far away from Xuria and when she did leave, she had to sneak.

The galaxy could be a dangerous place but she had Farka. She looked back one more time. Here she was officially exiled from her homeland.

FOURTEEN

Lenala knew of only one place that she could go, and that was Danix Point. This was the place she and her siblings used to sneak to when they were younger. They flew there on their Dragons. No one else traveled there because it was too far to risk getting caught, and too dangerous to go on foot. It was a small, beautiful planet hidden in the in-between that they had learned about from stories of the times when Xurians had no home. They had stayed there for a small period of time before they found Xuria. Her brother found it when they were young and it quickly became their secret place. They used to sneak out of Xuria together and stay for hours. The king never knew his children were sneaking out of Xuria. Interplanetary travel was forbidden. Danix Point wasn't far away and she knew it would be a safe place for them to stay while she created a plan.

"Ok, Farka," she said, letting out a big breath. "Let's go." Farka was an excellent flier. She had big, strong wings that allowed her to move very fast and make accurate turns. She loved to fly and could carry a lot of weight. She liked to play around when she flew. She would go up as fast as she could then dip and make sharp turns. If she was alone, she would spin until she was dizzy. It was a spectacular sight. Farka lowered her head so Lenala could climb onto her back. They had done this so many times. Lenala loved to fly just as much as Farka. There was no greater freedom she had ever felt than that of flying. As she climbed up and got in the ever-familiar position on Farka, she closed her eyes, relishing her favorite part. Farka began to trot and gain speed. Then she spread her wings and began to gallop as she flapped them with each stride. The sound of the wind pushing under her wings and the feeling of her taking off were magical. Gravity played no role as they sprang into the air. Lenala held on with her legs and her hands as she gripped tightly to Farka's neck. For a moment, she forgot about what she was leaving and what she may be facing. She felt only bliss. The wind rushed through her hair as they climbed higher and higher. The sound of Farka's wings beating was almost deafening but she loved it. Nothing mattered when they were in the air. Every thought and every worry succumbed to the joy she felt. Part of it was Farka's happiness. She loved to fly so much and Lenala could feel it. A magical experience was created as their happiness bounced back and forth between them. If only this feeling could last forever. Soon they reached the elevation where it felt like they were gliding. She opened her eyes and she relaxed her grip on Farka. The sky was bright with the colors of the stars and the glowing planets far away.

The path to Danix Point was one they knew very well, and it wasn't long. With the right wind conditions and lighting, it would only take about thirty minutes to fly there. Luckily, Farka flew fast and powerfully. Haruelio was just starting to rise and the light began to spread around them, revealing the land beneath. They were flying over the Outer Path, which was known to be treacherous. It was mostly dark and unkept. Especially the stretch near Xuria. It was very rarely traveled. There are different types of creatures that lived there. Some of them were dangerous. She was thankful they could fly over it. Once again, she thanked Draygon for giving her Farka.

Before long, Danix Point came into view. The light of Haruelio radiated around it, giving the planet a beautiful purple, hazy glow. So many happy memories of coming here flooded her mind. Memories that seemed far away and so lost. Soon, she and her Dragon arrived. Farka landed gracefully and lowered her head so Lenala could slide down to the ground. She felt a sting of bittersweetness as they landed. She took in the beauty; it was just as she remembered. The grass was green, and the trees were tall and flourishing. There were colorful flowers every-where. The smell of the wildflowers rushed her senses as the warm breeze blew across her face. She had always loved it there. To her, it was an escape, a sanctuary in the middle of nowhere.

She made her way to one of the small huts the Xurian nomads had built for themselves many years ago. It was the one she and her siblings always used.

It was still in perfect condition. *Too-perfect condition,* she thought. Her eyes narrowed as she got closer. *Who has been here? Perhaps the prince?* Something felt unsettling as she walked around checking out the grounds.

Nevertheless, she would stay there and get some rest. It

was her only option. At least until she figured out what she was going to do. She made her way to the little bedroom and lay down. Before she knew it, she had drifted off to sleep, a deep and restless sleep. Semian's passionate kiss, swordfights, and ravenous creatures ran through her mind.

Hours had passed when suddenly, Farka jumped up, jolting Lenala from her sleep. "What is it, girl?"

Farka bolted to the door. She didn't seem scared, but rather excited.

She ran outside, jumping around happily. Lenala was baffled. Farka never acted like this. What had come over her?

Suddenly, darkness spread around her. She turned her head to the sky and saw a huge shadow descending upon them. She quickly grabbed her sword. Heat flowed from her hand into the blade. The rush of power from Escitalo surged through her. She glanced down and saw that it was glowing again. The rays from Haruelio blocked her view for a moment as the giant shadow got closer. Her eyes widened as she gasped. It was Onepa, her sister Anala's Dragon. Onepa was the sibling of Farka. They were the same size, but different colors. Onepa's scales were a light creamy shade while Farka's were bronze.

Lenala sheathed her sword and laughed.

Onepa landed and before her head was lowered completely, Anala came jumping off. Lenala rushed over to her and threw her arms around her. She had not hugged her sister in over a year. Her familiar smell flooded Lenala with memories and made her long for the old days. Back when they had no cares in the world. Anala had grown even more beautiful over the past year. She had just turned sixteen. Their birthdays were only days apart. She stretched out her arms, putting some distance between herself and Anala so that she could get a better look at her. The ache of missing her sister was almost unbearable. As soon as she laid eyes on her, she sensed a flicker of emotion before it was quickly concealed. Lenala's body tensed, her brow furrowing with concern.

"What are you trying to hide from me"? she asked. Even though she hadn't been around her sister for quite some time, she knew her well enough to sense that something was wrong.

"Lenala, stop that," she said. "Stop trying to get in my head. This is about you, not me," she said with a frown.

She felt her shield go up even further. Anala knew how to block her sister from reading her but Lenala wasn't buying it. "You are doing something dangerous, aren't you?" she asked, looking into her sister's eyes.

"Lenala, please. I promise you I am being careful." There was hesitation in her voice as she studied her sister's face. Then she let out a big sigh. Lenala would keep pressing until she broke through the wall. "I met a boy. That's all. I'm just having a little fun with him before I go to the Castle of Nahkei," she said dismissively.

"A boy?" Lenala echoed. "From where? Does anyone know about him? You've been meeting him here, haven't you?"

"Please, it's nothing. I met him once when I was playing around in the Inner Path."

Lenala gasped. "Wait, you mean he's not Xurian?"

"No," she said as she raised her eyebrows. "He is

Pitian." A smile spread across her face. "And he is the prince." Lenala let out a heavy sigh. The look on her sister's face told her it was too late to try to stop her. Anala was just as stubborn as she was. "Oh Lenala, stop being so dramatic," she said, laughing. "We've already called it off. We both have our duties to uphold, and we know we can't take any more risks. Especially with me going to the Castle of Nahkei next month."

Lenala hesitated for a moment. Usually, she would take this as a challenge and get all the information she could, but she was emotionally exhausted and would have to work very hard to pry any further. "Just promise me you aren't doing anything to jeopardize yourself and that you won't see him anymore," she said. She couldn't help but be worried. Anala could get into a lot of trouble with the king and the Dragons. Not to mention, being in the Inner Path alone was dangerous. Anala wasn't skilled with any fighting or weapons. *At least she has Onepa*, Lenala concluded.

"Already done," Anala said.

"Ok so, what are you doing here and how did you know I was here?" Lenala gushed out.

They went inside the cabin as Anala proceeded to explain that she had eavesdropped on the meeting and heard the whole thing. She had been worried sick about her sister, and she came as soon as she could sneak off. "I brought you some supplies," she said as she pulled several items out of a large bag. "I wasn't sure if you packed anything." She handed Lenala a sack filled with food.

"Mother packed me a bag of food, but I will need as much as I can get. I don't know where I am going and Farka needs food, too. Thank you."

Her sister let out a deep breath as her face relaxed. "Ok, good, well I want to help you make a plan. We can figure this out together and bring Brantog down," she said as she began pacing. Her voice was stern. "I've been thinking that as soon as I join the castle, I will find witnesses and secretly gather evidence."

Lenala listened to her as she kept going. Everything she said was with absolute resolve. As thankful as she was to have a sister who was on her side, true to her word, and perfectly capable of doing anything they needed, Lenala feared for her sister's life. "If you get caught, you will be in my shoes, or maybe even worse. I need you to stand by and wait for my word. I will contact you as soon as I have a plan."

Anala sucked her teeth and scowled at her sister. "I want to do more than just wait for your word. I want to help you make a plan. In fact, I was thinking, why don't you go to Analicia? It's the most populated planet in our galaxy. Maybe you can get some help," Anala said. "Then you can come back and set things straight."

"I wish it were that easy," Lenala sighed as she plopped onto a chair. She knew that would be too difficult, as the Xurian army was a force to be reckoned with, and no other planet would agree to help her with such a small matter. Most of the other planets were afraid of Xurians. She'd never stand a chance.

"Maybe I can set up a meeting with the Dragons," she brainstormed out loud. "I could tell them what is happening. But..." She paused before she continued. "If I do, it will be the end of Father, and I don't think I can do that. I don't even feel right praying to Draygon right now. Anala sat down, her brow furrowed. Lenala stared out the small window inside the cabin.

"I have to find a way to kill Brantog myself. Undetected, you know? I'll make it look like an accident."

"How?" Anala asked.

"What if I were to go to Analicia and find a potion that could kill him?" She felt a sudden rush of excitement. Maybe that would work. Analicia was known to take in people from other planets. If there was any hope of her getting into a planet, it would

be there.

"Yes," Anala said, "that might work. It will be risky but I think you can do it." Anala sat there for a moment thinking. Then she stood. "You will have to find a Murke to communicate with me and to let me know any updates."

The Murkes were the only secret way to get messages back and forth. They were interplanetary dwellers who knew their way around the galaxy. They knew the Inner and Outer Paths like none other and knew how to sneak onto every planet undetected. They could turn invisible in an instant. They could also disguise themselves to blend in with the locals. These traits made them the perfect option for smuggling goods, sending messages, or sneaking around the galaxy. The only problem was finding them. One had to know where to look or know someone who did. They were very elusive but would do just about anything for the right price.

They mainly lived in the hills of the Outer Path. They kept to themselves unless they were needed or looking for work. A lot of times, they immersed themselves in different planets and listened to gossip, news, and anything they could get their ears on. Sooner or later, someone would need a Murke and the information they had.

The two sisters sat discussing her plan. A feeling of dread hung in the air. This was going to be a tough task that could take a while to complete. Neither of them knew when they would see each other again or what may happen in the meantime.

The day was coming to an end and Anala had to leave before it got dark. She needed to get back into Xuria safely and undetected. They bade each other farewell.

As Lenala watched her sister and Onepa fly away, she felt a pang of sadness overtake her. She and Farka watched them until they were out of sight. Farka sat with her wings limp and her head low. Once again, they were alone.

"Come on, Farka," she said, rubbing her head. "Let's get some sleep. We have a long journey tomorrow."

Morning came in what felt like seconds. Lenala awoke with adrenaline. She was rested and motivated to get to Analicia and find the poison.

This plan may just work and she felt good about it.

Analicia was a well-known planet in their galaxy, and very sophisticated. She had only heard stories from Hivey and learned about it in her studies. Xurians were never allowed to visit other planets, and kept their culture private from everyone else. Most of this stemmed from their origin on Xuria—many of the other planets had given them the cold shoulder while they were nomads.

Excitement and nerves ran through her body.

She and Farka said goodbye to Danix Point and started on their journey.

The flight through the galaxy was long and the paths below were rough. She shuddered at the thought of being down there. She would never make it in a timely manner if she had to walk. It could take weeks through the Inner Path and much longer through the Outer Path. She looked back to see Xuria's aura. It was a magnificent red. Her face grew hot and she clenched her teeth as she turned her head away. Her own planet had now become a bad memory. It felt like she was living in a nightmare.

A while later, they passed by a beautiful green glowing planet. *This must be Piatees*, she thought. Piatees was renowned for its extravagant beauty. The people were known for being peaceful and welcoming to visitors from other planets. Unlike Xuria. Lenala had always wanted to go there. She had only heard stories of the beautiful lands. There were lush green mountains, an abundance of flowers, giant ancient trees, and cascading waterfalls. There were rumored to be hidden caves in the ground that opened up into beautiful pools of water. The water was said to be sacred and had magical healing powers. Other people traveled to Piatees for healing and to absorb the natural cleansing powers of the water. Part of her longed to go there now. She wanted to forget everything and hide away. She promised herself that she would go to Piatees one day once this was all over. Thinking of Piatees reminded her of her sister and the Pitian Prince. *Anala better not get caught with that boy*, she thought as she squeezed her eyes shut and shook her head.

More time passed as they continued to fly. They were surrounded by planets and stars. Some were nearby and some were far off in the distance. Some were way above them and others were far below. The surroundings were so beautiful. There were different colors floating off of each planet, and the stars were twinkling. Haruelio was still bright but not so bright that they couldn't see everything. Every now and then, a star would shoot across the sky and leave a trail of shimmering dust. She loved looking at it all and dreaming. The beauty of the sky and the stars always gave her peace. The Inner Path below them was connected to each planet. From the air, she could see how it was suspended in the atmosphere and it appeared to float. It truly was a stunning vision. For a moment, she forgot the troubles she was immersed in and she soaked in the beauty. There she was, in the middle of the galaxy, flying on her Dragon. She had never been this far from Xuria, and it was far more beautiful than she could have imagined. She was thankful for Farka once again. She would never be able to see the galaxy like this if it weren't for her.

Soon, Lenala began to see the faint golden aura of Analicia in the distance. They were getting close, but Farka needed to rest after flying all day. It was already almost dark and they were both hungry. They could still see the roads below and decided to land and look for somewhere to sleep. There were known to be inns and places along the way for travelers to stop and rest, and she could see smoke rising in the distance. "That must be an inn, Farka. Let's land."

When they landed, the ground beneath them was parched and dry, and the wind from Farka's wings kicked up a cloud of dust, creating a dramatic entrance. For a brief moment, their view was completely obscured, and Lenala felt a sense of disorientation wash over her. It wasn't long before she could hear the sound of footsteps approaching, the sound growing louder with each passing moment.

She placed her hand on Escitalo. She squinted but was unable to see because of the lingering dust. Gradually, shadows began to emerge as the dust settled, and she realized that she was surrounded by a group of sinister-looking men. She was startled at the sight of them; they were all short and built very stocky. Farka let out a blood-curdling screech, spreading her wings and dropping her head low. She was ready to spit fire at them at any moment. Lenala was ready for whatever these men were bringing to her.

The men were terrified by Farka's screech and jumped back a few feet. "A Dragon!" one of the men managed to splutter out, wide-eyed. His voice was deep and had an accent she had never heard. Lenala said nothing. Her eyes moved from face to face but she didn't move, and held her stance. She was weighing the threat. One of the men regained his composure and stepped forward. "Identify yourself and state your business." He was gruff-sounding with a long white beard and the same accent as the first man. His head was shaved slick and he spat after he spoke to her.

She disliked him immediately. Farka's energy told her she felt the same.

"My name is Lenala and I seek, food, lodging, and passage to Analicia," she replied.

"You are going to Analicia?" he questioned, stroking his beard. He didn't wait for an answer. "Wait here," he barked. The men retreated and seemed to be arguing amongst themselves.

This is odd, she thought. *Don't they usually have travelers?*

"Maybe it's better if we just leave," she said to Farka under her breath.

A few minutes later, one of them returned. "We will allow you to stay here tonight, but the Dragon must stay outside in our stables," he said in a deep, scratchy voice. "We have never had a Dragon here before, and some of the men are scared to have her inside," he continued. "She can stay in the barn. She'll be comfortable out there and we can give her food." The thought of being separated from Farka didn't sit well with Lenala. She was used to having the dragon by her side at all times. However, she knew that Farka was a strong and capable creature who could defend herself if necessary. Besides, they were both in need of rest and sustenance, and Analicia was still at least a day's journey away. Reluctantly, Lenala agreed to the temporary separation. It wasn't an ideal situation, but she knew that she had no choice.

"Right, then," the man exclaimed. "Come on in and get something to eat."

Dinner was not the type of food she was accustomed to, but the hot, filling stew and bread were a welcome sight for Lenala. The aroma of the food was enough to make her realize how hungry she was. Soon, Farka made her way to the stable area that had been prepared for her, and settled down. Lenala could see that Farka was comfortable and content, so she left her to rest.

One of the men eating in the inn grew chatty with Lenala after he had a couple of ales. He asked her bluntly about her business in Analicia, to which Lenala responded firmly that it was a private matter. She found the men intimidating and was cautious about revealing too much to them.

The man let out a cynical chuckle and replied, "Well, my dear, the queen may let anyone in, but only if they have a valid reason or something she wants. So, your private matter better be worth her while."

"A valid reason?" Her eyebrows shot up.

"Yep. You can't just go into Analicia and expect to fly below the radar. Or have a 'private matter,'" he said again, this time with a hint of sarcasm. "Queen Halice knows what every citizen of Analicia is doing and why they are there. She has to approve each citizen who comes from another planet. She knows everything going on in that kingdom. She has eyes and ears everywhere." He finally stopped talking long enough to take a sip of his ale.

"Oh, I see," she replied, and took another bite of her food. She couldn't just say she needed poison or that she was exiled. That would never work. She wasn't prepared for this and now, she had only a short time to figure it out.

"So, what is your reason?" he questioned her, as his eyes narrowed. "You running away from home or are you running from a man?" He raised his mug with a half grin as he looked around, eliciting laughter from the other men. "Or maybe you did something very bad and got kicked out." He laughed deeply as he stepped closer to her. "Maybe you killed someone. Are you a killer?" He leaned in. His eyes were hollow. Lenala crossed her arms and scowled. He was drunk and probing her. The other men were encouraging him by laughing and waiting for her to answer. She knew she needed to tell him something before things got out of hand. Her stomach churned as she shifted in her seat. All of a sudden, the food wasn't sitting well. *We never should have stopped here.*

"I am joining her army," Lenala lied. The idea came to her suddenly. "Where I come from, women are not allowed to serve, so I was granted exit to come to Analicia," she continued guardedly and proud of her lie.

"Ha," he shouted, slapping his knee. "A woman in the army?"

The other men laughed as well. "That'll be a day to remember." He snarled.

"Well, you know," another man chimed in. "That queen is so kookie that she probably would let that girl in her army, especially because of her Dragon." A knowing nod passed around the room as a hush fell.

"What do you mean, especially because of my Dragon?" Lenala asked.

"Rumor has it the queen loves Dragons," he said as they chuckled.

"Men, I think she's had enough excitement for the night. Go home and leave her alone," the innkeeper said abruptly. He stood and began gathering the empty plates and mugs. Several groans echoed through the room. "This young lady needs some rest and you all are harassing her."

"We are just having a good time," the gruff man defended them. "Anyway, she's used to it—she's a soldier," he said as they trailed out of the inn, laughing raucously.

"I'll show you to your room," the innkeeper said. Although he was kind and gentle, she couldn't shake the uneasy feeling she had. She barricaded the bedroom door just to be safe. Escitalo was right next to her as she lay down. Her mind was spinning as it replayed the evening's events. *Maybe we should just go ahead and leave.* She checked in with Farka using their mental connection; she was fine and resting peacefully. Before she knew it, she had accidentally drifted off to sleep.

No telling how much time passed before she was jolted out of her sleep to the sound of Farka's screeching.

FIFTEEN

Brantog poured another glass of wine. He could never forget the anger that consumed him that day. He took a big swig as his mind continued to relive the Day of the Dragons.

Once the drawing was complete, Trayana was off-limits to him. She only had five days left. Those days were reserved for her to say her goodbyes and prepare to be sacrificed.

"If only I could get my hands on her," he growled under his breath. *Who helped her? Surely, it was Kineah.* "I'll have to pay her a little visit tonight." He snarled under his breath as the shadows from the fire danced across the floor. He sat there for a long time seething in anger. His mind was racing. He had never been taken for a fool like this. He felt betrayed and even worse, his pride was hurt. "Those ungrateful, selfish rats," he spat.

He stood and drank the last drop of wine from his

bottle. Then he slung the glass bottle into the fire. It shattered, the noise echoing as the excess wine residue burned, popping and crackling. The smell of burning wine engulfed his nose as he wiped his mouth. He stormed over to his dresser and placed his hands on either side of it as he leaned forward, studying his reflection. His tattoos looked distorted under the bulging veins in his arms. His eyes were glossy and his head was shining from the sweat. He shook his head and let out a groan. With a compulsion, he slung open the drawer and grabbed the bottle. *Damn it.* It was getting low. His mind drifted to Farka for a moment. He shuddered. He was afraid of Dragons, but their blood was what he needed. Especially tonight. His gaze was glued to the bottle as he swirled it gently. The blood was dark red and it was thick. It practically stuck to the sides of the jar as he rolled it in his hands. It shifted slowly as he moved it in different directions. *Such a magical little bottle.*

He unscrewed the cap and placed a small drop on his pinky. He had discovered through experience that taking too much would make him feel manic and crazed, so he had to experiment to find the right dosage. There had been instances when he had to lock himself in his room until the effects wore off. Even the amount he took last night had lingered, causing him to feel off during the ceremony. Maybe it was the blood or maybe it was because deep down, he knew something bad was about to happen. He convinced himself it was his senses and not the blood. Not his precious Dragon's Blood. He looked at himself in the mirror as he licked the drop off his finger. As soon as it touched his tongue, a rush of euphoria shot through him.

His head lowered as he closed his eyes. His insides became alive with a tingling sensation. He felt himself smile. He opened his eyes, locking in on himself in the mirror. He loved the feeling of the blood rushing into his body. This was the best part. When it first hit his system, the intensity was a feeling like no other.

The next stage was a surge of energy where he felt invincible and young again. His hip didn't hurt, his back felt strong, and he could stand completely straight with no pain. Most importantly, he didn't think about any of the things that weighed him down. He felt free. "If only I could feel like this all of the time," he mumbled as he carefully closed the lid to the bottle and tucked it away.

He turned his gaze to the window. Haruelio was long gone and the stars were shining in their full glory. They looked even more spectacular when he was on the blood.

It was late enough now. The city's buzz from the excitement of the night had finally died down. It was time to pay Kineah a little visit. He slipped out of his room and crept through the castle. He had to sneak carefully in the dark. The castle was sleeping.

He knew his way to her room very well. He could walk to it blindfolded if he had to. He was even more stealthy now that he had DB in his system. He made his way to her room. He wasn't in a rush. He had the whole night if he needed it. He gave three rhythmic knocks—this was his code. He didn't wait for an answer as he let himself in.

Kineah was sitting straight up in her bed. Her eyes were puffy and her hair was messy. She looked afraid and vulnerable. He hated when they looked afraid. Scared was ugly. His mother taught him that. When they were scared of him, it made him feel like he was some kind of terrible monster. They knew to hide it. If they showed any fear, he always made things worse for them. His eyes became cloudy and his face reddened as he stepped into the room.

She quickly replaced her look of fear with a mask of toughness. She knew better. "Good, you are up," he spewed as he closed the door.

"*I am now,*" she said with a raspy voice and a dismissive tone. He knew she was trying to disarm him.

He didn't mind the attitude. He liked it when they talked dirty. *No, I'm not letting her distract me.* He shook his head as he walked closer to her.

"Tell me, Kineah," he jumped right to it. "What happened today? Why did my Trayana get chosen without my knowing or my consent?"

Her eyes widened briefly as he let out a groan and rushed over to her in two long steps and shoved her back onto the bed, holding her by the neck. "Why do you look so afraid?" he hissed at her. "Do I still scare you? Even after all of these years?" She shook her head no as she regained composure. "Good," he said, loosening his grip.

"Don't you know this is the Dragons' will?" His eyes moved over her as he spoke. "You are my gift from them."

"That is what you tell yourself, she replied boldly. This wasn't the little attitude he liked.

She was being hostile and defiant. Anger shot through him. "Who do you think you are, talking to me like that?" he said as his fingers tightened around her neck with one hand. His face was right in hers.

She was shaking but her face showed no fear. "I'm sorry," she said confidently.

"That's my girl," he said as he let go of his grip.

He reached into his pocket and pulled out the vial of

blood. He was glad that he had remembered to bring it in his rage. This was going to be a long night.

She looked down at his hands as he unscrewed the lid.

She took a few deep breaths. He watched with pleasure as her eyes fixated on it for a moment before quickly looking away. He knew her. She needed the blood and that was just how he wanted it. She was compliant when she was high. When he hit her, she barely reacted. She even seemed to like it.

She glanced at the blood again. "Oh, is this what you want?" he said with a smirk.

He stood up tall and put it back into his pocket. "Let's see what you can tell me first."He leaned in to her again. His breath was hot against her cheek and reeked of wine. Brantog was relentless in his efforts to get her to confess, demanding to know how Trayana had outsmarted him. Despite her repeated denials of any involvement, his anger continued to escalate. He slapped her hard across the face each time she refused to yield. The force of the blows caused her to wince in pain, but she fought to maintain her composure, knowing that any sign of weakness would only fuel his rage further. She had learned this lesson the hard way, when her tears and pleas had only resulted in him taking his anger out on Trayana. Now, she remained silent. Suddenly, he yanked her up from the bed and pushed her against the wall, looming over her menacingly. But still, she refused to betray Trayana. Each blow he dealt her only strengthened her resolve, and although tears streamed down her face, her expression remained stoic. He shoved her to the ground and towered over her, demanding answers that she would never give. "Ugh," he said, looking down at her. "You look pathetic lying there." His hand disappeared into his robe. He sighed heavily. "Is this what you want?" Despite taunting her, he hated to see her lying there looking like his victim. At least when she was on the blood, her effort to be tough was much more believable and she seemed to enjoy his violence. He wasn't done with her yet and was tired of seeing her try so hard. He knew she wasn't likely giving up any information tonight.

He opened the bottle and dipped his pinky in. He put his finger right over her lips. He didn't even have to tell her to open her mouth. She closed her eyes, took his pinky, and desperately sucked the blood off it. "Open your eyes," he said as he looked at her with a twisted smile. Instantly, her eyes opened wide. Her face relaxed, and she was fearless and angry. She looked him right in the eyes. A look of satisfaction crossed his face. "That's better," he said.

He pulled her off the ground by her hair. "Let's try this again. Did you help her?"

This time, the blood was full force in her system. *"No."* She laughed a little bit while she spoke. It was a crazed, maniacal laugh.

The blood was surging through her body. He continued to hit her, in an effort to get her to talk before forcing her back on the bed. She was drenched in sweat and breathing hard. It was only a matter of time before he started mixing his punishments with pleasure. Just like he always did. He pulled her face in and kissed her. She was so high that she didn't even fight him. "One more tiny dab." He stood over her and dropped a half-sized drop of blood onto his lips as he leaned down. Instinctively she kissed him—she needed more blood.

The blood instantly made her body react to him. He knew exactly what he was doing. He didn't care if she hated him as long as she didn't show it—and she knew better than to show it.

After a long time of him taking out his rage on her, he finally stopped.

"I'll be back every night until you tell me what happened," he said as he stood over her.

"You promise?" She snarled. She was starting to come down from the high.

"That's my girl," he said. "That's how I like to hear you talk to me."

She detested him and he knew it. As long as she didn't show fear or disrespect him, he didn't care how she spoke to him. He thrived on that.

He left her room and sneaked back to his chambers. Although he didn't get any answers, he was confident that he would eventually break her. He felt a sense of relief wash over him after his visit. For a moment, he felt free. He no longer felt burdened by the memories that had been haunting him. He clung to that moment as long as he could and that night, he slept like a baby.

CHAPTER

SIXTEEN

Farka had not screeched out loud; it was an internal call to Lenala. Something was wrong and Farka either knew not to or wasn't able to scream out loud. *She must be in danger.* Lenala jumped out of bed and quickly gathered her things. She wasn't coming back. She sneaked out of the room and hurried down to the stables. As she got closer, she could hear men's voices. She crept around the corner. To her horror, Farka was trapped in a huge net and pinned to the ground. They had somehow managed to tie a rope around her snout so she couldn't blow fire, and her tail was bound. Lenala quickly sent her an internal nudge, letting her know she was there.

She could see there were two men. They were hovering over Farka and draining blood through a small clear tube inserted into her leg. They had a large jar that was almost full.

Dragon's Blood users. Of course, she knew about them but had never actually encountered any or had any experience with them. Aside from her recent knowledge of Brantog using it on the girls.

Many years ago, there was a period of time when the people of Xuria had quite a few Dragon's Blood addicts. Of course, the Dragons did not put up with this for long. They made haste to destroy these people. They were angry with King Byreon.

The king stopped the use of DB for all medicinal use and made an example of the addicts by burning them on the high mountain for everyone to see. The problem was eradicated and further deepened the people's fear of the Dragons.

Dragon's Blood, if used properly, could be a medicine. If used improperly, it made people high and was very addictive. Initially, they would feel intense pleasure and eventually become crazed. They would stay awake for hours, sometimes days. Many times, they would roam around and talk nonsense. They would become violent if they couldn't find their next fix. The blood was hard to come across and very expensive. No wonder Farka was a jackpot to them. Lenala became flushed as her eyes darted around. There were only two men, but they had already gotten quite a bit of Farka's blood and she was probably weak. Lenala carefully drew her sword, taking small steps into the stable. Immediately, Escitalo came to life. A hum buzzed through her veins and flowed into the sword. It was an amazing feeling that she was beginning to love. Her mind became clear and her body felt strong.

Her grandfather's smile enveloped her, and a vision flashed through her mind. This time, it was more than a vision. It was also a feeling. She knew what was going to happen. She saw the sword moving and felt herself following it. The men spun quickly as she stepped closer. She used the element of surprise, thrusting her sword into the man closer to her and causing him to drop to his knees. The other man reacted quickly, delivering a forceful kick that struck Lenala's back, leaving her breathless and sending her hurtling forward into the side of the stable.

The air felt thick and heavy as she got up and moved her sword into a ready stance. The orange glow of Escitalo illuminated his face as she pointed it toward him. He had a crazed look in his eye. Lenala shuddered. *He is clearly using the blood,* she thought as he lunged toward her with no weapons. Just bare hands. She swung her sword at him and he intercepted it with one hand. He did not even flinch with the blood it drew. Red blood poured down the glowing sword. Visions of the dripping blood and his wounded hand flashed in her head. She blinked. She saw a flash of a dragon bearing a sword in her mind. Realization hit her: These visions were not hers. They were Escitalo's. They were from the souls taken by this sword. She was seeing how this sword had killed others before and she was following its path. The visions were faint and all black and white. Except for the blood. That was red.

She didn't hesitate and drove the sword inward, pushing past his hand. Then with a quick upward motion, she sliced right through his chin, sending him stumbling backward. He wasn't even fazed. He looked terrifying. His face was gaping open and bleeding. His hands were torn and covered in blood. She jumped forward, knowing she would have just one shot to take him out. Just as she jumped toward him, something grabbed her foot, almost tripping her and making her fall. She looked back. It was the first man, who was still alive and grabbing at her leg.

With one shot, she severed his hand from his body then sank the glowing sword into his skull. A strange calm settled over her as she pulled her sword out of him. She hurried to Farka and quickly cut the rope and net away. The other man was coming toward her fast. Suddenly, Farka, who was now free but still weak, appeared behind him. Farka lowered her head and took a deep breath before exhaling a massive burst of flames that engulfed the man's body from head to toe. Before he could even scream, Lenala swung her sword, severing his head from his body.

"Three," she muttered under her breath, coldly. She hardly recognized her own voice. She was in a trance as she stood there looking around. Her sword was orange again and pulsating in her hand. Three souls she had now added to Escitalo. There was no telling how many souls were trapped in that blade. Every time she used it to kill, she felt more composed. Escitalo's powers were strong. She was mesmerized by the glowing blade. *The fire.* She snapped out of her trance and came to her senses. The fire was spreading. She swiftly removed the line that was attached to Farka's leg before shattering the bottle on the ground. Despite Farka's weakened state, she was still able to move. The barn was now almost entirely consumed by flames, and without hesitation, they ran as fast as they could, never once looking back. They continued to run until they reached a heavily wooded area where they could finally stop to catch their breath and rest. Lenala knew that they needed a safe place to hide until Farka was strong enough to fly again, which could take hours. Luckily, they found a densely forested area that was well-hidden from the road and concealed from view.

Farka's exhaustion was evident as she limped toward

Lenala, and with a heavy sigh, she lowered her head into Lenala's lap. Lenala had now killed three men in the past two days. She felt a fresh wave of guilt and remorse wash over her, as she lowered her gaze to Farka. "I didn't want to do it," she said quietly. "But I didn't have a choice. They would have killed us." Farka gave her a nudge. It was comforting to know Farka understood her. "I guess we did what we had to. May Draygon rest their souls." She let out a deep breath. She was a Xurian exile and she had a Dragon that people would try to steal for her highly addictive blood. She needed a plan to enter Analicia, and it would have to be solid. She would need protection for Farka and for herself. She sat for a while, rubbing Farka's head and thinking of a good plan to enter Analicia. Her sword was still glowing next to her. She stared at it as she replayed Semian's and her grandfather's words. The sword was special. Her grandfather told her this and gave it to her knowing she would use it for the good of Xuria. Little by little, it was becoming clear to her. Maybe fate had intended for her to become a Hite, and her purpose was to bring justice to her planet.

She recalled her hasty idea about joining the army in Analicia, and it actually began to make sense. What if she really did present herself as a soldier to the queen? Perhaps then she could gain entry to Analicia. Nobody would know she hadn't ever served before. Her heart rate increased as the plan continued to play out in her mind. She could join the army and pledge to serve the queen. This would give her access to protection for Farka. She could integrate into the army and find the herbs to make the concoction she needed. This would keep them safe while she planned her attack on Brantog. It felt like an idea that could actually work. As Kineah's face entered Lenala's mind, waves of sadness radiated through her. The harsh reality was that there seemed to be no way to save her from suffering. Despite this, Lenala resolved to never give up hope. She believed that if Kineah could persevere and endure the pain, there might still be a possibility of setting her free. However, if Lenala failed to help her friend, she made a promise to herself that she would do everything in her power to prevent Brantog from inflicting such torture on anyone else in the future. Exhausted from the day's events, Lenala decided that the best thing to do would be to sleep on her thoughts. She desperately needed to rest. She placed her sword back into its sheath before settling down next to Farka for the night.

Restless sleep overtook her. She dreamed of Brantog and the queen. She dreamed of the man on fire chasing her. She dreamed of Semian's kiss and of Escitalo.

Morning came too quickly. Farka was already awake and seemed to be back to her usual self. After a quick splash-off in a nearby stream, the two began the last part of the journey to Analicia. Farka was able to fly and seemed strong. As they flew away, Lenala looked back and could see the smolders of smoke in the distance from the burning barn. Shuddering at the memory of it, she nudged Farka to fly faster.

Five more hours passed. Farka could cover ground very quickly and made great time flying. This last leg of the trip would have been many days by foot. The whole journey had taken her three full days flying across the Inner Path.

On a horse, this could take weeks, on foot even longer. Dragons were fast, and she was one of the three people in Xuria who had their own.

Analicia's brightly glowing lights shone ahead. Even from afar, Analicia was a stunning planet that shimmered in the radiance of Haruelio's light. As they approached the border to enter, she realized it was actually the entry gates that were shimmering. They were giant, elaborate golden gates.

Two very tall guards stood at the gates. They looked menacing. They wore all golden armor and helmets. They were both Analician. Many of the people here were from other planets, but these two were natives. They had mocha skin and white hair. A beautifully striking contrast. One of the guards had blue eyes and the other's were brown.

"State your business, girl," the blue-eyed man demanded.

His deep voice and commanding presence shook Lenala inside, but she didn't hesitate. "I am here to pledge my service to the queen," she stated boldly.

"In what manner?" the other one asked.

"By serving in her army." A look of bemusement and surprise crossed over his face for a split second. The two guards traded glances. *Of course, they get ridiculous requests all the time*, she thought. Just as a nagging feeling of doubt began to creep into her mind, Farka reached out to her and sent a wave of confidence. A sense of relief came over her.

"Very well," the guard said, "we will present you to the queen and she will decide if you are welcome here." She felt a flutter rush into her stomach as she gave a small curtsy to the guard. Two other guards emerged from behind the gates. "Right this way," they said, ushering her to a carriage. "We will take you to sit before the queen."

The ride to the castle was long and Analicia was huge. The planet's streets were teeming with life, with a diverse array of people walking in every direction. Vendors could be seen on every corner, selling their goods, while the sounds of children at play echoed throughout the city. The ground was paved with bricks, and the network of roadways and walkways extended as far as the eye could see. This was in stark contrast to Lenala's home on Xuria. There were horse-drawn carriages everywhere, adding to the lively atmosphere of the planet.

Lenala was fascinated. She had always wanted to come to Analicia and so far, it was living up to everything she had ever learned about it. The castle came into view, and her jaw dropped as she took in the sight before her. It appeared to be suspended in the clouds. It was golden just like the gates. A deep gold. The steeples and arches were high and commanding. As she got closer, she could see that it was surrounded by water. There was only one bridge that allowed anyone to enter, and it was protected by guards.

The water was clear and blue, the land around it green and vibrant.

The guards had her wait while they approached the palace doors. After exchanging words with the men at the door, they summoned her to come.

As she entered the palace, her heart was pounding. She was taken aback once again by its beauty. Everything inside was accented in gold. The floors were white marble and the windows were huge, letting in an abundance of light. The inside shimmered with light and brightness. It was something else. Lenala was momentarily speechless. This palace made Xuria's palaces look inferior.

There were statues of what looked like gods and goddesses displayed by the stairs and windows. "Wait here," the guard instructed. Lenala continued to take it all in. Farka also seemed amazed as she stayed close to Lenala.

The grand room where she first entered the castle was huge. There were several hallways to the left and right with one beautiful spiral staircase that was protected by a guard. The man was quite massive, she noticed. He wore all black but his shirt was sleeveless, showing his well-defined muscles. He was clearly a well-trained soldier guarding an important area of the castle. *That must be where the queen's private quarters are*, Lenala thought, quickly losing her train of thought when the guard returned. "Come," he said. He led her down one of the hallways on the left to a room where there were others waiting to be seen.

"The queen has a full schedule of cases to review this morning, and her time is limited to just a few hours today," he stated matter-of-factly, his tone suggesting that he had delivered this message to many others before.

"She may not get to you today, but you will be provided lodging if this is the case," he continued as he led her into a large room with a huge throne set in the middle. The throne was no disappointment. It was solid gold with a white marble seat. The floors were the same white marble as the rest of the castle with a small staircase leading up to it. Nothing about Analicia was underdone. "Wait here." He extended his arms toward a chair. "She will be in shortly." She could only imagine how the queen must be in person.

She must be spectacular with her castle and city being so beautiful and well-kept.

As she surveyed the room, her heart sank in her chest. There were at least ten others waiting to be seen when she arrived. She sat down. There was nothing she could do but hope she would be seen today. She felt a knot in the pit of her stomach. What if the queen did not buy her story? What if she would not allow her to stay in the kingdom? What if she did not allow Farka to stay there? Lenala's mind raced with thoughts. She knew she had to get it together. She took a deep breath and closed her eyes. "You are Princess Lenala of Xuria, you are a Hite, you have killed three men, and you have a mission to kill Brantog. Now get it together," she whispered to herself. A surge of determination welled up inside her. She heard the rhythmic pattern of footsteps approaching. She took a deep breath and released it, opening her eyes. She was ready. It was now or never.

SEVENTEEN

As the footsteps became louder, the queen came into view. Lenala's breath hitched. The way she moved was mesmerizing. She appeared to glide above the ground as she walked over to her throne and nonchalantly sat. Lenala was taken aback by the energy in the room. She knew she wasn't the only one who was enthralled by the queen's presence.

There was a hush in the room as everyone there watched in awe. She had high cheekbones and big, amber eyes that were reminiscent of the Xurians', but with a darker tone that made them all her own. Her skin was a rich shade of mocha and her hair was platinum white, cut close to her head. It was as if she were covered in a fine layer of golden shimmery dust that danced and shifted with every movement. She was tall with a commanding presence, and her tattoos only added to her allure. Intricate patterns cascaded down both her arms, shimmering in the light. They seemed to come to life with her every gesture, as if responding to her will. She was the epitome of an

Analician woman and her presence was incredibly bold. Lenala could feel that about her immediately. This woman intimidated many people just by being in the same room with them. Lenala could tell the queen was not afraid of people and was the type of person who was perfectly fine speaking her opinion. This was a good trait in a leader and Lenala liked that about her. Despite Lenala not having seen her up close yet, the queen's aura told her that there was something troubling about her. She couldn't quite put her finger on it, but she could sense it nonetheless. The queen was the type of person who could hide anything from anyone. Lenala knew she would need more time to figure her out. As she watched the queen, she was taken aback by how much she knew by looking at her. It wasn't a guess or assumption, but a deep knowing that came from inside. She realized that her gift had grown much stronger. The feeling of unease hung heavy in the air. She wasn't sure why but assumed it must be the mix of emotions in the room. All of these people were there with their own stories, hoping to be granted entrance to Analicia.

Lenala waited patiently as the queen saw person after person. A few more people were brought in before they closed the doors for the day. She couldn't hear anyone's stories or the reasons they wanted entry, but most of them looked like simple peasants to Lenala. So far, it seemed like the queen was granting them all entry. *The queen lets anyone in,* she remembered the gruff man from the inn's words. She shuddered at the thought of them and reached out to touch Farka, who was lying on the floor drowsily.

Several hours must have passed. Finally, there were only eight people left in the room including her.

The four men ahead of her were, much to Lenala's

relief, in a group. She would be after them and the three after her would likely be seen as well. *Looks like we will all be seen today.*

As the four men approached the throne, her heart rate quickened and a wave of nervous energy passed over her. Thoughts of Brantog played through her mind. She had rehearsed her lie over and over. She inhaled, closing her eyes. She could see his wicked grin and she could feel Kineah's pain as if it were her own. Anticipation of revenge burned like a fire inside her. He was so vile and to make matters worse, her own father had sided with him. As far as she was concerned, he was just as repugnant. She took another deep breath and opened her eyes. Her attention was suddenly drawn to a glint of silver, jolting her back to reality. As she focused, she realized it was a sword, poorly hidden underneath one of the men's coats. She sat up and leaned in closer. The sight of the blade sent a chill down her spine. Farka was watching Lenala closely. Lenala reached down to make sure her sword was where she needed it to be. Pulsing energy shot through her hand as she grabbed the handle. Instant calmness. *Every time, Escitalo,* she thought. As the men approached the queen, she could see there was some mixing of words. The queen looked upset and stood up, pointing at the men angrily.

The man with the sword abruptly drew it, followed by the other three. The four of them made a circle with their backs to each other and their swords drawn. Instantly, the queen's personal guards jumped to action. There were six of them and they were lightning-fast. Two of them jumped in front of the queen. It was clear that their sole job was to protect her.

The other men and the guards continued to battle as

Lenala watched and tried to make sense of it all. The men seemed to be overwhelming the guards. It was apparent that these men had formal training. They moved swiftly and had an answer for each of the queen's guards' threats. Suddenly, the three men behind her jumped up and ran toward the throne with swords drawn.

This was a full ambush on the queen and her guards, and they were outnumbered.

Without a moment of hesitation, Lenala jumped into action and bolted toward the queen. Farka was already standing with her head lowered. She was ready to ignite the whole place and Lenala could feel it. "Stay put, Farka, until I need you." Farka let out a low snort and stamped her foot, but she obeyed. She was proving to be very feisty, always wanting in on the action. As Lenala closed in on the men, she sized up the situation. The two men guarding the queen were now fighting off two of the new attackers, leaving the queen unprotected. The third attacker was advancing on the queen fast. Lenala quickly unsheathed her sword as she charged at the man. She had the element of surprise. He certainly wasn't expecting her to be a threat. The queen's eyes widened at her advance as well. Lenala positioned herself in front of the queen, shielding her from harm, and assumed the stance of a Hite. She could feel the adrenaline coursing through her veins. Her grip tightened around Escitalo, heightening her senses and sharpening her reflexes. Escitalo was glowing the same shade of orange she had seen at the barn. The attacker engaged her and back and forth, she fought with the man. He was strong and very skilled. Out of the corner of her eye, she could see the other men had overtaken the queen's guard. She was able to maintain her stance between him and the queen for a while. However, he was fast and his footwork was more advanced than hers. Soon, she found herself having trouble keeping him back. With one fast jump and a swing of the sword, he locked his blade with hers, pushing in close. "Mighty fancy sword you've got," he said with a sinister grin as he pushed her back with a powerful shove. Then with one strong swing, he flung her sword across the room. His sheer power sent Lenala flying back, right into the queen. They both hit the ground hard. The queen was knocked unconscious immediately.

As he approached, he looked down at them with that same evil grin. Lenala sprang to her feet in a swift motion and assumed a ready stance, her hands held out in front of her. While she had some training in hand-to-hand combat, she was at a severe disadvantage without Escitalo. She knew that this man was far more skilled. Despite knowing that she should call on Farka for help, Lenala held back. Farka was tough, resilient, and fierce, but Lenala felt a deep sense of obligation to protect her innocence. Farka was Lenala's companion, and she had never been involved in a fight before the events of that night at the inn. Lenala didn't want to subject her to the violence unless absolutely necessary. She still had a few moments before she would be outmatched, and she wanted to give it her all.

Suddenly, Farka emerged and positioned herself behind the man. She stood tall with her wings fully extended. She threw her head back as she let out a menacing screech that pierced the air. The room fell silent as everyone stopped abruptly and turned to face her. With each deep, growling breath she took, her body began to grow larger before their eyes. She lowered her head and began to flap her wings, causing a thunderous roar to echo throughout the room. With every beat of her wings, she grew bigger, her body expanding in girth and length until she towered over the man she was confronting.

Lenala watched in awe and fear as Farka unleashed a massive fireball from her mouth, engulfing the man in flames and incinerating him. The sound of his screams barely registered over the roar of the fire. Farka then unleashed a wall of fire, shielding Lenala and the queen from the other men. The heat was intense, and the flames licked at their skin, but they were safe for the moment.

The distraction gave the queen's guards the opportunity they needed to subdue the other men. As they brought the situation under control, Lenala and Farka locked eyes, their gazes filled with newfound respect and gratitude for each other. They both understood that they were no longer the innocent royals they once were, but Hite who would do whatever it took to protect each other.

Lenala turned to assist the queen, who still lay unconscious on the ground. As soon as the guards had the assailants secured, two of the guards came rushing over. They quickly grabbed the queen and carried her away. The other guards took the men out and Lenala was left alone. She stood there in silence with Farka. Once the guards were far away, Farka shrank back to her usual size. Lenala ran over to her. "Oh, Farka, you saved me, again," she said as tears streamed down her face. She rubbed the sides of Farka's head and placed her forehead on hers. "Where did you learn to do that? You never cease to amaze me." She wrapped her arms around her. Farka was tired but still very alert and probably able to keep fighting if it meant protecting Lenala. There was nothing she wouldn't do to protect her. They sat there for a while in silence. The fire had simmered down, leaving behind a pile of smoldering ashes. As Lenala replayed the ambush through her head, she found the adrenaline rush that came with the fighting invigorating. In the last few days, she had been in three battles. It was scary but with Escitalo and Farka, she felt invincible and more alive than ever.

The thunder of footsteps approached, snapping her back into the present. One of the guards had come back. "The queen wishes to speak with you. Follow me," he demanded as he motioned for her to follow him.

The adrenaline continued to surge through her as she followed him through the castle.

He led her up the strange set of stairs she had seen when she first arrived.

He was taking her to the queen's private wing.

When they entered the wing, the queen was lying on a small, cushioned couch. She looked very pale compared to when Lenala had first seen her. *She must have taken a pretty hard hit when I landed on her,* Lenala concluded. She felt the queen cautiously watching her as she approached. Lenala did not want to show that she was royalty. Instead, she tried to walk like a warrior and did not hold her head as high as royalty would. A lifetime of training to walk like a royal was not easy to forget.

As Lenala came to a halt, she gave a slight bow.

The queen looked weak but hid it well.

She looked at Lenala with slightly narrowed eyes. "First of all, I want to thank you for saving my life from those traitors." Her words were rhythmic and slow. Each word was enunciated with precision and clarity. She continued to explain that the two Analician soldiers were working with the other attackers. They were seeking revenge for their brothers, who had been in a group of bandits who were exiled for crimes against the planet.

"Secondly, who are you?" She posed the question without pausing long enough for Lenala to answer. "And where did you get this warrior Dragon?" she continued in her rhythmic, mesmerizing way of speaking. A sense of pride welled up in Lenala. It made her proud to think of her sweet Farka as a warrior. Farka had lived a plush royal life and had never received any formal training. Even so, she was beginning to surprise Lenala daily and becoming a force to be reckoned with. She could see that her Dragon instincts were nothing to take lightly. "Are you here to seek citizenship?" She finished her questions, fixing her gaze on Lenala, who took a deep breath as she carefully spoke.

"Your majesty," she started. "Thank you for seeing me. My name is Lenala of Xuria and I seek to serve in your army in return for sanctuary for myself and my Dragon in your kingdom." Her words came out effortlessly as she had rehearsed that line over and over.

Lenala lowered her head after she spoke as a sign of respect. She knew precisely how to conduct herself in the presence of royalty. The queen did not speak right away as she studied Lenala from her couch. Her intense gaze moved tiredly back and forth between her and Farka. "Well, you certainly have caught my attention." She leaned back and laced her fingers. She took a couple of deep breaths, shifting in her seat. She didn't say another word.

Lenala could feel Farka getting nervous during the queen's silence. She sent her a calming energy. It worked.

"You seek to serve in my army? A woman?" she mused. Not really asking but stating. "You would be the only woman to serve in the history of my armed services. What makes you think you can survive in such a male-dominated environment?" She paused and then continued. "You did show courage today." She used her hands to accentuate words like *only* and *services*. Her voice was melodious and smooth, the tone deep. "Oh," she stated and then paused, "right, you have your Dragon to protect you," she concluded with a nod. "It's possible this may work, but it would be taboo." She continued to speak and her words began to sound like a song. The rhythm of her voice and the movements of her hands were captivating. Lenala was not sure if she should interject or just let her continue. She started to speak but the queen raised a hand. "I do love taboo, but you would need to learn to be able to fight independently—without your Dragon," she continued, as if she had come to a resolve. "I love Dragons and I love a woman who is bold enough to step into my kingdom and ask such a thing of me." She continued speaking with a gleam in her eye. "It takes courage." She dragged out the last few words gracefully. "And after all, you did save my life. Both of you," she said as her gaze moved to Farka.

After another long, calculated silence, she sat up tall and clapped her hands. "I have decided. You can stay and join my army, but do know I will be watching you," she said, pointing her finger at Lenala. "Welcome to Analicia."

"Thank you, Your Highness," Lenala said, hardly able to contain her excitement.

"Call me Queen Halice," she interrupted. "Your Highness was my father. Guard..." Her voice soared across the room. "...grant her entry and enlist her in the army." As she sang out the order, her hand moved in a sweeping gesture.

The guard stumbled on his words as he bowed to her request. "Yes...Queen Halice," he managed to get out.

Lenala almost laughed at how flustered he appeared to be. Then, as his gaze turned toward her and Farka, it was clear that he wasn't sure how to react, torn between anger and fear. "Follow me," he commanded in a flat, emotionless tone.

EIGHTEEN

Lenala's heart pounded in her chest. She could not believe this was happening. Everything she had planned completely changed with the ambush. Little did she know the rendezvous with the attackers would actually help solidify her case and get her into the army. Although she wasn't happy they had attacked the queen, she was grateful that she and Farka were there, and that the outcome had been in her favor. Farka had stepped up to the plate and shown what type of Dragon she was truly capable of being. Lenala's mind was racing. The adrenaline was still running through her. Her hair was still sweaty and she had soot and ashes on her clothes and body. She followed the guards for what felt like a mile before they got to the grounds for the soldiers. They were located far behind the castle and off the castle grounds. They had to cross the main bridge and take a road that led around the water to the back side of the castle. She could see there were several large fields and barracks even farther back. There must have been hundreds of men in formation training. Some were doing footwork or working with swords while others were doing hand-to-hand combat training. It was loud; with grunts and stomps echoing through the fields. There was the sound of swords clashing and men yelling. It was exhilarating. She caught a few stares as she was led through the men, but most of them were staring at Farka, who was doing an incredible job of looking mean. Lenala simply looked ahead, trying to do her best imitation of a soldier's walk. The farther they went, the more the intimidation began to creep in. She was enlisting in the army on another planet. She knew nothing of actual military functions. She knew how to fight and use a sword, but formal training? Only what she had been shown on the sidelines growing up. It was enough to get by and survive with. The last few days had proven that, but this was going to be different and she had a cover to keep up. She was a fast learner and kept reassuring herself that she could do this. She wanted to do this more than anything. She knew she would have to work hard to fit in and not show her true identity.

"Captain Chander," the guard said as he approached a large Analician man.

Chander turned. With a towering height and a lean, muscular face, he had the same blue eyes and mocha skin as the guard. His large frame was defined by thick muscles, his veins bulged in his arms, and his legs resembled tree trunks. His shoulders were etched with layers of muscles.

He exuded a commanding presence. The scars on his arms and his weathered demeanor were a clear indication that he had seen his fair share of combat and hardship. "Yes?" he said. His tone was clipped.

"Captain, this is Lenala. She has been granted entry by Queen Halice, and has been placed under your command."

"My command?" he scoffed. "Is this a joke?" His voice was low and gruff.

"No, sir. I was given the orders myself. She's all yours," he said as he walked away.

Captain Chander stood there studying Lenala for a moment before he spoke. "Well," he said, "this is a first for me. I must say I don't know exactly what to do with you or where to place you. What experience do you have? Are you a medic? A cook? A housekeeper?"

Lenala couldn't help but feel a sense of amusement once again at the reaction of the Analician soldiers. But she kept her expression neutral. It was comical to see a man of even his stature thrown off so much by her presence. "No," she replied in a deliberate and measured voice. "I have extensive training with the sword, and I have defeated three men in combat," she said, a little too boldly and proudly.

"Three men?" He laughed a deep belly laugh. "Is that all? Well then, we have work to do. How old are you?"

"Eighteen," she said...*ugh,* she thought, I *should have lied.*

"Eighteen? I see." He studied her for a moment longer. There was a sense of uncertainty in his eyes. "Well, who am I to question the queen? I don't have time to worry about this," he grumbled. "I am going to start you out with the other recruits. Give you some time to see where you stand, and you can work your way up. If your skills are sharper than those of a recruit, we will adjust you accordingly. I hope you are as tough as you think you are," he said, looking at her with a furrowed brow. "It's rough out there. Especially for a pretty girl like you." Farka gave a low growl. He took a small step back. "Keep your Dragon with you at all times," he said, looking Farka up and down, "and remember, I am not your babysitter."

Farka was doing a good job portraying being tough. Her eyes were locked on Captain Chander as he spoke.

This journey had been hard on them both but they were proving themselves to be resilient. She held onto hope that she had what it took to do this.

The captain led them to the recruit barracks, which were surprisingly nice. Of course, she was used to luxury, but this was better than she expected. She was given a small, private enclosed area with a bed and an area big enough for Farka to lie down in.

There were at least ten other enclosures for the other soldiers in these barracks.

"Dinner will come soon," Captain Chander said. "Come on with me and I'll introduce you to your unit."

Once they arrived at the dining hall, he led her to a table of young-looking men. All of them were eyeing her and Farka. She couldn't tell if they were afraid or suspicious. After all, she was a woman with a Dragon being added to their unit.

Captain Chander introduced her as she bowed slightly. Lenala squared her shoulders and nodded, trying to give off an air of confidence. She kept her face impassive, hoping that her true feelings weren't giving her away. Despite her best efforts, her heart raced in her chest. She felt a gentle touch on her leg and looked down to see Farka's wingtip resting there. Lenala felt a wave of calm spread over her, and she let out an internal sigh of relief.

She resolved to show no emotion until she had a better feel for this unfamiliar environment.

The men in her new unit were polite, and they all introduced themselves as small talk went around the table. She didn't say much and mostly answered trivial questions about Farka. She was so thankful for her. No one would mess with her with a Dragon by her side. Even though Farka was one of the sweetest Dragons in Xuria, she had a commanding presence that contradicted her gentle nature. At just six feet tall and lean, she was considerably smaller than the other Dragon species who towered over her at twelve to fourteen feet in height and were far more heavily built. Yet, Farka held herself with an air of confidence that made her seem even larger than she was. Her posture was straight and her movements deliberate, every gesture conveying a sense of power and authority. The men avoided making eye contact with Lenala and kept their conversations with her brief. This suited her just fine. The less they knew, the better. She decided that it was good for them to be afraid of Farka as it gave her an advantage in the situation.

That night, back in her new barracks, she lay down with Farka at the foot of her bed. This was a new beginning for them. They had made it to Analicia and joined the army. Not without a lot of tribulation, but they had made it.

~

The morning bell rang in what felt like seconds, and everyone was up and jumping into action. Training started right after breakfast and did not stop until nightfall.

Day in and day out, she trained morning to night.

Her sword skills were more advanced than her counterparts, but her hand-to-hand combat was about the same and needed much improvement.

Analicia was very different from Xuria. Haruelio felt farther away and the night sky felt different. The weather changed over the months. The leaves turned from green to orange and the grass became dry and brittle. The days were getting cooler and training outside had become easier.

Before she knew it, six months passed by. She had become completely caught up in the lifestyle of the army and training. She had fallen into a routine and found herself loving it. This was all she had ever wanted to do growing up.

Now she was gaining skills and becoming who she was portraying herself to be. She found herself obsessing over her training, making sure to ask questions and get the details right. Her fellow recruits had become somewhat closer to being friends, but she still kept her distance. Despite her new passion, never did a day go by when she didn't find herself thinking of Brantog and Xuria. Thoughts of his bony hands, scarred face, and nefarious eyes were her motivation to push through hours of grueling training. She was excelling and becoming relentless. She constantly spoke Kineah's and Trayana's names under her breath. She often grappled with the guilt of leaving Kineah and hoped she could stay strong until she could go back.

This hard work would not be in vain. She would bring justice to Brantog and set things straight.

She still had not gotten the freedom to go out and look for the herbs, but she had been asking questions and she knew where to find the ingredients to make the poison. She just needed to wait for the right chance to go.

The army was very strict with its rules and did not allow the soldiers to leave without permission. The recruits were not allowed to leave at all.

As soon as Lenala moved up in the ranks, she would be allowed one day free per week to do as she pleased. Until then, she would work hard and train as much as she could.

Months continued to pass.

The army was preparing to give promotions, and Lenala was confident that she would be advanced to the next rank and be allowed a free day. She had been patient and worked hard, waiting for this day to come.

As the day drew to a close and training came to an end, Lenala carefully sheathed her sword and took a moment to admire the sky. Haruelio was beginning to set, casting a warm, golden glow over the training grounds. The sky was painted with a breathtaking array of pinks, purples, and oranges. Lenala couldn't help but feel a sense of awe as she watched the sky transform. The Analician sunset was truly a sight to behold, and she cherished every opportunity she had to witness its beauty.

Lenala's mind wandered back to Xuria. She longed to see the familiar red and orange hues of the sky and the mesmerizing spectacle of the nightly volcano show. However, her once cherished memories were tarnished; every time she thought of Xuria, a wave of anger ran through her, the feeling still as fresh as the day she left. Her sword was pulsing in her hand. She snapped out of it. "There, there," she said. "Don't get caught up in my drama." She had developed a special relationship with Escitalo. It was as if it knew her and reacted to her feelings.

It was unique. She had always known this. She just didn't fully understand it yet.

Lenala sensed a stirring of energy that rippled through the air. Soon, the clanking of armor and swords clashing came to a halt. The grounds were silent. Lenala's gaze snapped to attention as she saw the queen approaching in the distance. The woman commanded attention without even trying. All of the soldiers lined up, standing at attention as the queen passed them by. She was closely followed by her personal guardsmen. There were five of them, all towering men with fierce expressions, and weapons at their sides. They were the best of the best, handpicked for this coveted position. This job was the most prestigious of all the army jobs.

The queen approached Lenala's unit and stopped. They were already in formation with their eyes down. The queen looked at them for a long time without saying a word.

Lenala could feel the nerves of her fellow soldiers. The queen was intimidating and her aura was strong and powerful. She turned and walked away, beckoning Captain Chander to join her. Lenala peeked out of the corner of her eyes as the queen spoke with him. He was slightly shifting from side to side for a moment, but quickly covered it up. As soon as she finished talking with him, she turned to the unit and stated in her low, rhythmic voice, "As you were," while walking away.

The queen was barely out of sight when Captain Chander approached. "Lenala, you need to gather your things." Her heart rate jumped up rapidly. Was she being cut? Had she done something wrong? Before she could stammer out any words or ask questions, he continued speaking. "The queen has somehow become impressed with you." He carefully measured her reaction as he spoke. "She wants you to serve on her royal guard at the castle," he continued. "I don't know what you did but somehow, she's decided you are up to the standard." Lenala's eyes widened and her mouth dropped open as he spoke. "This is going to make a lot of my men mad," he said, shaking his head. "They won't take it lightly."

She was dumbfounded, unable to utter a single word. *The queen wants me to join her royal guard? Is this a joke?* Her thoughts were running wild, jumbled and chaotic. All she could do was stand there.

"Well? She said she wants you there before dark. Are you just going to stand there, soldier, or are you going to move?" he barked, snapping her out of her daze. "Go get your things!" His voice was sharp and laced with annoyance. "If you act like this in there, she'll send you right back to me and have my head for sending her an idiot."

NINETEEN

The bed was hard underneath him as he sat reeling in his thoughts and emotions. Flames flickered in front of him, casting shadows that moved across the walls. He felt like his life was spiraling out of control. He was still the product of other people's decisions.

His mind drifted to his parents. They had forced their ambitions and desires on him, never allowing him to pursue his dreams. Anger, frustration, and resentment boiled up inside him like a volcano. Then there was Mina, *the one who messed everything up, and now Trayana too?* Suddenly, he felt an urge. The blood was summoning him, calling out to him. *Just one drop.*

He dabbed his pinky into the bottle and fell back onto the bed, his gaze fixed on the ceiling. The room began to swirl around him. The walls danced with the light of the fire. For a moment, everything was euphoric. He squeezed his eyes shut, waiting for the anger and pain to dissipate. But they didn't. The feelings were getting stronger, and he needed more to drown them out. All he could think about now was her. She was his new obsession. He just wanted to sleep and forget. Soon, he drifted into a restless dream of his most recent nightmares.

Nights had quickly turned into weeks. Trayana was gone and Kineah was still silent, despite his efforts.

Trying to get her to talk had become a game to Brantog. He didn't care anymore. He just wanted her to be afraid to ever try to pull anything like this again. Trayana's defiance triggered something deep inside him. He had sworn to himself long ago to never be taken for a fool, and to never let anyone get the upper hand on him. This whole situation had really thrown him into a spiral. He was taking his anger out on Kineah just about every night. He had her confined to her room as extra punishment. He also didn't want anyone to see the marks he had left on her body. Nobody had ever questioned him in the past when he punished the girls. So, he wasn't concerned about them being suspicious. They just didn't need to know the severity or the reasoning.

Aside from everything going on in his head, he felt less stressed after his reckless nights with her. He had been using more DB than usual and he felt lighter; he wasn't as weighed down with his emotional baggage.

He soon found that he was burning through it too fast and there were already issues getting enough. Supply was limited. He relied heavily on the Murkes to bring it in. Getting DB was dangerous in Xuria. If the Dragons found out, the penalty was death. To avoid detection from the guards at the portal, the Murkes had to make themselves invisible. After gaining entry, they used their abilities to blend in with the Xurians by altering their physical appearances. With their extensive experience and expertise in disguise, they were able to blend seamlessly into the crowd without being seen. They were professionals.

The idea of getting caught with DB was both scary and fascinating to Brantog. At times, he found himself wanting to be caught so he could escape the life that had entrapped him. But he was too much of a coward to run away or allow himself to be caught. He desperately needed to find a way to get a bigger supply. He had been brainstorming ways to get more. His mind kept drifting to the Dragon living right in his castle. "If only I could get my hands on that Farka," he mumbled to himself. He had been giving it some deep thought and decided to begin gathering intel on her. He needed that Dragon but in order to get to her, he needed to get past the princess, and that would take some planning.

Lenala had been keeping busy with her duties and Farka was almost always with her. He began watching her in secret, very carefully. He had many places where he could hide and see what was going on in the castle. He had been watching the people in the palace for years. He found it entertaining and he wanted to make sure no one was doing anything behind his back. He maintained order by knowing everything. He knew that people would take advantage of any opportunity they could find. He trusted no one.

Lenala was a quick one—he observed that immediately. She noticed everything. Something about her still stirred up discomfort inside. He wasn't sure if it was because of Farka or if it was just her. As he studied her and

Farka more and more, he began to see deeper into her. She was strong and had a backbone. Although she tried to hide it, he could see that she was holding back. There was something about her that made her stand out. Not only was she beautiful; she was smart, too. He could see that in her eyes. As he observed her and Farka more closely, he found himself increasingly drawn to Lenala. He was an intuitive man, and it didn't take long for him to see that beneath her beauty, there was more. He could sense a strength and determination in her that he envied. Her willful and confident demeanor hinted at a depth of character that he found alluring.

When she looked at people, it was as if she was peering into their very souls. *Reading them.* Suddenly, it dawned on him that this must be what really made him uneasy. He could always feel her trying to read him when she looked at him. *She may be smart, but she's not smarter than me, and she won't be able to see through me.* He had developed a wall over the years and it was very strong and hard to break through, but even though his wall was tough, he had never encountered someone as gifted as her. He felt a sliver of worry run through him. *Get it together; she's just a girl.* The more he watched her, the more intimidating and interesting she became. In everyday life, she seemed to avoid him at all costs. That was good for him. He really didn't want much to do with her. Especially if she could see through any portion of his wall. He knew he had to be very careful so that she wouldn't become suspicious of him or catch him spying on her. She was too smart. Still, he needed to figure out how to get Farka away from her.

If he could capture her and keep her locked up in a secret place, he'd have an unlimited supply of blood. He just needed a plan that would work. She wasn't a small, weak girl, but he could overpower her easily. *Maybe I can sneak into her room and kill her in her sleep.* Plans began to form as he continued to watch her. Soon, he began to see a side of her he'd never seen before. Every time she was alone, she would do what looked like dances—but he knew better. These were moves and footwork that only soldiers knew. "Interesting," he muttered under his breath as he observed her from one of his many hiding places. She moved with both speed and grace, holding her hands as if she were using a sword. Her eyes were closed and a radiant glow surrounded her. It was clear that she was truly passionate about what she was doing. Watching her movements was almost hypnotic. He shook his head to snap out of the trance. He knew the moves she was making, as he had practiced them himself to keep his own skills sharp. *Where did she learn this?*

He had become obsessed with watching her. The idea of stealing Farka and killing Lenala was all he thought about. He watched her as often as he could, studying her and learning her. Many times, when she was alone, she would sit by the window in her room, staring out into nothingness. Expressionless and emotionless. The only time she showed emotion was when she was doing her footwork. He soon began to realize the emotionless face was actually her true face. Anything else was just a mask. *Of course the princess wears a mask.* A small smirk spread over his face. *Why wouldn't she? She's one of them, one of us.*

He recognized that look all too well. It was the look of loneliness and defeat, a reflection of her desire for something more. As he observed her, it became increasingly evident that she resented being there. The more he watched her, the more he realized that she was not so different from him. She was a victim of circumstance, forced to live a life not of her choosing. Just like him.

It was clear that she had a passion for fighting, yet she was here against her will, her true desires stifled by the plans of others. In her misery, he saw a reflection of him. They were both prisoners in their lives, longing for something more but unable to break free from their chains.

He felt a twinge of sadness as he watched her. He remembered that feeling. He was still haunted by it every night. He saw in her what he hated about this place. He was about her age when he started really hating Xuria and came to realize he had no choice in his future. Those were the hardest times. He was young enough to care but could not do anything about it. She would realize soon enough that she was stuck. Xuria was not the place where dreams came true. Not for him and certainly not for anyone else. This planet of fire and Dragons was a living hell.

He concluded that his plans to kill her would set her free. He'd be doing her a favor.

He had been studying her for over a week now. He had enough of a plan to make this work. That night, he decided that after he finished with Kineah, he'd sneak into her room with two darts—one to tranquilize Farka, and the other to kill Lenala. It would be simple. He would take care of Farka first. He certainly didn't need her interference. Then he would use the other dart on Lenala, and find a way to make that look like a sudden illness or accident. He would then take the tranquilized Farka to his parents' old cellar and confine her with chains and a muzzle. He knew there were many Murkes in need of money, so he would hire one to keep a watchful eye on her.

He spent the rest of the day going about business as usual, but his mind was completely preoccupied with his plans. The darts were already prepared and in his chambers. He'd never needed them before but he kept them around just in case. Especially after what Larsen had pulled, and now Trayana. *"You can never trust anyone"* was a phrase he used often.

The fireworks display felt different; he almost enjoyed it for the first time in years. The clay in the soil emitted a bright glow, while the lava shimmered orange and gold as it cascaded down the mountain. The sky was illuminated with a stunning array of red and orange hues that were mesmerizing. He couldn't help but feel a sense of excitement. His plans were finally ironed out and he was ready to execute them.

His visit with Kineah proceeded as usual, but he didn't feel angry. Instead, he was preoccupied with a mix of excitement and nervousness over his plans. Kineah didn't seem to notice anything out of the ordinary.

She looks different, he noticed. She was looking haggard and rundown. "For Draygon's sake, clean yourself up, girl," he said, looking her over scornfully. "Are you even eating? You look ill."

She scoffed at him with little energy. *Pathetic*, he thought. *Look at her. She has let herself go.*

"You did this to me, so I figured this is what you like."

Usually, this may have angered him, but tonight it didn't. "You are blaming me?" His tone was accusatory. "If anyone deserves blame, it's you. Lord Draygon would not be pleased to see his gift in such a worn-out and unkempt state. Remember, you are a Nahkei, chosen to serve me until your time comes. This is your destiny, as chosen by the Dragons themselves." He gestured toward the door. "You may leave your room now. Get yourself together before I see you again. And for Draygon's sake, eat something," he said as he left the room.

He made his way back to his chambers, his thoughts dark and brooding. He couldn't shake the feeling of disgust at Kineah's appearance. Perhaps he had been too harsh on her, and she needed time to rest and recover. He resolved to leave her alone for a while after tonight, giving her some space to clean up and regain her composure. Right now, he had more pressing matters to attend to.

He indulged in a long, hot bath and poured himself a glass of wine as he meticulously reviewed his plans. The poison darts were his potent weapon, small but deadly. He had fashioned a tube to hold them, which he could use to eject the dart with a single, powerful breath. He had practiced this maneuver countless times, perfecting his aim and technique.

As the night grew late, he decided that the timing was right. With his darts ready, he stealthily made his way toward Lenala's chambers, his every step measured and deliberate.

He eased the door open. The room was silent.

It took a moment for his eyes to adjust to the darkness. He peered toward the bed. He blinked a few times, but he couldn't make out anything in the room. He crept closer, listening intently, but there was nothing. Only silence. He let out an angry grunt as he realized that she was not there.

He sneaked back to his chambers, wrestling with his

frustration. He wanted to take action right then and there, but now he had to wait

The next day, he made it his mission to track her down. He was determined to keep a close eye on her so that he would know exactly where she was when the time came. To his dismay, she was nowhere to be found and no one in the castle seemed to know where she was. She had vanished without a trace.

He woke up drenched in sweat and gasping for air. He threw himself out of bed and stood in the middle of his room his fists clenched tightly. Everything had gone down-hill since the Day of the Dragons and he couldn't keep living like this. Day after day.

He needed that Dragon and her infinite supply of blood. It was the only thing that would make things right again.

He would get to the bottom of this and find her wher-ever she had gone. He would take her life and claim that Dragon for himself.

TWENTY

Lenala turned away immediately and ran so fast to her barracks, she was practically skipping. Her mind was racing, her thoughts running wild. By the time she reached her room, she was dripping in sweat. Farka sensed her energy before she arrived and was waiting for her; her eyes were wild. She knew something big was happening, and she was standing up tall with her eyes locked on Lenala intently. All of a sudden, Lenala burst into laughter and flung herself onto the bed. "Farka, we got promoted." Farka let out a snort of relief and did a little hop with a sidestep in excitement. "This is the break we have been needing," Lenala said in one breath. She lay on the bed letting it all sink in. Now she would be able to have the best training with the most elite soldiers in Analicia. Most importantly, she would have access to whatever she needed to carry out her ultimate plan.

She knew the captain was impatiently waiting on her, so she frantically packed up her belongings. There weren't many. She only had the training uniform and the few small grooming supplies they issued her upon arrival. She quickly scribbled a note to her unit, promising to return and say goodbye properly. She barely looked back as they rushed out the door.

As expected, the captain was waiting for her, his impatience reeling. "Come on now," he said with a sigh, gesturing for her to get into the waiting carriage. She climbed aboard, but before she could express her gratitude for all the time and training he had invested in her, the carriage lurched forward.

From the window, she managed to wave and shout a pitiful, "Thank you for everything, Captain" as the cart sped away, leaving the training grounds behind in a cloud of dust. A strange mix of emotions welled up inside her—a blend of sadness at leaving behind what had become a second home, and excitement for what lay ahead. She was leaving well before she thought she would. She had become comfortable there, and she was learning and excelling. She knew the men and felt a camaraderie with them. She knew how things worked, and she was used to the routine. She loved training and was devoted to becoming a warrior 100 percent. This was going to be yet another new chapter for her. She had advanced in the ranks, and now she was going to be one of the queen's elite guards. She was filled with pride. She wished her father could appreciate this part of her. She wondered what Semian and her siblings would think. Without a doubt, they would be proud of her. They knew how much she had always wanted to be a soldier. *One day, they will see me,* she thought.

As she rode in the carriage, doubt began to creep in. The buzz of the excitement was waning and she started to feel worry setting in. *Why am I getting promoted to such an honorable position? Is it my skills? I mean, I know I'm getting good, but that good? Well, maybe I'm good enough,* she thought. *Or, maybe it's because I'm a woman and I can be of better assistance than a man can when it comes to certain things. Then again, that's what the handmaidens are for.* Realization sank in as she grappled with her thoughts and concluded that there really wasn't a good reason for her to be there. *What would the queen want with a newbie like me?* A feeling of unease began to gnaw in her stomach. She had been so dazzled by the excitement of getting promoted that her logic didn't even kick in. She was now also coming to realize that, though she had enlisted for her own reasons, she was feeling a deepening loyalty to her fellow soldiers and the queen—and a duty to embrace her new responsibilities. The carriage came to an abrupt halt, jolting her out of her thoughts. They had arrived. The carriage had escorted her directly to the back of the castle. She hadn't been back to the castle since that first day. This time, she was taken through a side door. This entrance was not visible from the front of the castle.

The hallway was nowhere near as glamorous as the main entrance, but it was still beautiful. It had marble floors, illuminated by soft yellow lighting. She was led to the private area for the personal guards.

It was an area with doors that led to different rooms, and it was very spacious. "Put your things here," the guard ordered, motioning to a corner in the open space. "You will be assigned a room later." She realized quickly he didn't like her. She could feel his energy and he was oozing jealousy. Perhaps he wanted the position she had been advanced to. She was used to people being jealous of her, but this felt different. Usually, she was confident and secure in her surroundings but here, she was unsure and intimidated. She covered it well, but she still felt like she was walking on rocky ground. Small nudges from Farka kept coming. She had been leaning on her a lot when the emotions got too intense. Farka was all she could count on. She needed to get it together and she knew it.

"First you must report to the queen," he huffed, snapping her out of it. "Follow me."

He was leading her to the throne room. Once again, a pit began to form in her stomach. Farka was with her, doing her best to help with the nerves. She sent Lenala another silent nudge. This time, it was a little stronger. Lenala felt it taking a moment to re-center and she let out an internal sigh. She glanced at Farka, nodding slightly. Farka returned the nod.

Soon she found herself standing in the beautifully familiar throne room. This time, it wasn't full of people seeking asylum or trying to kill the queen. The queen was waiting for her. "Come forward, Lenala," she called out melodically.

Lenala approached her and gave an appropriate bow. So she hoped. Although she was trying her best to control herself, she was trembling with nerves and adrenaline. "I'm sure you are wondering why I have chosen you to be in my personal guard," she stated rather than asking. "I've been watching you. Just as I said I would," she said deliberately. As she spoke, she brought one hand up to her face to rest her chin in it. She moved with grace. Her amber eyes were locked on Lenala.

"I have enjoyed watching you excel. Your determination and motivation are unmatched, and I need this kind of dedication in my guard." Her voice was low, rich and mesmerizing. "Not to mention it would be nice to have another woman around," she said with a small smirk. "The handmaidens are afraid of me and they have terrible conversational skills," she continued, waving her hand dismissively. "Your work ethic has proven to be most impressive." She paused just long enough for Lenala to start to thank her. Then she interrupted and continued, saying, "Do not disappoint me. You will be living a finer life than before now that you are within the castle walls, and you will be given much privilege." She paused and her expression tightened. "Remember, it can be taken as fast as it's given." She was an intimidating woman, but not to Lenala, who was raised by the most intimidating man in the Hamanan Galaxy. The queen's demeanor was mild to her, even though Lenala could see how she used this to her advantage.

"Are we in agreement"? she asked, fixing her eyes on Lenala's.

This time, Lenala knew she needed to respond. "Queen Halice, I am honored to be given this privilege and oppor-tunity." As she bowed her head, Lenala felt her stomach turning. She had never kissed up to royalty—she *was* royalty and people had always kissed up to her. A sweeping feeling of rage passed through her but it was stifled as quickly as it came. Farka. She knew, she felt it. As Lenala lifted her head, the feeling had passed. She smiled at the queen. She was playing a part and she had to remember. Stick to the plan. Kill Brantog.

The queen was watching her closely. Her work ethic and her confidence made her stand out from the rest. She was strong and determined. However, she carried herself with the poise of higher-class citizens. Her eyes shifted over to Farka. She was studying her intently, as if she was mesmerized. Lenala let out a breath as she waited for the queen to speak again.

"Very well then, welcome," she sang out. "Show her to her quarters and for goodness' sake, have the handmaids get her cleaned up." Lenala almost laughed out loud. She knew how dirty she was and how bad she must smell after living primitively. Instead, she stifled the laugh, nodded, and said, "Thank you, Queen Halice."

As soon as she arrived in her room, her face lit up. Finally, a nice bed and actual quarters suited for a woman. The room was large with a big bed and huge windows. The view from the window was beautiful and overlooked one of the gardens. There was a bathroom with a big tub that had plenty of space for Farka. The room was perfect for her to roam around and be comfortable.

The guard instructed her to report the following morning for training. Until then, she was to rest, get cleaned up, eat, and learn her way around the castle. The handmaids came in right away. They showed her around the room and the general area. They explained to her the protocols for meals and daily duties. They brought her clean clothes and a uniform that only the personal guards wore. The uniform was beautiful. It was solid black and had slim-fitting bottoms with a sleeveless top and gold shoulder plates stitched in.

It was more extravagant than what the Xurians wore, but Xuria was a very hot place—the soldiers would burn up in anything more than the thin garments they wore.

She would be more than happy to trade in her raggedy, brown training clothes for this.

The handmaidens showed her to her bathing room. Much to her delight, they already had a large bath drawn for her with bubbles and fine oils for her hair. The steam from the heat of the water clung to her skin. An invigorating, strong, sweet aroma filled the air. She submerged herself, allowing herself to relax until her fingers and toes became wrinkled from the water. This was the first proper bath she'd had in over a year. She took her time grooming herself. She felt refreshed and revived. Her skin felt soft again and her hair was smooth. She stood in front of the mirror and hardly recognized the reflection staring back at her. She would be nineteen soon. She let out a deep sigh. So much had changed since her last birthday. Mentally, she had grown up and felt more confident than ever. She was stronger and she was able to think fast in tough scenarios. She had been tested in both mental and physical situations that were exhausting, and she had succeeded. She couldn't help but notice how her body had transformed. Her abdomen had become etched with muscles, and her arms and legs were more defined and firmer. Looking at herself in the mirror, she realized that she looked like a Hite, and more like a woman than a young girl. Her hair had grown longer, and her face had become leaner. She still retained her curves and femininity, but now she looked fierce, and most importantly, she felt powerful.

In the reflection in the mirror, Farka leaped joyfully into the bath. Water splashed and sloshed everywhere as she dunked her head in and out of the water. Lenala couldn't help but laugh at her. She knew exactly how she felt. Once again, a sense of pride welled up as she looked at Farka. She let out another big sigh. They were both exhausted; it had been a long day of excitement and changes. Even though Farka didn't require much sleep, Lenala could tell she was tired. She wished they could just go to bed, but it was time for dinner, which meant it was time to meet the unit of guards she had been placed on.

She tied her hair up and put on the casual wear they had provided—a pair of sleek black pants and a crisp white top with gold stitching and buttons. The short sleeves revealed her newly defined muscles and tattoos. She stepped back and examined herself in the mirror. She felt a sense of confidence. She had worked hard to get to this point. She looked the part, she felt the part, and she was ready for this new step.

TWENTY-ONE

The dining room was grand and elaborate. Just as everything in the castle was. The off-duty guards were all seated around a big rectangular table talking. As soon as she entered, the room became silent, and all eyes were on her. Her heart rate soared but her face showed no emotion.

There were six men seated there, six men staring at her. The queen had a total of nineteen guards in the castle now including Lenala, and the others were on duty, enjoying their day off, training, or sleeping. They were divided into teams of five to eight. There were dedicated day and night guards. Lenala was on a day unit.

Wide-eyed, the men all watched as she and Farka approached. Lenala knew their awe was because of Farka. She was a few feet behind her and must have been giving her best impression of a soldier's walk.

"Welcome," one of the men said as he stood.

"My name is Enhan." He was very tall and strikingly

handsome. Lenala kept her eyes on his face to keep from sizing him up too obviously.

"Nice to meet you," she said cordially as she looked around the table at each of them. Enhan continued and introduced the men one by one. "My name is Lenala, nice to meet you all," she said, offering nothing else as she sat down. She knew she had to play her part but she hated introductions. "This is Farka," she said in a monotone voice.

The men acknowledged her with nods and their muttered greetings. Their attention was captivated by the Dragon, who sat tall and alert a fair distance away. It was evident that they had never seen a Dragon before. Coming from Xuria, a planet where Dragons were the cornerstone of their culture, she still wasn't used to the way people reacted to Farka. It was a reminder of how different her world was from theirs.

It was hard to focus on anything because the intoxicating aroma of food was causing her stomach to betray her. She hadn't had a proper meal in a long time. The small talk was graciously interrupted as dinner was served. Much to her delight, it was far better than anything she'd eaten since the Castle of Nahkei. She could get used to this. Conversation remained minimal as they ate. She hoped these men weren't boring. Especially since she would be working closely with them. They were all notably handsome, she admitted to herself. Clearly, the queen picked them for more than just their skills. Lenala took a little time to feel each of the guards out. While she was eating, she pressed into her gift and observed their behavior.

First there was Enhan, who stood out as the most handsome among the group. He was a tall Analician with deeply tanned skin and bright blue eyes that seemed to sparkle with life. His hair was cut close to his head and was almost white in color, which made his features all the more striking. Enhan had a light-hearted and cheerful demeanor that was contagious. He frequently cracked jokes to get a laugh out of the men, and Lenala couldn't help but be amused by his antics.

To Enhan's left sat the second guard, Tion, who was just as tall and imposing. He had the look of someone who could defeat any man in hand-to-hand combat. His rugged appearance showed that he had seen his share of battles. Unlike Enhan, Tion was quiet and reserved. He was not Analician, and his soft yellow hair and light brown eyes set him apart from the others. His skin was also tanned, but with a different hue than that of the Analicians'. Tion kept to himself, hardly looking up from his food. There was a heavy, dark aura around him.

The third member of the group was Doran, who was slightly shorter than Enhan and Tion but still quite tall. He appeared to be the youngest of the group, apart from Lenala. Doran was too busy talking to take a bite of his food, and his high-pitched voice got on Lenala's nerves. He spoke through his nose and had a whiny tone, making it difficult to get used to him. However, when he finally stopped talking, his good looks were hard to ignore. Like Enhan and Tion, Doran had blond hair, but his skin was fair. His green eyes were striking and vivid, and his lean, muscular build gave him an athletic appearance.

Her eyes drifted over to Quade, who appeared to be at least five years older than the others. He had a commanding presence that marked him as the leader of the group. There was something about him that garnered respect and authority. As she watched him, she couldn't help but be reminded of Semian, who exuded a similar level of confidence. Quade had black hair, dark skin, and piercing, almost black eyes. His sharp and etched features and his massive, muscular body added to his intimidating aura.

Quade's voice was deep and husky, and every now and then, he smiled a confident smile at one of Enhan's jokes, revealing a perfect set of teeth. *Ok, Queen,* Lenala thought, stifling a chuckle.

The last two were brothers, Crand and Drac, who were identical twins and clearly Pitian. Like all Pitians, they had creamy, tan skin, green eyes, and green hair. The gas produced by their home planet, Piatees, caused their hair and eyes to turn the same unique shade of green. It was an incredible sight to behold. Lenala had never seen people from other planets before her journey to Analicia, and she couldn't help but be especially intrigued by the Pitians. She hoped she wasn't staring at them like people had been staring at Farka. They were both strikingly good-looking men, with tall, muscular builds that suggested they were skilled fighters.

As she studied the brothers, her mind drifted to her sister Anala and the Pitian prince. A flash of worry crossed over her features as she considered the amount of time that had passed since she'd been gone. *It's been over six months. I hope she is safe and being smart.* The sound of laughter brought her back to the present. Enhan had made another joke. She laughed on cue as she continued to study them.

She felt a little silly noting their looks so much, but she couldn't help it. Shaking it off, she took a deep breath and decided to push past the surface and look deeper.

She quickly noticed that the twins had a combination of kindness and loyalty, traits that were highly valued among the Pitians.

Quade exuded a fierce energy that commanded respect. But beneath his tough exterior, she could sense a deep loyalty and patience that made her feel like she could trust him.

Enhan was the lighthearted one, always ready with a joke or a laugh to lift everyone's spirits. His happy-go-lucky attitude and kind nature made him instantly likable.

Doran seemed to be the newest member of the group. He exuded a peaceful energy and had a warm, boyish charm that reminded her of her brother, Tyralon.

And then there was Tion. At first glance, he seemed like a quiet and reserved man, but she could sense that he was hiding something. There was a darkness in his eyes that hinted at a troubled past. She decided to give him the benefit of the doubt. The queen had chosen these men to protect her. Obviously, they were the best. The one thing they all had in common was their loyalty. She could see that clearly after studying them.

A wave of relief flooded her body, giving her a sense of hope. Small talk ensued as they finished their food. "Lenala?'? Quade's deep voice boomed over the chatter.

A hush fell over the room as all eyes turned to her. Lenala's relief was quickly replaced by doubt. *I wish I had Escitalo with me.* Even with Farka there, she longed for Escitalo. She wanted the assurance that she could defend herself fully. She didn't know these men and even though they seemed to be ok, they could turn on her at any minute. *I'd hate to have to have Farka torch them,* she thought, taken aback at the amount of intensity she had.

"Dragons are hardly ever seen here," Quade continued. "Forgive me for asking but where did you get her?" His question seemed sincere. "Most of us have never laid eyes on a Dragon before. In my homeland, Dragons are considered creatures of myth, and we only heard stories about them when we were children. It wasn't until I arrived in Analicia that I discovered they actually existed."

Lenala relaxed a little as she realized Quade meant no harm. His tone was just intense. "She was a gift, when I was a child." Her words were slow and cautious.

"Are you Xurian?" he pressed.

"I am," she said.

"I've never met a Xurian," he continued.

"Well," she replied slowly, but her mind was racing. "We don't get out much," she said with a shrug and a smile. This elicited an unexpected eruption of laughter from the men. She burst into laughter as well. It felt amazing to let go and laugh freely—something she hadn't done in a long time. As the laughter settled, the air was lighter.

"Is it true that the king of Xuria is a tyrant?" Doran asked. She felt herself tense up.

Even though what he asked was true, she was not prepared to smudge her father's name. She thought for a moment before replying. "It depends on who you ask."

"And there are Dragons living amongst the people?" he continued.

It was clear to her that the history of Xuria was not well-known to others. Just as her father wanted. "Well, not exactly among us. They keep to themselves in the mountains," she offered.

"Is the problem with DB bad there? Like it is here?"

"DB?" she asked as her eyes moved over their faces. Some of them shuffled uncomfortably.

"Dragon's Blood," Tion answered with a raspy, deep voice. He cleared his throat as he looked up from his food. There was something dark in his eyes.

A chill ran down her spine. "Oh, right," she replied. She had never heard of it being called DB. "Is it bad here?"

"Very," he retorted. His voice was cold like shards of ice. The men all nodded in agreement.

"Well," she continued, "there was a time when it was bad, but now it's only a few here and there." She chose her words carefully, though she was beyond angry with her father. She didn't know these men and didn't want to tell them the inner secrets of her planet.

"DB has become a huge problem in Analicia," Enhan continued. "The people get crazy on it and they get sick if they don't have it," he said with a shrug. "Now that you are a part of our unit, we will make sure Farka stays safe. She is a part of our team now, too," he said. His gaze landed on Farka and softened. "We just can't have word of her getting out to the public just yet." Lenala felt a little bit of comfort in this. He was being genuine and if Farka was going to be safe, she was happy.

"I'm sure she makes one hell of a soldier," Crand interjected, his green eyes lighting up. "Is she trained in battle?"

Poor Farka, Lenala thought. *She's a domesticated Dragon who has had to become a fighter to save my life.*

"She is very tough by nature and has killed before," Lenala replied. "But she is not a trained soldier."

"Great," Crand said before she could finish her statement. "We can train her." He jumped up quickly. Drac rolled his eyes and shook his head at his brother's dramatic display. "Just imagine, the first army with a Dragon."

Lenala balled her fists under the table. Farka was hers and was not going to be exploited. *Is this why the queen brought me here? To use Farka as a weapon?* All of her instincts were on high alert and she knew she needed to intervene immediately.

"No," she said cautiously as she stood up. "Farka is my Dragon and she will not be a weapon for you to use at your convenience." Her tone was firm. Sensing Lenala's sudden change in emotion, Farka stood up right on cue, adding to the intimidation.

"Whoa," Enhan said with a shaky smile. "No one is trying to make her a weapon. I think Crand means that if she is here, she could be training with you and she could be of service."

"I have her trained exactly how she needs to be trained," Lenala snapped. "End of discussion."

Quade, who was meticulously studying Lenala's reaction, shifted forward in his chair, locking his eyes on her.

"It's her Dragon, now drop it." Enhan and Crand were instantly silent as they nodded. The room was frozen with tension for a moment. Lenala gave him a slight nod and sat back down. Had she not been so hungry, she would have left dramatically, but she needed to eat. Although she wanted to maintain a good rapport with the men, she wasn't going to let anyone get their hands on Farka. Farka was much too precious to her; she was a part of her. She hoped this would not be an issue again. Out of the corner of her eye, she saw Drac eyeing Crand with narrow eyes. "Look what you did, you idiot," he whispered. She smiled inside and relaxed a little. They were harmless and she liked their dynamic. Small talk continued around the table. The men were pleasant and Farka was at ease around them. They didn't mention her anymore and kept it light-hearted. They laughed a little more and ate a lot. Enhan gave her the instructions for the next morning. Breakfast would be early, then they would have a short briefing before relieving the night crew.

As she walked back to her room, a feeling of anticipation rushed through her. The day had been a rollercoaster of new emotions and it had left her feeling exhilarated and drained.

Once she reached her room, she decided to take another long, hot bath to unwind and think about everything that had happened. The steamy water enveloped her, and she let out a deep sigh of relief as the tension began to melt away. She couldn't help but feel a sense of expectation for what was to come. The next day, she would be directly serving the queen.

TWENTY-TWO

Guarding the queen was far from what Lenala had anticipated. Instead of excitement, her duties were mostly patrolling doors, shadowing her, and accompanying her all day long. Some days were even more monotonous because the queen would stay in her room for most of the day, not even emerging to eat. She would have her meals delivered to her. The queen's schedule was far from predictable. Some days, she would attend to the asylum seekers, and listen to the issues amongst the civilians. Other days, she would stay up late into the night strolling through the gardens. She did as she pleased.

Occasionally, the queen asked Lenala to walk beside her. She asked Lenala all kinds of questions about Dragons and her homeland. Her fascination with Farka made Lenala unexplainably uneasy. Despite her discomfort with all of the probing questions, she answered every one, though with a certain degree of caution.

The guards were never sure of what the day may have

in store for them. The only consistency in their schedule included their training days, days off, and days designated to guard the queen. The units never changed, even if someone was sick or if they were fired. If they were fired, Queen Halice would replace them. Just like she had done with Lenala.

She had replaced a guard who was fired for sneaking handmaids into his chambers while on duty.

Lenala was in Quade's unit. She had gotten to know the men better and found herself fitting in. Once again, she was becoming immersed in her new way of life. The queen had taken a special liking to her. Even the guards began commenting and teasing her about it. They said that it was because she was the newest toy. They told her to enjoy it because it would only last until the next one came along. She shot back, telling them that they were just jealous and upset because they weren't the center of her attention anymore. This had become a good way for them to joke around.

Lenala finally finished her training phase and was now eligible to have days off. Days when she could leave the castle alone. She had been patiently waiting and working hard for this ever since she joined the army.

She had been to town a few times before but never alone. She had a specific list of the things she would need to make poison. This list had been diligently constructed over time and hidden in her room.

She knew that she would not be able to get all of the ingredients at once because of the risk of alerting the herbalist. Surely, any skilled herbalist would know the ingredients for the concoction she was planning to make.

She would have to take her time getting the ingredients a few at a time and purchase other unrelated items as well.

Lenala's first solo trip to town was invigorating. The city was alive with energy, bustling with people from all over the galaxy. The cobblestone streets were immaculately clean, and there were numerous shops and bakeries lining the roads. The aroma of food in the air caused her stomach to growl. It didn't take her long to discover a few places that offered delectable breads and pastries. She even picked up a treat to bring back for Farka. She couldn't take Farka to town with her because she would draw attention to herself, and it wasn't safe because of the DB problem the men had warned her about. There were a few spots on the outskirts of town where the addicts were known to hang around. The Analician citizens tried to avoid interacting with them but sometimes, the users would wander into town. Most of the time, they came to steal goods to sell for money to buy more blood. They didn't even want food when it was offered to them. All they wanted was blood, which was hard to come across; if anyone knew about Farka, she would be in grave danger. The guards told her that blood was smuggled in from other planets. They told her stories of Dragon farms where they collected and sold the blood. Lenala was suspicious that Xuria had some dealers, even though they would have to be extremely careful to get it past the king. She could only imagine how angry he would be if he caught anyone doing that. She shuddered at the thought.

The herbary was huge. The aroma of various herbs and oils filled the air. The herbalist was an old man named Calcius. He was a short and portly man with a long, white beard and round, thick glasses. He hobbled around the shop as fast as he could, helping his customers with a smile on his face. "Hello there, and welcome." His voice was warm and endearing. She liked him immediately. He was friendly and had a trustworthy essence about him. "Let me show you around and if you need anything, just ask." He had one entire wall of shelves filled with various potions. The other two walls were lined with shelves that were stocked with a variety of herbs. There were rows of tables with an array of plants all neatly labeled for easy identification. After the tour, he hurried off to help other customers. She was glad the shop was busy. She blended right in and hoped she could get a few of the items without him noticing exactly what they were. She needed ten items to make the mix. After careful consideration, she decided three items would be safe to start with. Sure enough, to her relief, he didn't even seem to notice what she was buying. Lenala exchanged a few more pleasantries with Calcius before stowing the herbs in her bag and making her way back to the castle.

The comforting warmth of Haruelio was a welcome sensation as Lenala basked in its glow. She closed her eyes and allowed the gentle rays to envelop her as she took a deep breath and inhaled the sweet fragrance of a nearby bush adorned with bright red flowers. She savored the aroma, allowing it to transport her to a moment of peaceful tranquility. Suddenly, she felt a dark shadowy presence very near her. Her eyes jolted open and darted around. Nothing. She slipped her hand inside her coat and onto the grip of her sword. Escitalo immediately came to life and began pulsating. It had become her favorite feeling. It seemed as though the sword was always ready for anything. She continued her trek back to the castle but could not shake the eerie feeling that she was being watched. She looked around once again and didn't see anything unusual. She was used to being looked at; she was beautiful and people had always stared at her, but this was different. She felt uneasy and unnerved. She wished she could bring Farka with her next time as she tucked her purchase in close. *Maybe I'm just being paranoid after buying supplies to make poison.*

Hurrying back to the castle, Lenala tried to shake off her apprehension, hoping that she was just being overly cautious. When she entered her room, Farka was waiting anxiously by the door, clearly uncomfortable about being left alone. Lenala knew that Farka would eventually adapt, but it was still difficult for her to leave her behind. They had rarely spent much time apart, but it was for Farka's own good. When Lenala was present, Farka was free to roam the castle grounds. But if Lenala left the grounds, Farka had to remain in the room.

That night, Lenala dreamed of being followed. She dreamed that she was free-falling in a smoky tunnel while Farka was being taken from her. The overwhelming feeling of coldness and emptiness consumed her. It took her a while to rip herself out of the dream. She sat up, gasping for breath, her heart racing. She was covered in sweat.

"Farka!" she screamed, desperately looking around. The room was dark and silent. She could usually feel Farka's presence but right now, she couldn't. Farka was gone.

In a state of panic, she leaped up and rushed over to Farka's bed. The room was so dark that she couldn't see anything. Fear gripped her tightly. Then suddenly, Farka stirred and jerked her head up in surprise, startling them both. "Oh, Farka.'' Lenala threw her arms around her as the fear and tension drained from her. "I thought I lost you.'' She gushed out, "Thank Draygon it was only a dream."

Farka, who was far less concerned than Lenala, sleepily nuzzled her to reassure her that she was ok before laying her head back down. Lenala went back to bed but still couldn't shake that empty feeling she'd had. Maybe Farka was just in too deep a sleep or maybe she was still being paranoid from the market.

The next morning, Farka was wide awake and lying nearby when Lenala woke up. Warmth flooded through her. This was the way she was supposed to feel when she was with Farka.

She shuddered at the memory of the night. She never wanted to feel like that again. She shook it off and hurried to get ready for her day. Out of the corner of her eye, she noticed Farka was licking her leg. "What is it, girl?" Lenala said, walking over to inspect. She had a tiny cut in one of her scales. "What happened?" Farka snorted in dismissal. Clearly, it didn't hurt and she didn't want Lenala making a fuss over her. Maybe the lack of sleep was causing her to overreact. She must have bumped into something. It seemed to be healing, so Lenala wrapped it up and left it alone. "That's better. Okay, let's go."

~

The strange feeling hovered over Lenala throughout the day. They spent most of the day guarding the queen in the garden.

It was a day when Queen Halice was very quiet and chose not to engage in conversation. Instead, she sat there for hours gazing at the sky.

Lenala didn't mind easy days like this. It gave her time to think and work on her plan. Her heart wrenched as her thoughts drifted back to her last conversation with Kineah.

They had discussed the possibility of Lenala being kept away from the castle of Nahkei. Death or exile had never even occurred to her. Which was why she was so shocked that the council suggested them.

She promised Kineah that she would do everything she could and that she would not give up on her. A pang of sadness passed over her as she remembered Kineah's deep sorrow and their long hug before she left. Lenala had been grappling with the guilt of choosing to leave her, even though she knew it was for the greater good.

Just then, as she was lost in thought, a cracking sound echoed behind her. She snapped her head around and caught a glimpse of movement near the entrance to the garden. She had to do a double-take because it was so fast. An eerie wave engulfed her. It was the same presence she felt in the city. She quietly moved toward the entrance to check it out. Her eyes darted back and forth. There was nothing. *Are my eyes playing tricks on me? Or is it the lack of sleep?*

"Everything ok?" Tion's deep voice startled her. He was right behind her. His piercing eyes fixed on her.

"I thought I heard something. But it must have been the wind," she said as she returned to her position of guarding. *He never misses a thing,* she thought with a shudder.

"Mmm," he said, turning and heading back toward his post. The queen and Tion had a close relationship. Tion was not only a member of the queen's personal guard, but also held the esteemed position of inspecting all shipments of supplies to and from the castle. This was a highly noble job, entrusted only to those who had proven themselves to be loyal and trustworthy. Tion's unwavering dedication to the queen and his impeccable attention to detail made him an invaluable asset to the guard. Lenala found him to be mysterious. He had striking features, including light brown eyes and long, dark blond hair tied back with a leather strap, that added to his allure. Although he had an intimidating presence, she was not one to be easily intimidated. However, there was a certain darkness about him that made her uneasy and hesitant to trust him. Despite Lenala's attempts to give him the benefit of the doubt, it was a challenge. So, she mostly avoided interacting with him, and was thankful that their encounters were usually limited to group settings.

She looked over her shoulder once more and decided it must have been a tree branch or something blowing the wind. Farka was alert, but she didn't seem worried. Lenala took a deep breath and told herself to quit overreacting. She really needed a good night of sleep.

As she shifted her gaze back toward the queen, she was surprised to see her looking right at her.

How long has she been watching? Is there anything these people don't notice? The queen summoned her forward. Lenala heard a stifled cough and out of the corner of her eye, she saw Crand, who was doing a terrible job at holding back a smirk. She rolled her eyes internally at him.

"Do bring Farka," Queen Halice said as Lenala approached. "I want to look at her a little more closely," she sang in her rhythmic voice. Lenala nodded and summoned Farka with her mind without turning her gaze from the queen. Tion shuffled slightly as they passed by.

The queen's eyebrows shot up as she said, "How fascinating: You can communicate with her through your thoughts?"

"That's amazing," she murmured. As Farka approached, Lenala sent her a nudge to stop her from coming too close.

The queen looked at her. "She is truly a magnificent and majestic creature. I would

give anything to have my own. A gift from your grandfather, right?" She continued talking without allowing Lenala to answer, something she often did during their conversations. "And what happened to her leg? Why the bandage? Is she injured?"

This time, she waited for an answer.

"It's just a little cut," Lenala answered.

The queen's brow furrowed. "May I see it? I used to dabble in the art of medicine and herbs before I became the queen," she sang.

Lenala was a little surprised at this news. *The queen is into herbs and medicine?* She summoned Farka closer and unwrapped the bandage. "There, there," said the queen as she looked at the cut, "I'll have our doctor bring her some ointment to fix that right up." There was a slight quiver in her voice and a single drop of sweat on her brow. "Tion, see to it that she gets some ointment. We don't want that getting infected," she called out.

"Wow, what a beauty," she gushed. Her eyes were fixed on Farka. For a moment, Lenala thought she caught a glimpse of envy in the queen's gaze. Or was it admiration? Then after a long pause, she dismissively waved a hand and said, "That's enough for today.

Night after night, Lenala would wake up in a panic, searching for Farka—only to find her sleeping soundly and without a worry in the world.

TWENTY-THREE

More than a year had passed since Lenala was exiled. She had now served with the queen's private guard for over six months. Another birthday had come and gone. She turned nineteen years old. Although she was excited at what she had accomplished in the past year, she could never get rid of the underlying darkness that loomed and lurked around her. This birthday only served as a haunting reminder that another sacrifice had taken place in Xuria. It gnawed at her knowing there was nothing she could do. She was so disconnected from her home that she knew nothing about the situation. She had tried to find a Murke to send word to her sister, but with no luck. Anala would be living in the Castle of Nahkei by now.

The thought of Brantog having another year of winning his deceitful, disgusting game ate a pit in her stomach. She couldn't be joyful until he was brought to justice. There he was, living his best life while playing the

Dragons and deceiving everyone. To make matters worse, her father and the council were covering it up. Every time she thought of the lies, it made her blood boil. Her anger was her continued motivation to finish what she had started. At times, she wished she could forget it all and stay in Analicia forever. She knew she could have a good life here. She was well on her way to being one of the most distinguished guards and maybe one day, she could study in the university. There was so much she wanted to learn. *If only I could forget it all.*

She found herself thinking about it more and more. Sometimes, she would get caught up in dreaming of the possibilities. There was so much out there that she could have if she never looked back at Xuria. However, the truth was sobering and she knew better. She had to get her mind right on several occasions. She knew what needed to be done. She had a mission to complete. No matter how hard it got at times, she kept on pushing. Day after day. Eventually, she would be ready and all of this would be behind her. So much time had been spent integrating into this new life. There were periods of time when she felt like she was just spinning in circles. Even though the progress had been gradual and sometimes it felt like she was wasting time, she was caught up in the process and devoted to her plan. No matter how long it took, she would patiently live out each day until it was time to make her move.

She had strategically gathered most of what she needed for the poison, but there were three herbs she couldn't find.

She recently learned from Calcius that they only came in once a year, and she would need to wait for them to arrive. Hurry up and wait seemed to be her new life motto.

It was her off day and she had decided to stay in her quarters after another long, restless night. She wanted to spend some quality time with Farka and relax.

Farka was still having trouble with the same cut that wouldn't seem to heal. The ointment helped a little bit, but it was becoming concerning because now, Farka seemed to be bothered by it. She acted as if it was tender and she licked it throughout the day.

They were having a relaxing morning when suddenly, there was a loud knock on the door.

Bang, Bang, Bang,

Lenala jumped up and hurried to answer. Much to her surprise, it was one of the soldiers from another unit.

"Good morning, Lenala," he said in a deep, commanding voice. "The queen has requested your presence immediately. She is in her throne room."

Lenala hurried and got ready. She was in her lounge clothes and couldn't go see the queen dressed like that. A pang of worry shot through her. It was uncommon to be summoned on one's day off. *What in Draygon's name could she want?*

With Farka in close pursuit, she set out for the throne room. When she arrived, the energy in the room was buzzing.

Lenala was taken aback by the appearance of a soldier standing before the queen, but it wasn't just any ordinary soldier. He had long, thick black hair and a towering, muscular build adorned with tattoos, unmistakably marking him as a Xurian. Her heart pounded as she continued to study him. Something was amiss and it took her a moment to recognize that he was wearing the uniform of the Analician soldiers. *Another Xurian in the*

Analician army? As she continued to move closer, she began to recognize the tattoos. They were the markings of a Hite. As Lenala stared at the Hite in disbelief, sudden realization and panic gripped her. She knew the man standing before her all too well. It was Semian.

He found me. What is he doing here? Lenala was barely able to contain the rush of emotions that flooded through her. She was unsure of what was happening and her senses were on high alert. Farka immediately recognized Semian and sensed Lenala's turmoil. Remaining calm, Farka sent a wave of tranquility to Lenala, hoping to help her relax.

Is the queen angry? Is he here to take me back to Xuria?

Before she could consider more options, the queen spoke. "Lenala, do you know this man?" Her heart rate was steadily climbing. *Do I say yes or no? What are his intentions?* The queen quickly continued, "He claims to know you." This was one time she was actually thankful for her run-on questions. "We already know he is a Xurian," she sang as her eyes moved up and down Semian.

"He wants to serve in my personal guard," she mused with a small smirk. "The only problem is that I don't have an opening for another guard." She leaned back in her throne as she continued to eye Semian. "And we all know that he's far too skilled to be a regular soldier—he's proven that over the past month."

Wait, what? He's been here for a month? How did I not know? What was he thinking? Is he spying on me? Although Lenala's mind was racing, her face was like a stone.

"Hmm," the queen went on, "perhaps I could use him as a personal guard." She emphasized the word *could*. "I'd have to make an exception. What is it with you Xurians? You seem to have a way of getting me to make exceptions.

"Lenala," she snapped, "on your word, would he be a worthy guard? Should I add him to my personal services? If he is a friend of yours, he is a friend of mine," she continued.

She then stared at Lenala, ready for an answer.

Lenala thought quickly. *Should I trust Semian? Or is he here to cause problems? Was he sent here to kill me?* So many thoughts were going through her head. Her eyes locked with Semian's.

Here goes nothing, she thought.

"Queen Halice, Semian is one of the best soldiers I know. He taught me much of my early training. It would be my honor to recommend him to you."

She knew there must be a good reason he was here. After all, he had infiltrated the army to get to her. She would find out soon enough, and he better not disappoint her.

The queen was silent, her expression grew pensive, and she appeared to be lost in thought for a long moment. "Very well, then, why not?" she suddenly exclaimed. "Welcome to my guard. You will join Lenala in Quade's unit." Semian gave a respectful bow, expressing his gratitude to the queen. Lenala followed suit and bowed as the queen rose from the throne.

"Go on now," she said as she waved them off.

They both bowed again and exited the room. The guards led them out. Lenala didn't dare say a word until they were far from anyone else. The walk down the hallway and away from the guards felt like it would never end. Finally, they were alone.

"Semian..." She rushed her words without thinking. "What in Draygon's name are you doing here? Why didn't you come to me sooner?" Her face flushed red with anger.

"Lenala," he started, his amber eyes locked on hers. His expression was emotionless and hard for her to read. His voice was warm and familiar, and just the sound of it sent a wave of memories and emotions flooding through Lenala. Her gaze moved over his face, and she felt an overwhelming urge to hug him tightly. Memories of the last time they were together spread through her, including the passionate kiss they had shared. Thoughts of that kiss had lingered in her mind ever since.

"I had to leave Xuria," Semian replied urgently. The king, your father, was planning to assemble a team to assassinate the Pitian prince!"

"What?" Lenala gasped. Her mind immediately went to Anala.

"He wanted us to sneak over there without the Dragons' permission and carry out the assassination," Semian continued, his voice filled with concern. "I refused to be a part of it. I told the king that I would not violate the Dragons and put our people at risk just to kill a man. But he didn't take no for an answer. He threatened to demote me, exile me, and even kill me for insubordination. He wanted to scare me into fulfilling his dirty little plan, but I won't be threatened, Lenala. After all the years I've given him in service, he thinks he can force me to do his bidding? I won't stand for it. So, I escaped and came here to find you."

Semian paused for a moment before continuing, "I had to find you because your sister is in danger..."

"If my sister is in danger, then why did you wait so

long to find me?" Lenala interrupted. Her face turned red and her voice trembled as she spoke.

"Lenala, I tried every day to find a way to get word to you and I wasn't granted leave until today. I had to be sure it was safe here without blowing my cover. I had to make sure you were safe, and that these people could be trusted," Semian explained earnestly. "I've been keeping an eye on you and the people here for a while now. Infiltrating their army was the only way I could fulfill my plan to safely get to you. I could not risk revealing your identity and putting your life in danger. Now please let me explain."

Lenala crossed her arms as she nodded for him to continue.

"Anala has been sneaking off to see the Pitian prince, and it's unclear how long this has been going on. The prince was spotted by our guards near the border, and a fight broke out between him and one of our men. During the fight, the bodies of the men we killed were found, and the prince was blamed for their deaths. Anala was nearby and tried to intervene, but in doing so, she gave away their secret. Word got to the king, and he was furious. Anala is now back in the castle being punished until the king decides what to do. He wants the prince dead, and I fear the worst for your sister."

Lenala was speechless as she listened. She had worried about her sister getting caught, but she never imagined it would turn out like this. The news hit her hard, leaving her breathless and stunned.

It would only be a matter of time before he sent the unit of men over to Piatees. King Byreon was not going to let this go. The gravity of the situation was intense. If he sent men to kill the prince, this would start a war with

Piatees. Even worse, the Dragons would likely banish the Xurians from their land or kill them for treason. Her brain was in overload. Another wave of panic hit her as she thought of her brother. What if the king sent him in to kill the Pitians? Then, he would be in danger of the Dragons' vengeance.

"Lenala, I told your father that I killed those men. I couldn't let their blood lie on innocent hands. He called off the assassination but he still wanted the prince arrested for trespassing. He wants to punish him for everything with Anala. He's obsessed with the prince and I believe he will he change his mind and kill him."

She looked at Semian, trying to find the right words. Her mind was racing. "They have to leave Xuria." Her words came out absentmindedly.

"Who has to leave?" Semian asked.

"Or else they will die."

"*Who* will die?" he pressed.

"My siblings." Lenala stuttered as she tried to find the right words. Semian was quiet as he looked at her. Suddenly, she felt self-conscious. His body language was different and there was a small glimmer of excitement in his eyes. She had changed in the past year and since the last time she saw him, when she had saved his life. Then there was the kiss, the kiss that haunted her. Did it haunt him the same way? Was he also obsessed with the memory of that night? *Wait, what am I doing?* She furrowed her brow.

Is Semian trying to scare me into returning home?

Is this some made-up plan to capture me? Did my father send him here??

"How did you find me?" she asked as she narrowed her eyes.

"The Murkes," he answered, almost too quickly. "I had them follow you."

Suddenly, realization hit Lenala as she remembered the feelings she'd had of being followed.

The more he spoke, the more she was able to read him. *Sincere,* she thought. She relaxed her arms and looked away. Lenala felt his energy. He was concerned and scared for Xuria. She could feel it.

"How did you get here? And what is your plan?" she pressed.

"I traveled on foot. It took me close to one month. To be honest, I don't have a solid plan yet. I need you to help me find a way to stop him. He's going to commit treason against the Dragons and our people will suffer."

"And how do you propose to stop him?" Lenala already had ideas running through her head. Poison darts for one.

Semian does not know of the Brantog case, and he certainly has no idea that I plan on taking him out. Now he wants me to help him stop my father. This is a mess.

"We will build a case against him and take it to the Dragons," he said, interrupting her thoughts.

"Or, we could just poison him," Lenala said flatly.

Semian's eyebrows shot up. "He will stop at nothing, Lenala, but do you really want to kill him?"

"He is a tyrant, Semian. Do you know why I was exiled?"

He stared at her blankly. "Exiled?" he repeated as a dark expression clouded his face. Nobody knew the real reason except the king, queen, the council, and her sister. Her brother didn't even know for his own sake. In order to protect him, Lenala had made her sister swear not to tell him.

Before Lenala could continue, Quade approached, clearing his throat as his eyes darted between Semian and Lenala. After briefly introducing himself to Semian, he turned to Lenala and informed her, "I've been instructed to show Semian to his quarters. Also, the queen wishes to see you." *Twice in one day? This can't be good.*

CHAPTER

TWENTY-FOUR

She stood there collecting her thoughts as she watched Semian and Quade walk away. Lenala's worry for her sister had now escalated to a full-on concern as her mind raced with questions. How long had Anala been under house arrest? What was her father planning? Had he already sent soldiers to Piatees? Was her brother safe? The situation could turn into a war, and it could spell the end for Xuria. How could her father be so stubborn and selfish as to put the whole planet at risk? And what was Anala thinking? How could she continue to engage in such dangerous behavior?

So many questions ran through Lenala's head as she made her way back to see the queen, feeling a lingering sense of darkness creeping in.

This time, she was sent to the queen's private quarters, which she had not been to since her first day in Analicia. Farka was emitting an aura of nervousness and sticking close to Lenala. Their energies were intertwining and amplifying each other.

She paused for a moment, waiting for the guard to leave. She needed to bring her and Farka closer together to soothe their energies. Farka placed her snout on Lenala's shoulder. They closed their eyes and she whispered soft, calming words. She'd had quite an emotional afternoon with Semian showing up. She knew she would have to process that more later but for right now, she needed to be calm and composed. She didn't like feeling out of control of her emotions. She took three deep breaths with her eyes closed. Farka did the same. Her breaths sounded more like deep growls. She and Farka let their minds clear for another few breaths. The tension finally released. Lenala knew she was in deep and needed to remain calm to maintain her position.

She approached the doors feeling a little stronger. A guard opened the door, motioning for her to enter the queen's dayroom. The room was a space where the queen would entertain her guests and unwind. Sometimes, she would spend entire days or even longer periods of time there. It had been so long since Lenala had been in the room that she had forgotten what it looked like. The dayroom was spacious and grand, with an elaborate sitting area centered around a magnificent fireplace. The tall windows were adorned with luxurious drapes woven with golden threads, giving the room an air of luxury. *Fit for a queen.*

She could envision herself or better yet, her mother lounging in here. The aroma in the air was so sweet that she could almost taste the fresh fruits and the fine wine. Her mother used to allow her to have wine on occasion. Now that she was old enough to indulge on her own, she wished she could. A stab of sadness hit her when she thought of her mother. Her warm, beautiful smile and her genuine love for others were undeniable. Lenala smiled for a moment, but just as quickly as she felt that sadness, anger followed. Her mother had ultimately sided with her father. The logical side of Lenala didn't blame her. She understood, as she knew how the political scene worked. Her mother's fight would never be won. She was power-less. She knew anger wasn't the feeling she should harbor, but it was there. She had ultimately chosen to cover for Brantog over listening to her daughter.

At that moment, Lenala felt a rising resilience inside. "You will never be powerless," she whispered to herself. Farka let out a small grunt of reassurance.

"Let's go," Lenala whispered boldly as she proceeded to the private sitting area.

The queen was waiting for her. "Sit down, my dear," Queen Halice demanded softly. Her piercing eyes were locked on Lenala. Those eyes didn't miss much but Lenala didn't worry. She knew her cover was rock-solid and she was excellent at shielding herself from other people's intuition.

"I want to talk to you about something important. I've been watching you closely, as you know," she started in her typical fashion. "But more so since you've been in my guard, and now that I've added another guard to my service, I wish to have you as my private guard." She paused briefly as she watched Lenala attentively. "I will have you accompany me on more personal matters." She made an effort to drag the word *personal* out. "You will still be a part of the same unit, but sometimes I will need you to do things for me. Things that don't suit a man," she said with a small smirk.

"You will be given more privilege and more responsibility. I need to know that I can trust you, and I believe I can." She continued talking with hardly any time to take a breath between words.

"You have quickly become someone I enjoy talking with, and I'd like to have you accompany me for visits more often. Farka as well," she said as she glanced over at the Dragon. "My, what a beautiful creature she is. I'd love to learn more about Dragons," she mused in her singy voice. Farka sat very still. She was sitting up tall and held her snout down just a little. Lenala almost laughed at how menacing she looked. She played her part well. Farka was fascinating and intimidating to others, especially the queen.

"So, what do you think?" she asked, looking back at Lenala pointedly. Her expression told Lenala this was a question that required an immediate answer. *I mean, what choice do I have?* she thought. *What am I going to do, say no?* She had no idea what this would entail but she knew she needed to say yes.

"I would be honored to serve you in whatever way you see fit," she replied. "Thank you for giving me this opportunity." She lowered her head, taking the bow that she hated so much.

As she rose from the bow, she noted the queen was looking at her. A slight smile was on her lips. Her eyes were soft as she nodded in approval. "Right then!" she burst out with a clap.

"Sit down, let's chat. I know you are educated and I long for a good conversation. Tell me more about your home. I know very little of Xuria, only what you've told me and I want to know everything about Draygon."

Lenala found herself relieved to get her mind off the matters at hand.

They sat and talked for hours. The queen wanted to know everything about her planet, even down to what the ground looked like, what the people ate, and what they wore. She wanted to know a lot about the men. Especially after seeing Semian.

"He is a gorgeous man," she said with a gleam in her eyes. Lenala couldn't help but agree. The men in Xuria were all handsome, and he was one of the handsomest.

She wanted to know all about the Dragons. Lenala gave her as much information as she could without telling her too much of the truth. She didn't want to tell on herself nor did she want to tell too many of her planet's secrets.

She said just enough to entertain the queen and not enough to ruin anything.

Farka was now completely out of character and lying in the corner, napping during most of the conversation. The queen was clearly infatuated with Dragons. She lit up when Lenala talked about them. Lenala had begun to accept that a lot of people were equally afraid and mesmerized when they saw Farka. Though many people from the different planets worshipped Draygon, most people had never seen a Dragon in real life. She had taken them for granted because of where she grew up. Xuria was the sacred land of the Dragons. She respected the Dragons, especially because of Farka. She even prayed to Draygon on occasion, even though her father had not raised her to worship Draygon. Her whole life had been Dragon-oriented right down to the architecture of the castle. The queen didn't strike Lenala as someone who prayed much but she was enthralled with Draygon. She asked question after question. The conversation continued until the queen needed to leave for a meeting.

As Lenala was preparing to leave, the queen made a request. "May I pet Farka?" she asked, her voice filled with curiosity. Lenala hesitated for a moment, unsure about someone touching her beloved Dragon. However, she decided to grant the queen's request. "Of course," she replied, her voice calm and composed.

She sent a nudge for Farka to come over and let Queen Halice pet her. Farka was stunning and invigorating. Her breathing was loud and almost sounded like grunts. She walked slowly with her tail swaying behind her.

When she approached the queen, Lenala could see several small beads of sweat had formed on her forehead. Lenala almost laughed at how nervous she was. Petting a Dragon must be nerve-racking.

She gave one or two small pats to Farka, who didn't seem to mind but just for show, made a low growl. "Whoa!" The queen snatched her hand away, wide-eyed. Lenala played along and pretended to calm Farka. Soothing her, she said to the queen, "She will get used to you." Lenala had a profound sense of pride. Farka was playing the part of a menacing Dragon so well. She was a natural.

The day had quickly passed and it was almost time for dinner. Lenala and Farka headed back to their room to get cleaned up and ready to meet the men for dinner.

Lenala released her tightly braided hair and flung herself onto the bed. This had been quite a day. She just needed a few minutes to let her mind work. She was over-whelmed with the thought of Semian being there and the information he had given her. A rush of emotions flooded through her.

Seeing Semian today had brought a whole wave of feel-ings back to her. Semian was five years older than her and had been her main trainer. She had trained with him since she was twelve and he was seventeen. He was the one who taught her how to use a sword. Most of her lessons from him were tactics he was learning at the same time. In return, she made sure his family had plenty of food and supplies. There were a couple of other young soldiers who had also helped her learn, but he was the one in charge. She had always had a crush on him, but she knew that to him, she was just a young girl. She also respected him and admired his abilities in military tactics. He had always been at the top of the class in sword yielding, hand-to-hand combat, wrestling, and every other aspect of training. She looked up to him and trusted him. If it weren't for him taking a risk with her, she would have had a much harder road in her training.

When she was about sixteen years old, Lenala began to notice a change in Semian's behavior toward her. He appeared to be more nervous and would stumble over his words when speaking to her, despite his usual strength. Though he tried to hide it, Lenala could sense the change in his demeanor. She had caught him looking at her once or twice with a certain kind of gaze, one that she was familiar with. As she grew into a beautiful young woman, men and women alike began to take notice of her. While most of them revered her, some were envious, and Lenala had grown accustomed to this attention. Just not from

Semian. Then, when she was taken to the Castle of Nahkei, she didn't see him for over a year. The next time she saw him was when he had to sneak her out of town. He had no idea what he was doing or why he was taking her away. That night still rang fresh in her mind. The killings, hiding the bodies, the kiss.

A wave of butterflies flew through her.

She thought about him often. They had never admitted to having affection toward each other. They never showed any real signs but that kiss told her differently, and now here he was, in Analicia.

Dinner bells jolted her awake. "Shit." She jumped up. This whole day had been a mess of emotions and surprises. She had fallen asleep.

She got up and quickly got ready. "No wonder I'm so exhausted. "Farka, I wish I could live like you and only sleep a little." Resting only at night, Farka never slept soundly and would often get up to pace around. This behavior was typical of Dragons, as they did not require much sleep in general.

"If only I could get away with a little sleep," she muttered.

Dinner was approaching, which meant that Lenala would soon be in the presence of Semian. As she felt the familiar flutter in her stomach, she took a deep breath and tried to calm herself before hurrying off to the dining hall.

TWENTY-FIVE

By the time she arrived at dinner, the men were already seated and having small talk. She sat in her seat, which happened to be directly across from Semian. She was doing her best to act natural and not nervous. She didn't want him to say the wrong thing and blow her cover.

He had already introduced himself to the group and seemed to be fitting in well. He was used to military men and knew how to blend in. He had a presence about him that commanded respect. Very much like Quade. The men all commanded respect but Quade and Semian were the type who automatically took the lead.

Semian was typically quiet and not the type to try to project himself on anyone. He had no problem speaking his mind, but he wasn't going to be the most talkative person in the room. He was generally shy as a younger man, but that only seemed to push him further in his training. He had quickly risen and become one of the top Hite in the Xurian army. His tattoos showed that. Lenala noticed that he had gained several more tattoos since she'd trained with him, all tattoos of mastery in the different arts of war. These took years to achieve and were a high honor. She was impressed but not surprised. He had always outworked everyone.

She felt silly sitting there with her royal tattoos. She had always wanted military tattoos. Here, only the two of them knew the meaning of their tattoos. She knew her skills were inferior to his, yet here she sat at the same table with him. As if she were his equal in skill. *If only they knew what kind of a soldier he really is.* She felt a strong desire to prove to him that she had done it. That she had used what he taught her and advanced in rank. She felt an urgency to show him that she wasn't an imposter. *Why do I feel so vulnerable around him?* she thought. Maybe it was because he was from her homeland or because of their history. Perhaps it was because he could out her and ruin everything she had worked so hard for. Or maybe she felt that way because he was there for her. He had fled Xuria and everything he'd ever known to find her.

Ugh, this day and these emotions are too intense. Suddenly, she felt his gaze piercing her. She looked up and knew immediately he was reading her like a book. He could see exactly what she was trying to hide.

"Semian," she said flatly, trying to deflect any more intruding eyes. "I hope you are finding yourself welcome here."

"Wow, two Xurians! This is great," Enhan said, cutting right through the tense air. "Yeah," Crand piped in. Lenala cringed inside. Semian's expression and energy lightened, but he didn't take his eyes off of her. He saw the cringe. He was amused at her nervousness. No one else seemed to notice it, but he did.

"We've hit the jackpot," Crand kept on.

"Do you have a Dragon, too?"

Semian cracked a small smile as he turned his gaze away from Lenala. Crand's lightheartedness was easy to like. "It's my honor to be here. And no, I don't have a Dragon," he said as he looked back at Lenala. She froze inside. Her eyes were pleading with him not to say the wrong thing.

"I guess I wasn't lucky enough," he continued, his gaze moving around the table. He must have known she was grappling with trusting him.

"You see, Dragons aren't available for everyone—you can't just buy them," he continued. "They are bestowed upon you, and only three of our warriors have ever been lucky enough to have been given one." Lenala glanced around the table. They seemed to be buying it. She was afraid this would go wrong, so she chimed in before anyone could start asking questions. "My father was a great warrior and Lord Draygon blessed him by awarding me a protector Dragon." This wasn't fully a lie, and it would suffice to shut them up. She looked at Semian, who seemed intrigued with her input. *Does he think this is funny? If he blows this, I will never forgive him.*

She gave Semian a look warning him to stop talking about her. She was thankful he obliged.

Small talk continued, mostly among the men. Lenala chimed in occasionally and laughed at some of Enhan's jokes. She tried to seem casual but deep down, she couldn't wait to get Semian alone and talk with him. They had a lot to cover. She'd have to be careful not to draw attention to them. They were in a precarious situation. Finally, dinner was finished and the guards began to go their separate ways. Semian took the opportunity to whisper to Lenala, "We need to talk."

"Come to my room in one hour," she replied barely above a whisper.

He gave a nod and headed off.

One hour seemed to take all night. She had smoothed her hair and looked in the mirror more times than she liked to admit. Farka watched from her bed as Lenala made a fuss.

She was clearly amused but could not care less.

Finally, a small knock on the door. *Rap, rap, rap.*

She hurried over and let him in, looking around to make sure the coast was clear before she locked the door.

"No one saw me," he said. "I made sure of it and I'll leave through the window later. I know a route."

"Ok," she started to say as she turned to face him.

Suddenly, he pulled her into his arms. "I have missed you, Lenala. I was so worried about you."

Lenala embraced Semian with equal force, feeling the depth of her longing for him. As she breathed in his familiar scent, memories of home came flooding back to her, and she relished the comfort of being near someone she had known for so long and trusted. "I missed you too, Semian," she replied, overwhelmed with relief that he had come. "I am so glad you are here."

They stood there for a few moments before pulling away. Neither of them wanted to let go.

"I thought you were sent away to see a healer," Semian

said in a low voice. "And now that I know the truth, I would have never been able to rest. Why were you exiled?"

"You better sit down for this," she said with a big sigh.

Lenala recounted everything to Semian—the involvement of Brantog and Kineah, the foul play, and his tampering with the drawings. She shared the details of her meeting with the council and her father's ultimatum, as well as her plan to join the army and create the poison. Lenala explained how she had to use the army as a cover to blend in and keep Farka safe while making the substance. She also revealed the killings that had taken place over Dragon's Blood. Semian listened intently, his emotions shifting visibly as she told each detail.

Semian's initial reaction was one of anger. "How could Brantog be allowed to get away with this? And worse, how could King Byreon permit it and even go so far as to cast out his own daughter for speaking the truth?" But as Lenala continued to describe the situation, she could see Semian's emotions shift to sadness. "Those poor girls," he said, shaking his head. "Their lives have been ruined by Brantog, and you and Farka have been forced to abandon your former lives and become rebels."

"It hasn't been easy," Lenala agreed. "But the crazy part is, I've actually gotten some really good training here and I've moved up in the ranks. In a weird way, this is what I've always wanted to do."

Semian laughed a heartfelt laugh. "Yes, you have and I don't doubt your ability. After all, I trained you," he said with a smirk.

"So, tell me more about this poison." The more she told him about her idea of using the mix to kill Brantog, the more he seemed to like it.

They talked for hours and formulated a plan.

They decided they would finish the concoction and continue with the plan to take out Brantog. Then they would take out King Byreon. They decided that the Dragons could never find out about Brantog because they would retaliate against all of Xuria in anger. So many years of being betrayed would be impossible to explain. The Dragons would likely kill whoever they felt was a part of the plan. And that could be anyone.

Their intention was to depart as soon as they made the poison. Lenala felt at peace around Semian. He was familiar and reminded her of home. So many years of training with him, and now here they sat on another planet, planning an invasion of their homeland.

She laughed out loud in disbelief.

"It's so good to have you here," she said, looking up at him. As he stepped closer to her, she could feel her heart rate increase and her breath hitch.

"I'm so glad to be here with you," he said, his voice soft and reassuring. He leaned in even closer, putting his forehead against hers and closing his eyes. After taking a few small breaths, he opened his eyes. "If only I had known you were in so much danger. Anything could have happened to you. The king is going to answer for this," he said, his face reddening with anger. He pulled away from her, shaking his head in frustration.

But Lenala couldn't let him go just yet. She pulled him back toward her and reassured him that she was safe now that she was with him. She was tough and capable, but it still meant the world to her to have him by her side.

His presence was balancing for her. Like Farka, he

made her feel grounded. She felt more in control of her gifts when he was near.

Before she realized it, she was kissing him. The same kiss she had been dreaming of over and over. His familiar scent rushed over her. It was intoxicating and flooded her mind with memories of all of the years training with him. She wanted to melt into him. She felt a rush of excitement go through her body as he pressed into her, hugging her tightly and kissing her. His kisses felt like warm honey on her lips, sweet and soft. She wanted to stay in this moment forever.

A loud creak echoing through the floor abruptly ruined their intimate moment. They quickly pulled away and listened silently.

There were footsteps approaching. Panic swept over her. Who could be coming into her wing at this hour? Semian hid, not making a sound, and she climbed into her bed to feign sleeping. Farka, who had been sleeping, sensed the panic and jumped up, making a clamor. She quickly realized something was wrong and she froze in place. The footsteps came to an abrupt halt, then scurried off.

Lenala jumped out of bed. "Who was that? Was someone coming to spy on me?"

"Maybe it was a maid," Semian said as he came out of his hiding place. I don't think you need to worry—you have Farka and she will always protect you if I am not with you."

Am I still being paranoid? she wondered. *I need some sleep.* She knew she was overthinking things. It was her nature to overthink and evaluate every possibility, especially after the whirlwind of a day she'd had.

"Lenala, I need to go. I'll see you tomorrow."

With one more hug and a lingering kiss, he left through the window. Lenala watched as he gracefully and athletically scaled down the outside wall and disappeared across the courtyard. She paused for a minute. He seemed to know this route a little too well. She let out a deep sigh. "Stop being so suspicious," she said out loud as she closed the curtains.

CHAPTER

TWENTY-SIX

Time continued to pass with no sign of Lenala. There were whispers spreading throughout the castle. One was that she had fallen ill and had been sent back to the castle. There was another that she had been sent away to another planet to study and learn the art of healing. Even though the people in the castle seemed to buy it, Brantog knew there was more to the story and those rumors were lies. *What has she done? Where is she?*

He hadn't seen Kineah in weeks, but he was not interested in her for the time being. He was obsessed with finding out where Lenala went. He needed that Dragon. His supply was dwindling rapidly. He had been trying to ration himself but had still been using much more DB than usual. He had to get control of himself.

A few more anxious weeks passed. It had now been over two months with no word and he was beginning to lose his grip. It was time for the charade. He put on his robe and went outside, just like he did every night. He was pleased to see that Kineah was out and about looking healthy again. *What nerve she had letting herself go like that. Maybe tonight, I'll go see her. After all, it's about time to replace Trayana.* This would give him some excitement and help get his mind off Lenala's disappearance.

As he was deep in thought, there was a sudden commotion and Senleah briskly approached them. "Your grace, King Byreon is here to see you," she announced. Brantog's heart skipped a beat. *What could he possibly want?* Before he could gather his thoughts, King Byreon was making his way toward him.

Brantog quickly bowed, showing respect to the king. "Your highness," he said, trying to sound polite. "To what do I owe the honor?"

The king, however, had little patience for formalities. "Oh, cut the royalty crap," he replied, his tone blunt and impatient. "You know why I am here."

Confusion clouded Brantog's mind. He did not know what the king wanted with him.

"You have caused me a lot of trouble at home," he started. Brantog was silent, waiting for further explanation. "With Larsen, it was no problem, but with Lenala, now we have a huge issue." He let out a deep sigh as he looked toward the mountains. "I have been having to answer to the queen." He furrowed his brow as he turned his gaze back to Brantog. "For some reason, she believes that I am protecting you," he continued. "Why would I protect you?" King Byreon asked, his tone sharp and accusatory. "Maybe it's because I've known you my whole life and you've always been a trustworthy high priest. Or maybe it's because I simply don't feel like dealing with the consequences when your little games come to light." His words were laced with a thinly veiled threat, and Brantog couldn't help but feel a chill run down his spine.

"Your Highness, I don't know what you are talking about," Brantog lied. He knew he had to tread lightly if he wanted to avoid angering the king any further. He didn't think the king actually believed Larsen all those years ago but now, somehow Lenala knew of his secrets. His mind was racing. *She must have found out and told the king, and of course he would believe her.*

"We both know what I am talking about. Do not make me angry by offending my intellect." The king's voice rumbled low and deep. "Because of your stupidity, I had to exile my own daughter for treason."

"She's been exiled?!" Brantog's heart sank as he asked the question.

"Yes, to protect our planet. How do you think that makes me look?" His face was etched in worry. Clearly, he had been dealing with the repercussions of this at home. "For years, I've been covering this up because as long as the Dragons are content, I don't care what you do," King Byreon said, his voice low and stern. "But I never thought you were capable of being so irresponsible. For Lenala to discover your misdeeds and report them to me is the worst possible scenario. Now, the situation has escalated beyond my control, and the queen is determined to investigate your actions. Consider this a warning: Clean up your act. I cannot protect you any longer." With that, he gave Brantog a pat on the shoulder and left without waiting for a response. The gravity of the situation weighed heavily on Brantog's mind. *How did Lenala find out about any of this and how long has she known?* he thought.

The sound of fireworks exploding jolted him out of his

daze. He darted his eyes around to see if anyone had been paying attention to his conversation with the king. Everyone seemed to be preoccupied. except for one person whose gaze was fixed directly on him. Kineah.

A wave of anger rushed through him. *She must have told Lenala,* he concluded as he narrowed his eyes, locking them on her. *The little traitor told Lenala.*

Her face lit up with hope and for a moment he was confused. Then it dawned on him. *Oh, she thinks Lenala actually did something to help her? She thinks that since I've been absent from her room, I'm afraid? All she did was get herself kicked out of Xuria.* Brantog was seething and his lips were curled into a sneer. She looked at him with a glint of defiance in her eyes. Her posture was upright and confident. *She thinks she has protection now and that I've been caught?* He shook his head from side to side as he continued to stare at her. Fireworks boomed all around them, their eyes locked on one another. Even though it only lasted a few seconds, time felt frozen. The thunder of the volcanoes sounded like a distant thud. Then he saw it, the crack in her armor. It was slight but it was there. Fear, deep down. *Maybe she is scared after all.*

Brantog sat in his room staring into the fire. He was halfway through a bottle of wine and he was still fuming. Had he not done what he needed to in order for Kineah to respect him? Even if she did not respect him, was she not afraid of him? Was she so unbothered by him that she had the nerve to sell him out? Perhaps he needed to change his method. He jumped up and began walking around in front of the fire. *These girls are getting too brave and now, the queen is going to be on my back.* He'd have to make sure Kineah kept her mouth shut. He hadn't been to her room in a while. Her bruises were healed, but now he couldn't risk putting any more on her until the queen was finished.

He sat for a while, thinking about his next move. He needed to get to Kineah to see what she had done, but he needed to figure out a new method first. Fear tactics obviously didn't work on her. Then it hit him. He would control her with the blood. If he forced her to take a little every day, she would become addicted to it quickly. Then he could use it to make her keep her mouth shut. Not just a little bit like he had been giving her. He'd give her a full dose.

At least until the queen was done with him.

As he thought about it longer, it became more and more of a good idea.

Time to pay her a visit. He put the tiny bottle in his pocket and sneaked out of his chambers.

Knock, knock, knock.

The door crept open.

She was wide awake and expecting him. She knew he would come to her, and she knew he was angry. "How is it that the king's daughter knows everything about our little secret?" he started as he approached her bed, talking as slowly as he was walking.

"He is angry with me because he almost had to have his own blood executed for treason."

"Executed for treason?" she replied, confused.

Brantog ignored her question.

"So, tell me, what did you tell her?" He was standing

over her now. He wanted more than anything to squeeze the life out of her. The ungrateful little whore.

Her face didn't show any fear but her body was trembling. Sweat began to form on her temples. *So, she is afraid of me*, he thought.

Then why did she tell?

Then it dawned on him. "Was it Trayana? Did she sell me out before she was sacrificed?" It began to make sense.

"Did she think she could make a difference in her absence?"

He scoffed. Kineah was still silent but trembling.

"Speak!" he barked at her.

She jumped. "I don't know how she knew. She seemed to just know."

He grabbed her arm and then let go. He sat there for a moment looking at her. She wasn't lying. *It was Trayana,* he thought *I'll be damned if she is my downfall.*

He pulled out the tiny bottle and took a full drop onto his finger.

Her heart rate was already increasing as he opened the bottle. She hadn't had any blood since his last visit and had been aching for it. She started to breathe heavily as she watched him dip his finger in. This was a big drop.

Watching her reaction, he realized she was already hooked. This would be easy. He held out his finger for her. She took it like a hungry animal.

"Now tell me everything." He sat back and waited.

The blood hit her with force. The full dose was more than what she was used to, especially right from the start.

As she closed her eyes, he could see a wave of euphoria running through her body—she appeared to be savoring the feeling of freedom. He knew that feeling all too well.

The few blissful moments, when the hardships and problems of life seemed to vanish. Suddenly, her eyes opened and fixed on his.

"She's going to win, the king will do the right thing for his daughter, and you won't get away with this anymore." She almost laughed as she said it.

It took everything within him to resist grabbing her by the neck and throwing her across the room.

"Oh, that's what you think? You think the king has sided with her? Didn't you hear what I said? He almost had her executed for treason."

"Yes, but you said *almost* executed, so she's alive." Kineah's voice was triumphant.

"Do you think the queen would allow him to execute their daughter?" he scoffed. "They exiled her instead, and she is gone forever," he said, watching her reaction. All of the color drained from her face as realization hit her. "The queen may be investigating me, but you and I are the only ones who know about this. They won't take a chance of the Dragons finding out based on one little girl's testimony."

He knew that wasn't true. If Kineah cracked, the queen would likely have him killed and bring her daughter back. She was no fool. If she wanted something, she'd stop at nothing to get it.

Brantog's voice was low and menacing as he spoke. "You will keep your mouth shut, or you won't be the only one who suffers. Your family will pay for your mistakes, too. And if the queen questions you, remember this: They exiled their own daughter because they didn't believe her. Do you really think they'll believe *you*?"

"Then why are they even questioning me!?" She was defeated even with all of the blood on board.

"To ease her conscience, of course. She feels very guilty for exiling her daughter," he lied.

"Go to sleep now. You need some rest."

She seemed confused; the blood was still coursing through her veins and she couldn't focus for long.

That was too easy. He had a stronger grip on her than he realized. His secret would be safe with Kineah. Lenala was gone. She had been a threat and he didn't even know it. With the king on his side, he felt confident that he would be protected. The king would do anything to protect his precious deal with the Dragons, including lying to the queen and exiling his own daughter. He laughed at the thought of it all. Brantog held the cards. He was proud of himself; he had done well.

TWENTY-SEVEN

It was finally her unit's day off.

Her plan was to head into town to check on the last few things she needed for the poison. She was so close to having all of the ingredients, and Semian agreed to accompany her. She wanted to look good for Semian, so she took extra time to get ready. He had only seen her in her uniform recently, so she wanted to look her best. She tried braiding her hair to the side, but decided against it and let it hang loosely instead. Although she liked the look, she felt a bit self-conscious about wearing her hair down in front of the other soldiers, as she was always professional around them. Nonetheless, she pushed the thought aside and focused on impressing Semian. Unfortunately, she didn't have any fancy clothes to wear, as she had only been given one outfit for her day off— a loose white blouse and black pants. She tucked in her top and studied herself in the mirror, deciding that it would have to be enough.

Farka was watching her from the corner of the room, once again amused at her fussing over herself. "Don't you judge me, Farka." The Dragon snorted in reply and lay down on her bed as if she couldn't be bothered with Lenala's nonsense.

She gave Farka a hug—much to her disapproval—and whirled out of the room.

Semian was waiting for her at the bottom of the stairs. *Ugh. these damned flutters need to stop.* She didn't like not being in control of her emotions. This was new to her. It was exciting but also getting her all worked up. *Why is he so handsome?* She had almost forgotten. He'd gotten even more handsome since she had seen him last. He was more mature and had gained even more confidence.

Most of the men in her unit had already left for the day. She was relieved that they wouldn't see her looking less soldier-like and more like a lady.

Semian's eyebrows shot up when she came downstairs. He was so used to seeing her as a princess all these years. She had always been in fine clothes with her hair and makeup done perfectly.

Seeing her now looking more laid back made her even more attractive. Despite always being beautiful, she had transformed into something impressive. She had grown into a warrior, with a body that reflected her strength and determination. Her lean and toned physique was accentuated by muscles that flexed with almost every movement. Though she had always exuded confidence, now there was something different about her demeanor. She was hardened and had learned how to take care of herself and Farka, no matter what obstacles came her way. They made their way into town and chatted about nothing important. They both understood that their public presence needed to remain professional. They were part of the queen's guard and had to maintain that cover.

Once they arrived in town, they decided to split ways so they wouldn't both be in the herbalist's shop at the same time. Despite the diversity of the city, two Xurians together would certainly draw attention.

Lenala went in first. As usual, the shop was bustling with people. Calcius had a beautiful display of flowers in the window today. Lenala stopped for a moment to admire them. Flowers were something she had learned to appreciate during her time in Analicia.

Flowers were scarce in Xuria. The climate was too harsh for them to flourish.

The herbalist had the two items she was looking for. "Ah, yes," he said, "those just came in three days ago." Lenala feigned surprise and smiled her most charming smile. The herbalist hurried to get her the plants. She tucked them away safely and hoped Semian would be able to get the herb.

The plan was to meet Semian back by the lake in two hours. She still had a little time to kill, so she decided to see what Analicia had to offer as far as clothing. All of a sudden, she found herself more concerned than ever about how she looked. *Thanks, Semian,* she thought as she shook her head. She was annoyed at herself for being so childish with her emotions when it came to him, but she couldn't help it.

The city had many options for clothes. She went into a few stores and quickly decided they were not for her. She was used to dressing in the nicest clothes back on Xuria. What they wore was usually not a whole lot of material. It was too hot there to wear a lot of clothing. Even Lenala's uniform in Analicia was more than what she was used to wearing. She never wore pants back home. Her dresses were usually very thin, light material. It was common for Xurian women to have open-backed or two-piece dresses made of fine, soft material. The men were typically shirtless and wore short-cropped pants made of thin material as well. The dresses in Analicia looked like something a child would wear. They had too many layers and frills, and women who wore them looked ridiculous. They looked like they were wearing costumes. Surprisingly enough, the queen didn't wear stuff like that. She usually wore something very sleek and fitted.

Lenala chuckled to herself thinking of Semian in his Analician uniform. The pants, the black sleeveless top. Butterflies again. She shook it off and decided she did not want to buy anything. She needed to stay in the mode, so instead, she stopped off at her favorite place to pick up some pastries for them to share.

She found Semian waiting for her by the lake.

"Did you manage to get it?" she asked with anticipation. This particular herb was crucial for their poison concoction.

"Absolutely," he replied, his gaze fixed on the small bag she held in her hands. "What in Draygon's name smells so good?"

"These pastries are divine," she exclaimed, passing one to him and settling down beside him. He took a bite and let out a satisfied "Mmm." A smile spread across his face as he stuffed another mouthful into his eager mouth. Lenala burst into laughter, taking a bite herself and relishing the sweet, warm, and flaky delight of the bread.

Semian took a deep breath and looked at Lenala, his

eyes filled with determination. "Let's review the plan," he said, his voice steady. "Once the poison is ready, we'll begin our mission to Xuria. We'll need a few more days for the herbs to dry out before we mix them in boiling water."

Lenala nodded. "Right. In three days, we'll sneak into the kitchen and create the substance. Once it's prepared, we'll request permission from the queen to attend a fabricated funeral back home. It's a daring move, but I hope it will sway her and allow us the leave we desperately need."

Semian leaned forward. "But we can't rely solely on that plan. We need a backup. We can't risk being denied our opportunity."

Lenala's eyes met his. "Agreed. If she says no, we will escape, and take everything we need to vanish without a trace."

They continued to strategize, their voices hushed.

"When we arrive on Xuria," Semian whispered, "we must be meticulous. We can't afford to be seen or raise any alarms. We'll split up, with you infiltrating the Castle of Nahkei and me infiltrating the main palace. We will each have our poison darts. Once darkness falls, we'll make our move and sneak past the guards. Once we reach the king and Brantog's chambers, we strike."

Lenala nodded, her mind already visualizing the mission. "And if our initial plan is compromised, we have a backup escape route. It's risky, but we have to be willing to take that chance."

"If we succeed," Semian said, "the queen and Tyralon will be in charge. I know they won't subject Anala to further punishment, and they'll work to rectify the situation in Xuria. We'll make sure of it. We just need to get there in time."

"Damn it, Anala. Why did she have to fall for the Pitian prince? She's put the whole planet at risk." Lenala squeezed her fists together as she vented to Semian. "Even though she made the mistake, my father's reaction is putting them at an even greater risk. Has he gone mad? Sending Xurian men to Piatees to abduct and kill people? All of this because of Anala? If he could exile me, he could certainly exile her." Lenala's words rushed out as her mind raced.

"Semian, why wouldn't he just exile her and leave the Pitians alone? Do you think he's afraid she will flee to Piatees? Why would he even care if she's exiled? Why must he retaliate and kill the prince?" She paused for a moment. "He knows they didn't kill those men and he still wants to bring war to our people. Xuria stands no chance against the Dragons."

"We have to put an end to this," Semian replied grimly. "Our country, our families, and our people are at risk."

Lenala turned to Semian, her voice filled with a mixture of sadness and determination. "Semian, my mind keeps going back to my grandfather. He would be utterly disappointed in his son. Grandfather dedicated his life to the people of Xuria, and in return, the Dragons treated us with kindness. But my father's repeated betrayals, allowing Brantog to remain in his position, are on the verge of undoing everything."

She paused, her gaze fixed on Semian. "You had every right to flee Xuria. The king wanted to send you on a mission that would have likely caused your death... it's unfathomable. But I'm so grateful that you are here. This journey won't be easy, but now, at least, we can face it together."

Lenala took a deep breath, her resolve growing stronger. "In the meantime, we must be patient and wait for the poison to be ready. Then, we move forward with our mission."

They made their way back to the castle as they continued discussing their plans.

As soon as they walked through the doors of the castle, Lenala knew something wasn't right. She felt an overwhelming empty feeling. It was the same one she had been feeling every night but this time, it was magnified. It was as if something was sucking the life right out of her.

There was something wrong with Farka—she could feel it. Without hesitation, she took off running to her room. When she stumbled into her quarters, Farka was nowhere to be seen. A sudden wave of nausea arose in her. The room began to spin and blackness crept into the edges of her vision. She tried to steady herself, but the dizziness was overwhelming. In an instant, she crumpled to the ground. Horrifying images flashed through her mind as her gut twisted and churned. Semian came bolting in after her.

"Lenala," he gasped, "what happened?"

Lenala's complexion turned pale. Panic gripped her. Her body trembled as he helped her off the floor and guided her to the bed. "It's Farka," she cried out, barely recognizing her own voice. "She's gone, and something is wrong." Springing to her feet, she began to pace back and forth across the room. Lenala had never experienced Farka disappearing or being away from her for long periods, and she could sense that something was amiss.

Semian scoured the room, actively searching for any clues that might help. "Lenala, could she be outside or in a different area of the castle?"

"I don't know, but I can still feel her and wherever she is, she's scared." Lenala also began to look around for any signs of a break-in or foul play. Nothing was out of place or disturbed.

"Could she have run away?" Semian asked, looking around.

Lenala instantly cut her eyes at him. "Really?" she practically hissed. "Run away?"

"Lenala, we have to explore all possibilities." He knew she was emotional but she needed to think of everything.

"That is not a possibility," she retorted. "Farka would never just leave like that, not even if she was afraid."

Semian continued to brainstorm. "Do you think she was abducted? A Dragon, taken against her will seems highly unlikely. How would they get her out of the castle?" he continued.

He was slightly sarcastic and Lenala did not like that. *Why can't he get it? Farka would never run away from me.* Doubt began to creep in. *Did he have something to do with this? He shows up and next thing, Farka is gone.*

Seeing her expression, he continued.

"I'm just trying to be logical. We can't just assume she was stolen because if she was, then that means it was by someone who knows she's here. No one in Analicia knows about her except for the soldiers and others in the castle."

Lenala sensed a sudden change in the energy around her, followed by an overwhelming sense of emptiness. She could no longer feel Farka's presence. There was no fear, sadness, anger, or any other emotion. Her feelings had been completely numbed. Shocked by the sudden realization, she sank back on the bed.

"I can't feel her anymore, Semian," she sobbed, overcome with grief. The absence of Farka's presence meant that she was too far away physically or even worse, dead.

Farka was as much a part of her as her own limbs were. Heaviness began to set in and overwhelming sadness took over her.

Semian moved closer to her. Her body tensed up. She didn't know whom she could trust. "Lenala, we will find her. Wherever she is. I promise you. We will find her."

Lenala was at a loss for words and remained silent. She was consumed by fear and concern for Farka, mixed with anger and confusion. She lay down on the bed, trying to process what was happening, and eventually drifted off to sleep. She didn't dream.

Hours later, Semian's entrance into her room jolted her awake. The harsh reality of the situation hit her once again; the nightmare was still very much real and not just a figment of her imagination.

"I have to look for her." Lenala sat up quickly.

"I've already asked Quade to do some intel. He wants to come talk to you."

"Quade?" she repeated.

"Quade is someone I believe can help us."

She knew Semian was right. She trusted Quade as well and agreed to talk with him.

Semian was all business. "Remember, this is a sensitive topic, because if someone took her, it's someone inside the castle." A look of understanding crossed her face.

"If anyone finds out there's a Dragon missing or on the loose, it could wreak havoc in the city. You are going to have to be patient and wait until we can gather some more information." As much as she wanted to run out into the streets and scream for Farka, she knew this was true. She could put Farka in more danger if she reacted wrongly.

Soon, she, Quade, and Semian were seated in her quarters. She filled Quade in on the details.

"Has anything out of the ordinary happened lately that you can think of?" he asked Lenala.

Lenala's mind jumped back to the night Semian was in her room. The noise at the door.

"I did hear something outside my door, but I didn't see anyone or anything."

As Semian and Quade continued to talk, she began to think back on anything unusual that may be related to Farka's disappearance. Suddenly, she remembered the empty feeling she'd been experiencing every night and wondered if this was relevant. She decided not to share this with Quade or Semian. Despite her efforts to tap into her gift and read them better, she found herself frustrated and unable to do so. The weight of her emotions and the stress was creating a fog that clouded her ability to perceive the truth.

She needed to decide how much she trusted them. Without Farka, she would have to sort out all of these emotions on her own, and she needed time to do that.

It was getting late and they all had to report for duty in the morning. Quade and Semian went over a few more possibilities and decided to call it a night. As Lenala thought more deeply about the situation, she began to feel increasingly suspicious. Had Semian been spying on her? The way he knew the route out of her room seemed too easy. Could he have had some involvement in this? She thought of how he had initially reacted to the news of Farka's absence, a little too nonchalantly. *Maybe he is here with ulterior motives. Is this all a front for him to bring me home for some form of punishment?* Thoughts were racing through her head. Anger began to boil inside her. It was just too coincidental.

Semian lingered after Quade left.

Lenala decided to confront him, specifically about his sudden exit from her room and his spying before joining the guard. He was either against her or he was on her side and would have no problem talking.

TWENTY-EIGHT

"Semian," she said. "I need you to be completely honest with me.

"All of a sudden, everything in my very unpredictable life has changed. You show up randomly and soon after, Farka is gone. You appeared out of nowhere after I've been gone for a year, and ask me to help you with a seemingly crazy task." She shook her hands in exasperation. "On top of that, you've been here for a while and I just now found out." She continued as she paced around the room, "You've admittedly been spying on me and now you are trying to get me to return to Xuria to help you overthrow the king." As she continued, her confusion began turning into frustration and anger.

"Now Farka is missing and I have no real allies here. I can't make up my mind about your intentions. What is really going on? Is there more than what you are telling me?" She paused before continuing. "Has my father sent you to bring me home to stand trial?" She knew some of what she was saying was a stretch, but she was confused.

She stood there with her hands on her hips. Everything was constantly changing for her. She couldn't help this feeling, even though she knew deep down she was wrong. She wanted more than anything to trust him, but she was overwhelmed and afraid.

Semian looked at her, expressionless.

His amber eyes were burning and Lenala knew he was mad. She didn't care. She needed answers and she needed them now before things went any further.

After a long moment of silence, he exhaled a deep breath.

"Lenala, everything I have told you is true. First of all, I came here to find you and to make sure that you are ok.

"Secondly, I needed to tell you about your father and his plans because I need your help to stop him." Lenala looked at him, deliberately reading him. "I had to leave Xuria and you are the only person I trust," he continued. "If his plans go through, all of Xuria could be destroyed by the Dragons or even other planets. That's it. No secrets, no tricks. I understand that you may not trust me right now, but do you really believe I would turn on you?" he asked flatly. Not begging or pleading. Just matter-of-fact.

She knew her emotions were clouding her judgment and she knew he was being honest. Closing her eyes, she let out a sigh of relief. His intentions were true. She just needed to hear it and clear her head a bit so she could use her gift.

"You must not doubt me. Lenala, it's true that I have been checking in on you by sneaking to your window on some nights, but I wasn't spying."

Watching me sleep? A sliver of embarrassment ran through her.

"I just needed to know that you were safe. I needed to see what was happening here before I could move forward."

He stepped in closer to her. *He is so gorgeous.* She couldn't help herself. She shook it off. *I need to get a grip.* "I only checked on you a few times until I knew you were safe."

"Well," she replied, taking a step back and attempting to snap herself out of his spell. "Did you see anything that looked suspicious? Was anyone following me or in my room? How did Farka not see or sense you?"

"Nothing out of the ordinary that I could see," he replied. "You and Farka were sleeping like babies every time I checked in on you." She smirked at that.

"I wish I could sleep like a baby," she said.

Her sleep had been so bad lately that she'd give anything for a sound night of rest.

At that moment, she realized what he actually said.

"Wait a minute, Farka was sleeping like a baby?" She had never slept like a baby. In fact, she was usually restless all night. She certainly didn't sleep deeply ever. She typically napped lightly and paced around but she didn't need much sleep. No Dragons did. It was part of their protective nature.

Then the pieces began to come together. She hadn't been connected to Farka in her sleep for a while. She had been feeling empty and unsettled at night, yet Farka had been sleeping all night. As she relayed this to Semian, she realized that maybe Farka wasn't actually sleeping—maybe she had been drugged.

"That is possible, but someone would have had to sneak in here and drug her. Why? What would they want with her? Were they trying to get to you?" Semian thought out loud.

Stress and anxiety began tightening around her once again. Then she started to feel that all-too-familiar pull. Escitalo was beckoning her. Without hesitation, she rushed over to grab the sword, and to her surprise, it was glowing with a pale red light. She placed her hand on the hilt and closed her eyes, allowing herself to be consumed by the sword's power.

In a few swift motions, she moved the sword, and then stood completely still. Like a sponge, Escitalo absorbed all the emotions she was feeling. Gradually, a sense of clarity began to emerge. She remembered the blood and the small cut Farka had. "Dragon's Blood," she exclaimed, turning toward Semian.

"What do you mean?" he asked, slightly startled at her outburst. "You think that someone has been drugging Farka and stealing her blood?" he asked.

Could this be true? Was someone stealing her blood? Did they have the audacity to steal it?

She was sickened at the thought of this. The story of the goons trying to steal Farka's blood flashed through her mind. She would never forget the sounds of Farka screeching in fear. Rage began to boil in her. Someone had her Farka and someone was going to pay. As she simmered in anger, her energy poured out across the room. The faint red glow of the blade became bright red and blazing. She closed her eyes again. Her body was rigid. Her grip was so tight on her sword that her fingers were blanched.

Semian struggled to contain his anger as he spoke through gritted teeth: "This is unacceptable." Their energies were combining. He began pacing. "If what you are saying is true, then we are dealing with something bigger than I thought. We have to find out who did this. We will get her back but we have to tread lightly. We are dealing with Dragon's Blood users and even worse, I believe we're dealing with dealers."

They had to find her before something bad happened. If the thieves were careless, she could die. They could drain her too quickly or she could get an infection. She could become dehydrated. These people didn't care about her well-being. They wanted her blood and would stop at nothing to get it.

Another whirlwind of emotions had Lenala feeling weak. She needed to get out. "I need fresh air," she said.

"Me, too." Semian was still pacing. "Follow me. I know a good spot."

Semian led the way. They had to sneak out of a window to leave the castle at that hour. The soldiers were guarding the doors.

He led her through the window and along the roof.

The fresh air was invigorating. There was a slight cool breeze rippling through the leaves in the trees. The sky was black and speckled with endless stars. The faint hues of other planets were glowing off in the distance. There were no lights in sight. Just the soft glow of a candle or two flickering in some of the windows in the different wings. Most of the castle was sleeping at this time. Everything felt bleak and dark to Lenala. Her heart was so heavy, and she was scared.

Semian took her over the rooftops and down into one of the gardens. This garden was small but it was one of Lenala's favorites. The queen liked to have her morning tea here sometimes. It was small and private. It was nestled within the castle grounds and hidden behind trees. They sat under one of the trees in darkness and total silence. Lenala rested her head on Semian's shoulder. He leaned his down onto hers. They sat like that for a long while. So much was happening in their worlds. And now here they were, together on another planet, serving in the army together and planning an attack on two of the most powerful figures on Xuria. She could feel his heart beating and the rhythmic sound of his breathing.

Semian reached over and pulled her chin up to his. The moonlight grazed his face. He was so handsome. For a moment, she completely forgot about Farka and all of the drama. She was lost in his eyes.

"We will find Farka," he whispered. "We will kill Brantog and we will bring your father to justice. Ok?"

"Ok," she replied without hesitation.

"But in order for us to do all of this, I need to know that you trust me. Do you trust me?"

Lenala was still mesmerized as she nodded. "I need to hear you say it." She looked into his eyes. She had always trusted him. Even when she had moments of doubt, deep down she knew he had good intentions. She could feel it. He was peaceful, loyal, and honest.

I trust you," she said.

He studied her face for a long moment. "Good," he muttered as pulled her face to his and kissed her. Lenala was swept away by a flood of memories of their past kisses, and she became completely lost in the moment, forgetting everything else around her. She kissed him back with a sense of desperation, turning her body toward his and running her hands over his arms and chest. His firm body and intoxicating scent filled her with euphoria.

He pulled her closer with his strong hands, and their bodies fit together perfectly. The butterflies overwhelmed her as she lay there, lost in him. In the moonlight, she could see the outlines of his muscles, the result of years of training and hard work. He was nothing but a beautiful man, and she loved every inch of him.

As she threw her head back, all she could see were the stars. Every worry, every thought, every frustration disappeared, and her mind was consumed by him. She had no fear, no shame, no worries, and no doubts. In that moment, she felt more alive than ever before.

Under that sparkling sky, time stood still. Lenala didn't want the moment to end. She didn't want to go back to reality. She wanted to stay there with him forever.

CHAPTER

TWENTY-NINE

As the days continued to pass, there was still no news of Farka. Time seemed to be paralyzed. The sadness was intense for Lenala. She found herself in Semian's arms almost every night.

Escitalo and Semian were the only escape she could get from reality, and she so desperately needed to rest her mind. Her time with them was the only thing allowing her to stop worrying about Farka. Semian was the only one who knew how she was feeling, and hiding her emotions from the others all day was exhausting. At the end of each workday, Lenala found herself completely overwhelmed and consumed by stress and anxiety about Farka's disappearance. Without Farka to help shield and balance her, she increasingly relied on Semian to bring her back to a centered state. She couldn't help but feel frustrated by how weak and dependent she felt without Farka's presence.

Every night, she spent at least an hour with Escitalo.

All of the plans they had been making were now halted. Several times, they postponed making the poison.

With no news or leads from Quade and Semian, Lenala was starting to come to the realization that they were going to have to move forward without Farka. They couldn't afford to lose any more time. The reality of that revelation was what was weighing down on her the most. How could she leave her Farka? She hated the situation she was in. Once again, she was torn between her own ethics. If she stopped looking for Farka, she knew she'd have to accept the fact that she would never see her again. It had already been so long—days had turned into weeks. Many times, she considered asking the queen for help. Maybe she knew something, but Quade was adamant about her letting him handle the investigation. He didn't trust that the queen or someone close to her was not somehow involved. Everyone was a suspect at this point. There were many times that they had to make up excuses as to why Farka wasn't with Lenala. Every person who asked about where she was immediately became a top suspect. Even the queen had asked about her several times. Lenala lied and said she was feeling sick and resting, but this couldn't go on forever. If the queen knew Farka was gone, she may not suspect foul play and in her mind, having a Dragon on the loose in Analicia could be a huge problem. The people would panic and chaos would ensue. Semian and Quade had already done days and hours of investigations. Quade had conducted private interviews with a few of the men he trusted the most. No one knew anything. Lenala was well aware that the situation was dire and that she needed to move forward. However, she couldn't shake off the guilt that was weighing heavily on her. She felt like she was giving up on Farka and leaving her behind. Despite these feelings, Lenala knew that waiting any longer could put both Anala's life and Xuria's safety in jeopardy.

It was time to move forward with the original goal. Farka would want her to finish what she had started before it was too late.

The herbs were completely dry now, and all she and Semian needed to do was sneak into the kitchen at night when the guards were gone and boil them.

They had already decided it would be best to go one of the nights when they were off duty. They would have to wait until the queen was sleeping. That way, they would know exactly where the other guards were and avoid having any surprises. They needed to move quickly and had already waited weeks looking for Farka. Semian planned to bring the remaining herbs to Lenala, and they would cook them the next night.

Later that evening, after dinner, Quade pulled Lenala aside. "Meet me outside in ten minutes," he whispered in a low voice.

A spear of excitement shot through her. She was trying her best to act nonchalant as she excused herself and went to find Quade. He was waiting for her along a walkway, partially hidden.

"I found a solid lead, " he said to her in a hushed tone. "There's a man in the city who is known as the Dealer. He is where the junkies get their Dragon's Blood from. I'm suspicious that someone in the castle took Farka and sold her to him. Just Imagine. He would have an infinite supply to sell to his users."

"Where did you find this information?" Lenala asked as she considered what he told her.

"The Murkes."

"You went to the Murkes?" Her breath hitched. "How did you find them?" Quade didn't reply and his dark expression told her he was not going to answer that question.

In order to use them, one had to know where to find them, and that was not easy. Lenala figured Analicia would be a perfect place for them to hide because there were so many different types of people living here. *There must be tons of them here*, Lenala thought. *Of course they would know something.*

"Thank you for getting this information, Quade. Where can I find this dealer?"

"They told me he is downtown in the alleyway behind the herbalist's shop," he said quietly. "There is an unmarked door about fifty feet down."

Lenala felt a surge of adrenaline. This could be the break they needed. "Ok, I'm going tonight. I'll take Semian with me."

"Please be careful. It's a dangerous area and if he does have Farka, he's not going to part with her easily."

Lenala felt a glimmer of hope. Maybe Farka was alive. She would definitely be much more valuable to a DB dealer if she was alive. Lenala needed to brief Semian on the plan, but it was late and everyone had already retired to their rooms for the night. She would have to wait for Semian to visit her room after everyone had gone to sleep. The plans for their lethal herb mixture would have to be postponed for a little while longer.

Lenala was pacing the room as he knocked.

She ran to let him in and quickly filled him in on the new details.

"We have to sneak out and go downtown," she said.

Semian immediately jumped into Hite mode. There was hope and he couldn't let her down. Lenala's emotions had been intense and the plans of moving forward without Farka had taken her to a new level of sadness. "Okay, here's the plan. Let's go scout out the place. If you can sense her presence, then we go from there. Sneaking off the grounds at night won't be easy, but fortunately, I've done it many times since I've been in Analicia, and I know a good route we can take. We'll go out of your window and onto the rooftop. The night guards will be on duty. We'll have to be patient and wait for the right moment to slip past them. Now, there are only three ways in and out of the grounds: the bridge, swimming across the guarded waters, or flying with a Dragon. Right now, the bridge is our only viable option. I know exactly how to sneak under the bridge by crawling through the boards. However, we still have to contend with the guards. We need to wait for the perfect moment to reach the bridge stealthily and get underneath it. Patience is key here."

Lenala let out a sigh. "Ok, let's go."

Timing was critical since they needed to report for duty the following morning and could not afford to be late. So, they set out on their mission. Once they made it closer to the bridge, Semian suggested creating a small diversion by throwing something into the water to make a splash. This would draw the guard away, allowing them to get under the bridge undetected. He had used this tactic before, and it had proven successful.

"Wait here," he instructed. Lenala lay in wait in the dark, belly down on the ground, watching the guards. They were all posted pretty far apart but the main concern was the one closest to the bridge. They could get past the others but this one needed to be distracted.

If only their day off were the next day. They could walk right over that bridge. Their next day off was five days away, and they couldn't wait that long. Farka could be dead by then and so could Anala. They needed to move fast.

Semian returned with two decent-sized rocks. If the rock was thrown just right, it just may work.

"Two?" Lenala questioned. "We have to get *off* the bridge, too," he said with a smirk. "Once I throw it, we have to make a run for the bridge. Go down to the left side and grab the rope. Pull yourself underneath and I'll be right behind you. Steady and quiet. As long as he is not looking our way, we'll be fine. Ok?" She nodded. "Let's do this. One, two, three." He threw the rock, causing an immediate reaction from the guard, who quickly turned away and started moving toward the ripples in the water. Lenala didn't hesitate. Adrenaline surged through her as she ran toward the bridge. She knew how to run without making a sound. This was a tactic they were taught in training.

Lenala ran as fast as she could across the open space between the guards, with Semian close behind, just as fast and just as stealthy. Once they reached the bridge, Lenala grabbed the rope and hoisted herself up under the bridge, landing on the support beams. She tossed the rope back to Semian, who followed suit and tied it off for later use. They sat there for a moment, making sure they hadn't been spotted. Semian was acutely aware of his surroundings, knowing exactly where each guard was stationed.

They cautiously made their way under the bridge, crawling and climbing from beam to beam, making haste while ensuring they didn't make any noise. Eventually, they reached the other side, where guards were set up in a similar manner. They would have to repeat the process with the second rock, but Semian anticipated it would be easier on this side since the guards were mainly on the lookout for people entering the area.

As they began to prepare to create the diversion with the rock, they heard footsteps approaching. Semian quickly raised his hand, signaling for Lenala to halt.

The footsteps were heavy and coming from the direction of the castle.

Had they been spotted? Was someone following them?

The footsteps thundered over their heads and approached the guards. They heard muffled conversation. The men walked away from the bridge and began to talk. They couldn't hear what they were saying but there was occasional laughter and coins jingling. They were obviously familiar with the man, and it was clear that he was paying them off to let him cross.

Semian directed his hand toward the edge of the shore, indicating for Lenala to move. This was a perfect distraction for them to get off the bridge.

They made their exit. In a hurry, they moved down the edge of the water until they got to the edge of the woods. They climbed up the bank and crawled to the woods.

Again, Semian put up a hand and they stopped a few feet into the woods.

"I want to see who that is," he said, lying flat on his belly. Lenala also lay flat and scooted closer to the brush line. They could see that the man was walking away from the bridge and along the road headed toward town. As he got closer, Lenala started to recognize his walk. Soon, his profile came into view. A pit formed in her stomach; she knew that face. She looked at Semian. His expression was stone-cold and a cloud of suspicion was practically radiating off him. They both knew exactly who he was and he was up to no good.

THIRTY

It was Tion. Lenala's heart and mind were racing. "What is he doing out here?" she whispered. He was definitely paying off the guards for passage. They had seen him giving the guards money. If this were a private mission for the queen, he wouldn't have to bribe them.

She looked again at Semian, who was still staring dead ahead at Tion.

Neither of them moved a muscle until he was too far away to see or hear them.

Lenala let out a sigh. Semian made no sound, but just motioned to move forward. He was all business in full-on soldier mode. They began moving along the edge of the woods.

He wasn't going to let Tion out of his sight. Something bad was happening. Tion emitted very dark vibes. "Semian," Lenala whispered, "what are we doing? Are we following him?"

"He's up to something and I have a strong feeling it

could lead us to Farka," he said without stopping or looking at her.

Silently, they followed him into town.

Once the cover of the woods was gone, they decided it would be best to split up. Semian would follow from the rooftops and Lenala would stay on the ground.

Step by step, they covered ground as Tion led the way.

Lenala recognized the path. They were crossing by the herbalist's shop and down the back alley. Could he be going to the Dealer?

Suddenly, he came to a stop and turned. He looked as if he had heard something. He peered out from under his hood. His light brown eyes looked black because of the shadows. Lenala sank farther into the cover of the darkness and froze. Time seemed to drag by as he looked around. She knew Semian was nearby, giving her a sense of comfort.

Then, Tion lifted a large, muscular arm and knocked on what appeared to be nothing but a wall, producing three sharp raps.

A few moments later, a door opened and he disappeared. Lenala moved closer to the door, hoping she could catch a glimpse or hear something. The sound of two men's voices carried through the door. She recognized Tion's voice but the other man's was unfamiliar.

She could tell the other man was angry with Tion. Their voices were muffled but she could still make out what they were saying. "You can't just come in here at all hours of the night!"

"This is the deal we had!" Tion snapped. "Anytime I come, you give me what I need. I supplied you with an infinite supply so that you could supply me with an infinite supply," he said. His deep voice cut like a knife.

"I paid you well for this supply, and I transported her," the other man said with a snarl.

"Besides, it's late. I was sleeping. Why can't you come at normal hours? When I said anytime, I didn't think you meant these hours," he hissed. "If anyone gets word of me opening my doors so late, I'll never get any sleep."

"Your payment was merely a deposit on a debt that will never be fully repaid, and you know why I come at night." Tion's voice was laced with frustration.

"You think you did me such a favor. You couldn't have kept her even if you tried," the man cut back.

"I also didn't have to choose *you* to keep her," Tion said. "I could have chosen anyone to be the dealer, and put you out of business."

"You should be grateful for my help," the man snarled, his eyes narrowed in anger. "Without my wagon, how else would you have been able to smuggle her out?"

"I have numerous connections and a vast network of resources at my disposal." Tion's voice boomed. "Don't you know who I am? I am responsible for every wagon that comes onto the castle's property, and my influence extends far beyond that. Don't forget, I could just as easily take her away from you as I gave her to you. Mark my words, old man. If you continue to give me problems, I'll end this." There was a long silence.

"How are you already out?" the man finally asked. Tion obviously didn't like this question. Lenala heard some scuffling and grunting. "Ok, ok, ok," the man said. "How much do you want?"

"Enough for another month for two."

"Very well."

Lenala waited as the man made a ruckus opening cabinets, slamming doors, and clanking around. After a few minutes and a few more words, Tion left.

Lenala quickly ducked into the alley to avoid being seen as she heard Tion coming out the door. As he emerged, he pulled his hood over his sweaty head and quickly scanned the area to ensure no one was watching. He then grabbed one of the bottles and dipped his pinky finger into it, causing Lenala's breath to hitch in her throat. In shock, she watched as Tion brought his finger to his mouth and sucked the blood off it. He stood there for a moment and took in a deep breath. He closed his eyes and a serene smile spread across his face. She had never seen him smile. He had a gorgeous smile and for a small moment, she pitied him. What led him to this? What was he trying to mask? Pity quickly turned into anger as she continued looking at him. Realization hit her. He had stolen Farka and sold her to this man for his own gain. He was a backstabber. He was the one who had been drugging her and stealing her blood. He had been planning this all along.

Disappointment, anger, and sadness weighed heavily on Lenala. Tion had never really sat well with her, but she didn't think it was because of drugs. She thought maybe it was because he had a dark past. Apparently, she was partly right. Casually, he began walking back toward the castle.

Seconds later, Semian landed softly in the alley behind her. His expression was cold. "He's our man," he said grimly. "I never trusted that guy. The moment I saw him crossing the bridge, I knew."

"That man inside has Farka," Lenala said. Closing her

eyes, she tried to call to her. She tried to feel her but she couldn't. Nothing. Just emptiness.

"I can't feel her. They must have drugged her."

"From the rooftop, I could see that there's a back alley and a possible entrance. Let's go up and have a look," Semian said.

Together, they climbed to the roof. They could see that there were several rooms but no door to get them inside. Lenala tried again to press into her senses and see if she could feel Farka. Nothing.

"Ugh," she sighed in frustration. "I know she's in there."

"We are going to have to break in," Semian said, looking around for a good option. There were a few windows but they were pretty high up and small.

"Look." Lenala pointed to a small window that was barely visible. "There's a window down in the back that's just big enough for me to climb through. I can sneak in through there."

The window was perfect. It was low enough that she would not have to drop too far to hit the floor inside.

"Lower me and wait for my signal."

With Semian's help, she reached the window with ease and pried it open. She wiggled through and disappeared.

Semian didn't usually get nervous in situations like this, but he couldn't help but feel a wave of nerves once he lost sight of her. He knew Lenala was capable, but she could also be emotional, especially when it came to Farka. If something had happened to her, he didn't know how she would react. He felt a strong desire to protect her. He loved her determination and passion, but he also worried about her safety. Maybe it was because they had known each other for so long.

He took a moment to thank Draygon that Lenala was a skilled fighter who could protect herself. He couldn't be with a woman who couldn't take care of herself in a fight. If he had to worry about another woman like he did Lenala, he would go crazy. He wanted her to be safe and taken care of, but he also respected her independence and strength. He had always been protective of her but now that they were older, those feelings had grown stronger, and he couldn't imagine life without her.

As Lenala crept through the dark and eerily quiet hallway, she peeked into each of the rooms, finding them all empty. She stumbled upon a room with shelves and cabinets lining the walls, filled with rows of empty bottles. *This must be where he fills his bottles with DB.* The room was dimly lit by a street light shining through a window high up in a corner. Lenala could see that the door leading to the alley was bolted shut from the inside; that confirmed this was the same room Tion had been in.

As she continued down the hall, she noticed that one of the doors was slightly ajar. She approached it with caution, opening it as quietly as possible. She could barely make out a set of wooden stairs leading down. She followed them. Her heart was pounding. The staircase seemed to go on forever. Finally, she arrived at the last step. It took her a minute to adjust her vision to the darkness. There was a small crack in the ceiling that let in a small amount of light from somewhere. Lenala cautiously made her way around the perimeter of the room, realizing it was much larger than she had initially thought. Suddenly, she stumbled and tripped over something, creating a loud noise that echoed throughout the room. Her heart pounded as she froze, listening for any indication that someone had heard her.

After a moment of silence, Lenala reached out to see what had caused her to trip. Her hand came into contact with a long, leather-like rope that was securely attached to the wall on one end. As she followed the rope's path, she realized it was leading to something and began to gently tug on it, feeling her way forward guardedly. After a few more steps, Lenala bumped into something. "Farka?" Joy and excitement filled her as she whispered Farka's name. However, Farka didn't move. She hugged Farka and pulled her head close to hers, but there was still no reaction. Lenala could tell that Farka was alive, but she was in a deep drug-induced sleep. The rope was connected to a net tied tightly around Farka's tail and body. Lenala looked around the room, trying to find the source of Farka's sedation, but she couldn't see well enough in the dark. The sound of creaking wood overhead halted Lenala in her tracks. They must have heard the racket.

The footsteps got closer. Someone was coming down the stairs.

She quickly hid behind Farka, praying they wouldn't see her.

A man entered with an oil lamp. "What are you doing down here, ol' girl? Making all that noise?" It was the voice of the man who was talking to Tion. The Dealer.

"Let's check those lines." He walked over and loosened the net to lift Farka's front wing. There he had a small line draining Farka's blood. And another line giving her a sedative.

"Let's make sure this line isn't loose. We don't need you waking up.

"This shit doesn't last long enough," he mumbled to himself. "Stupid beast," he said as he kicked her and walked out.

Rage began rising inside Lenala. She wanted to jump out of there and rip that man's head off, but getting Farka out safely was her priority. She would deal with him later. She waited to make sure he was far enough away before she sneaked out from hiding. The lines were under Farka's wing. She quickly disconnected both the sedative and the line draining the blood. It was probably Orez. That was a strong sedative but should wear off quickly. It was one of the herbs she had been waiting on for the poison.

As she moved quickly in the dark, she accidentally kicked one of the bottles, sending it spinning across the floor. It made a horribly loud noise when it crashed into the wall and shattered.

She froze in fear. She knew he had heard the clamor and would come running back.

She hid by the door and waited. Moments later, he was back and angry. "What are you doing, you stupid Dragon?" The man's voice boomed through the room as he saw that the lines connecting Farka to his DB supply had been disconnected. He started cursing and swearing in frustration. He set his lamp down on one of the shelves and began to kick Farka again, but Lenala had seen and heard enough. She emerged from the shadows, her voice sharp and commanding. "She's not a stupid Dragon," she declared, her eyes flashing with anger. "And you're not going to hurt her anymore."

"What the..." he started to say as he spun in horror. Lenala stepped into the light and before he had time to react, she lunged and smashed a jar over his head. The glass shattered into pieces as she shoved him to the ground and began kicking him with all her might. *I could really use Escitalo right now.* She and Semian had left their swords behind on purpose, knowing that it would have been difficult to be stealthy under the bridge while carrying weapons. This would serve as a lesson to never leave Escitalo behind again. He tried to get up and charge at her, but she countered with another kick. She pinned him to the ground with one knee planted firmly on his neck and the other extended beside her on the ground to balance her. It was a strong stance she had learned in hand-to-hand combat training. She reached over and grabbed a glass shard, and shoved it to his neck. "Where is the antidote for what you gave her?"

He was sluggish and not a savvy fighter, but he was cocky. He snickered. "You'd love to know, wouldn't you?" She drove her knee into his neck a little harder. He whimpered but didn't speak. She dug the shard in deeper. Blood was beginning to spill.

"Wrong answer," she hissed at him. "Tell me where it is and I'll spare your life."

"It's only Orez and it will wear off in a few minutes and she'll be good as new," he said through ragged breaths. Blood continued to pour down his neck. "You can't have her. She's mine. I paid a fortune for her and she's making me more money than I've ever made before. "I'm tired of everybody else having the finest things while I live in filth. Now it's my turn."

White heat filled Lenala. She wanted to crush his neck right there. How could someone be so diabolical? Unbeknownst to Lenala, the Dealer had reached into his pocket and pulled out a tiny jar of DB. Just then, Farka began to stir and lift her head. He was right—the Orez was wearing off quickly. Just as Lenala turned her attention to Farka, the man took the opportunity to take a dab of the DB.

Suddenly, he was invigorated and shoved her knee off of him. The rush from the blood gave him the strength to send her flying across the room with one push. She slammed hard into the wall, knocking the wind out of her as she hit the ground. He jumped up off the ground and charged after her with a crazed look in his eyes. The same look as the men she had killed in the barn.

She kicked at him but missed, kicking his lamp over instead. The oil spread to the corner of the room, creating a trail of flames.

The Dealer lunged at Lenala, knocked her to the ground, and grabbed her by the throat, his hands squeezing tightly around her neck. Although she was foggy from the impact of hitting the wall, she managed to hang onto the broken jar shard. She began stabbing him in an attempt to free herself. However, he remained unshaken, a crazed smile spreading across his face as he continued to strangle her with increasing force. Suddenly, Semian appeared behind the man and snatched him off of her. He grabbed him with his bare hands and slammed him against the wall. It took Lenala a few breaths to regain her wits. The man was strong and powered by the blood. She shook her head and looked around. The room was getting brighter with the spreading fire. "Get Farka and get out of here!" Semian shouted.

Lenala nodded and quickly made her way over to Farka, who was now awake but looked frightened and disoriented. Lenala knew that this was a common side effect of Orez, which could leave a person feeling confused for several minutes after waking up. She approached Farka, speaking in a calm and soothing voice to reassure her and help her regain her bearings.

"I'm here, girl, it's ok." Lenala embraced her. "Come on, Farka, let's go." Semian had the man pinned to the ground. By now, the room was almost fully in flames. "Semian, leave him. Let's go."

"Go, I'm behind you!" he shouted.

She and Farka began running up the long staircase. The effects of the Orez slowed Farka down, making her clumsy. Semian was on their heels when the man suddenly grabbed hold of his leg, tripping him and pulling him down. He was on top of Semian in a drug-induced frenzy. Semian kicked at the Dealer and pushed his face, causing him to stumble backwards. Taking advantage of the moment, Semian lunged and grabbed the Dealer's head, slamming it repeatedly into the stairs. Blow after blow rained down on the Dealer's face until he was left bloody and battered, lying motionless on the ground. Semian stood over him, panting, his fists clenched tightly at his sides.

Fire rushed up the bottom of the stairs as Lenala screamed for him to hurry.

He ran up as fast as he could. Lenala had made it to the front and unbolted the door. Smoke was pouring into the hall. She and Farka rushed out into the alley, waiting for

Semian to catch up. Just as he made it to the door, the fire roared behind him, engulfing the room. They ran through the alleyway. Farka was getting faster but she was still a little wobbly. They continued to move, staying hidden in the dark alley until they reached a safe distance. Smoke was billowing up into the air and all of a sudden, a massive explosion erupted.

CHAPTER

THIRTY-ONE

Six more months had passed since Lenala's exile.

The queen's investigation had gone exactly as Brantog expected. Smoothly. Kineah had proven loyal by keeping her mouth shut. She gave the queen no evidence to move forward with. For her loyalty, he had rewarded her with more blood and fewer beatings.

A few empty threats were all the queen had for him. She had tried her hardest to prove everyone wrong but in the end, she lost her case. The king had not said another word to Brantog, but he was still uneasy about moving forward with recruiting another girl.

Brantog had become fixated on maintaining a steady supply of DB to sustain his and Kineah's habit. He was well aware that he was consuming too much too quickly and needed to start cutting back. He decided to start by reducing Kineah's intake, she was becoming increasingly expensive and risky. Obtaining DB had also become more challenging, as the Murkes were lying low.

Lenala almost really messed everything up for him.

The more he thought about her, the more he began to hate her. Even though she had been exiled, he couldn't help but feel jealous of her. The reality was that she was the free one now. Free to live out from under the thumb of this hellhole. *Only the princess could get away with something like that,* he told himself time and time again.

If only I could have gotten to her one day sooner, none of this would have happened.

Things had become hopeless. The only thing she looked forward to was when he brought her the blood. Everything else in life had lost its meaning. What little meaning it ever had. The hope she had in Lenala had long faded. She was gone forever and there was no chance of beating Brantog at his game. Every day, she hated herself more and more. She constantly dwelled on the fact that she should have told the queen the truth. Maybe there was a small chance that she would have believed her despite Brantog's threats. Maybe she would have rescued her from this prison. The thought of what he would do to her family was the only thing she held on to. It wasn't worth it. She had accepted her fate. To anyone else, being in the Castle of Nahkei was an honor and a privilege. To Kineah, it was a death sentence. Day after day, it was the same thing: Pretend to be like the other girls, act happy, keep it together, smile when he was around in public, and keep her mouth shut. Then wait in her room for him to come. Every single day. Nothing ever changed.

She detested when he came but now, she needed him to. She was fully addicted to the blood and he was her only source. She had thought about running away, but she worried about her family and what he would do to them if he thought they were involved. There was no escaping. Not until she was eighteen and freed from the castle. She dreamed of that day but it felt so far away. If she could just hang on and endure a little longer, she would eventually get her freedom.

Night after night, she stared at the small knife she had hidden in her room. She imagined what it would be like to plunge it into Brantog's neck. But she was too afraid to act on her thoughts. She also entertained the idea of using the knife on herself, but her fear held her back from taking such drastic measures. The weight of her self-loathing had become overwhelming, and she felt trapped with no way out. The only glimmer of hope was a distant light, seemingly impossible to reach. She felt lost and alone, with no clear path to escape the darkness that had consumed her.

He had begun decreasing the amount of blood he'd been giving her, and she blamed her increasingly dark thoughts on this. She needed her own supply and was sick of him controlling every aspect of her life. Once, he inadvertently left a small vial in her room, but that was long gone. After much consideration, she decided to sneak into Brantog's room and steal some of his supply. She didn't need much, just enough to get by when he refused to give her any. It was the only thing that kept her from losing her mind, the only escape from the pain. She knew it was a dangerous and desperate act, but she felt she had no other choice. It was the only thing that made her feel alive and gave her relief.

His schedule was predictable and she could easily

sneak into his room. She would take just a little at a time, and he'd never notice.

Morning was the best time to get into his room. He never missed breakfast and no one would think twice if she wasn't there.

She quietly made her way to his chambers and sneaked inside.

The smell of burnt wine and fire pierced her nose. The fire was smoldering, and the room was cold. She looked around, quickly observing the area.

Brantog's room was luxurious with a high bed adorned in dark brown linens and matching dark brown furniture. Two large chairs were strategically placed by the fireplace. The walls were decorated with his impressive collection of military medals and an extensive assortment of weapons, highlighting his passion for combat. The assortment included swords of various sizes, along with an array of knives, ranging from large fighting daggers to small throwing knives. Brantog's collection even included long spears, arrows, and shields, all meticulously displayed on the walls and shelves, showcasing an expertise with weaponry. It was quite impressive. The thought of him using any of those weapons sent chills down her spine and prompted her to hurry.

She quickly went to one of his dressers and began searching through the drawers. There were papers and old medals stuffed in them. She searched every drawer and couldn't find anything. It must be hidden. *Of course he would hide it—he trusts no one.*

She continued looking around the room for any sign of a hidden box or drawer. *Where is it?*

She was beginning to get nervous, as she had already been in there too long.

Out of desperation, she went back to the first drawer and felt around once more. Then she felt it. It was so small that anyone could miss it if they didn't know what they were looking for. There was a tiny notch that her finger barely ran across. A change in the pattern of the wood along the bottom of the drawer. A surge of adrenaline shot through her. She tapped it a couple of times. Nothing. Then she took one of her tiny hairpins and poked at the seam. It burst open. There was a small hidden compartment containing four vials of DB and four darts. She grabbed the bottles and took five drops from each one, placing them into the tiny vial she had kept. This would last her for quite a while. She could at least have some on the days he was cutting back. She would take her weaning into her own hands. He would never notice such a small amount missing from each bottle. She hid her vial and sneaked back to her room. She didn't leave a clue and there was not a soul in sight.

She was elated. *That was too easy.* The next week or so, she supplemented what he gave her. He had drastically cut hers back and she was supplementing more than she had planned.

Her plan to cut back only backfired on her. The more she had access to it, the more she wanted it.

Her obsession with Dragon's Blood had intensified, and she found herself sneaking into his room more frequently. Some nights, after Brantog had left her, she would sit and stare at the swirling, thick liquid in the bottle, mesmerized by its hypnotic movements. It had become her savior, the only way she could numb the pain and cope.

As weeks passed, her supply of Brantog's blood began to dwindle once again. Her plan remained solid, and she had become faster and more efficient at sneaking in and out of his room undetected. She crept into his room, careful not to make a sound. She tiptoed to the dresser and opened the drawer. As she dropped the drops of blood into her bottle, the only sound in the room was the soft plop of each drop hitting the bottom. Suddenly, there was a creak, and her heart skipped a beat. She froze, holding her breath and listening intently for any other sounds. Then, she heard it. Breathing. It was soft and rhythmic, and it seemed to be coming from right behind her. She slowly turned, her eyes widening in fear, and there he was— sound asleep in his bed.

Panic flooded her body as she clutched the bottle tightly, her knuckles turning white. *Why is he still here? Why didn't I check? How could I be so careless?*

She was so used to him being gone, and he had never missed breakfast before. She slowly turned back, tucking her bottle of blood away. With a sense of unease, she placed his bottles back in the dresser and closed the drawer as quietly as possible. She didn't make a sound as she tried to keep her breathing under control.

Suddenly, a presence surrounded her, and she knew he was standing behind her. Before she could react, darkness enveloped her, and then everything went black.

"The little whore is trying to steal from me?" He hissed the words out as he looked at her body lying there on his floor.

"How could you? Have I not given you all that you need?" He grabbed her and threw her into one of his chairs. She moaned as her eyes fluttered open. Her body was shaking and she was sweating.

"You sneak into my private chambers and take from me? The one who feeds you, the one who takes care of you?"

She had a pit in her stomach as she listened to him. He was speaking in an angry yet calm tone. Suddenly, she began to feel nauseated, and before she could react, she started to vomit. Her body shook with the force of it, she felt sick and stressed beyond measure.

As she sat up, she struggled to catch her breath, she knew she needed more blood.

"Clean it up," he barked coldly as he grabbed a small towel and threw it at her. Slowly and shakily, she got up. Her head was throbbing from the impact of the blow. "Throw it in the fire," he demanded after she had cleaned it up. *The fire, why didn't I see the fire? His fire is always out when he is gone.*

He stepped closer to her. Suddenly, without thinking, she pushed him with all her might toward the fire. He stumbled back a few steps but managed to grab her arm and regain his balance. His robe licked the edge of the flames and caught fire. He shoved her down hard as he took his robe off and slung the burning garment into the fire. The fireplace was huge and the flames raged as they engulfed the robe.

He let out a laugh as she sat there helpless once again.

With a malicious glint in his eye, he strode over to the

wall where he kept his arsenal of weapons, and began to run his fingers along the razor-sharp edges of the knives.

"Which one of these would shut you up?" he taunted. "Perhaps this one?" He grabbed a big sword with a black blade and swung it through the air a few times. He pointed it at her. "No, too big," he said, putting it away. "This one?" He grabbed a smaller one. That one had a smooth handle with a jagged blade. He ran his fingertip along the sharpest point, drawing blood. With a twisted grin on his face, he put his finger in his mouth and sucked the blood off.

He then walked over to her and squeezed his finger, drawing more blood. *"Go on,"* he said, holding it out to her. She didn't oblige him. He shoved it into her mouth. "Not quite the same effect, huh?" He smirked.

She was angry now. She bit down on his finger, drawing more blood, and spat it on him.

He yelled and yanked his hand back. He narrowed his eyes at her but remained calm.

As angry as she was, she knew this was bad. He was sober and had nothing to soften his mood. "Hmm, not this one either," he said as he walked back to the wall. He picked up a small knife with a short, sharp blade. "Yes, this is the one," he said, dragging out each word. "This one will cut out that tongue of yours. If you can't speak, you can't tell, and if you can't tell, you don't need the blood." He stood there for a long moment watching her. "Or maybe I will just kill you. I am beginning to feel like you are ungrateful and causing me more stress than pleasure." He paused, placing his hand on his head and squeezing his temples. His eyes were closed as he rolled his neck in small circles. His body was beginning to ache for DB. Kineah watched him. She knew exactly how he felt. His eyes opened and focused on her. "As a matter of fact, I think I will just kill you, or better yet, I will bring your family here and kill them in front of you to teach you a lesson. Yes, that is precisely what I will do," he decided. He turned and put the small knife back and grabbed a much larger one. He swung the sword into a ready position and turned back to face her. To his surprise, she was standing up and looking at him.

"You can't kill them. I have been quiet and I have kept my part of the deal." Tears were streaming down her face. "They have nothing to do with me," she pleaded.

"Oh, but I can, and I will do it, " he said as he stepped forward. "Today, right in this room." He was serious.

"Kill me instead," Kineah begged, her voice shaking with fear and desperation. "They are innocent."

But there was a dark, menacing look in Brantog's eyes that cut right through her, and she knew that he would not spare anyone, not even her. Fear filled her, but she refused to give up. With a quick movement, she grabbed the small bottle of DB that she had concealed in her pocket.

As Brantog began to move toward her, she opened the bottle and held it up as a weapon of defense. "You can never hurt them, and you will never hurt me again," she declared, her voice trembling with a mixture of fear and determination.

Brantog lunged at her with his sword, attempting to knock the bottle out of her hand, but he was too slow. In a moment of panic and desperation, Kineah poured the entire contents of the bottle into her mouth, feeling the effects of the powerful drug surge through her veins.

"You will never win," she spat out, her eyes blazing with defiance. With a sudden burst of strength, she smashed the now-empty bottle on the ground, shattering it to bits and stopping Brantog in his tracks. For a moment, he stood there, stunned.

Euphoria took her over within seconds. She felt herself fall to the floor but it didn't hurt. Brantog was standing over her yelling at her, but she couldn't hear him. She closed her eyes. Memories of her childhood flooded through her mind. Her parents, her siblings, and all of the happy times. She would do anything to make sure they stayed safe. There were no regrets for what she had done. Even if it meant that she was throwing away any chances at ever living a free life. She had to protect them. She would rather sacrifice herself than see anyone else suffer at his hand. She felt Brantog rolling her over to her side and telling her to breathe, but she was in another world. She felt peace and happiness for the first time in as long as she could remember. A light was shining ahead of her. She could see her family standing there waiting for her. They were laughing and motioning for her to join them. As she soared toward the light, she glanced back and saw Brantog hovering over her, frantically trying to revive her. She knew she had moved past the point of no return. She turned her attention back to the light; it was beautiful and warm just like Haruelio. It was as though the light was wrapping around her and she felt like she was glowing from within. It was wonderful. Tears of joy streamed down her cheeks as a deep sense of serenity overtook her. Kineah was finally free.

THIRTY-TWO

Thunder rumbled through the streets, causing the ground to shudder and debris to swirl through the air. Lenala couldn't help but wonder if the townspeople had heard the commotion and would soon emerge from their homes to investigate. The three of them ducked into dark alleyways so they would be out of sight. They hurried along, neither one saying a word, barely making a sound. Farka was keeping up even though she was still groggy and weak. They had to cover a good bit of ground to get to the woods. Finally, they made it. The dense woods provided a safe cover for them. Lenala hoped that Farka would regain her strength soon. Every passing moment became increasingly critical as they had only a few hours left before they were expected back at the castle to report for duty.

"We will give her one hour to let the sedative wear off," Semian said flatly. His face was stone-cold and dark. In the distance, they could see the smoke faintly. Lenala knew that once Farka was strong enough, she would be able to fly them high enough to escape detection. They needed to reach the castle before sunrise.

While they waited, Lenala recounted the events of the night. *How could Tion be an addict when he is one of the most elite soldiers? Maybe he is some kind of functioning addict who can hide his addiction and still perform his duties?* She never would have guessed that he was a DB user. He always had a darkness about him that didn't settle right with her, but DB? He almost always kept to himself, so maybe there were signs that she just didn't see. *I wonder if the queen knows,* she thought. Surely, the queen knew. He was one of her longest-serving guards.

Lenala was unsure of how to approach the situation. Should she confront him directly or bring it to the attention of the queen first? She knew that the queen would need to be informed eventually, and Lenala knew that she needed to tread carefully. Farka was not safe until Tion was out of the picture.

Relief and thankfulness were at the forefront of her emotions right now. Her world felt right again, even though there was so much craziness happening. With Farka by her side, she was able to deal with it. She laid her head on Farka and waited for the Orez to finish wearing off.

An hour had passed and Farka was finally beginning to perk up. Her black eyes were still glazed over, but she was moving around. She would be able to fly soon. Semian had not said a word since they got to the woods. He was smoldering. Lenala could only imagine what was going through his head. He was extremely unsettled and she could feel it.

"You need to report this immediately to the queen," he

said to Lenala. "Before Tion has a chance to hear about the explosion." He paced back and forth as he spoke, his voice low and direct. "The queen may not believe our story, and we need to be prepared for that," he continued. "She could become angry and side with Tion, who is one of her closest guards. We need to be cautious and present our evidence."

Lenala considered his words. He had clearly put a lot of thought into this.

"She may already know about the whole thing and choose to take his side. Anything could happen," he continued.

"Do you think she will dismiss us?" Lenala asked. She felt nervous thinking about all of these possibilities.

She didn't know what the queen did or did not know. The queen could have been in on the whole thing for all they knew. She had never liked all of the questions and the overenthusiasm the queen had about Farka. Semian stopped pacing and stood next to Farka, who nudged him with her head, sensing his stress.

She was trying to calm him. Farka wasn't usually fond of people aside from Lenala and her immediate family, so it was clear that Semian had gained her trust. After all, he had just helped save her life, and they had known each other for years.

Lenala felt a surge of warmth in her heart as she watched Farka thanking Semian in her own way, by trying to ease his emotions. Semian took a deep breath, and as he exhaled, his body relaxed. He and Farka locked eyes, and Lenala could see the calmness settling over him as Farka let out a small grunt. Semian smiled at her and gave her a gentle pat.

"This throws a pretty big wrench into our plans," he

continued in a determined tone. "We still need to get the poison done and we need to move with haste."

Lenala agreed and interjected, "Semian, we have to make the mix before we tell the queen. Because if she dismisses us, we aren't going to be able to make it at all."

"Right," Semian agreed. "We get through today and we sneak away and make it tonight."

There was still darkness for a short while longer, and they only had a small window of opportunity to make it back to the castle undetected. Farka was showing signs that she was ready to fly.

She stood and dipped her head low to the ground, allowing them to climb onto her back. Despite her smaller size, she could carry a large amount of weight. She spread her wings wide and began to flap them. Her wings were long and powerful. In order for her to get the momentum to fly, she had to do several large, rhythmic flaps before she started running for takeoff. The wind she created with her wings was a magnificent feeling. Lenala loved this part. Semian had never flown on a Dragon before. Lenala could sense that he was excited and nervous. The roar of the wind under her wings was almost deafening. It sounded like drums being beaten. He let out a startled cry as Farka began running for her takeoff. Lenala erupted in laughter. "Oh, you think this is funny," he said as he held onto Lenala tightly. Farka, who sensed his fear as well as Lenala's amusement, didn't miss a beat. As soon as she was high enough in the air, she dipped quickly and made a few sharp turns, causing Lenala to laugh even harder and Semian to yelp a couple of times. "At least she is feeling better," he grumbled with a smirk as they flew higher into the sky.

It was still dark and the sky was bright with stars and glowing planets. Semian had never seen anything like this. He'd never been so far off the ground. There was so much to see and explore in this universe. Maybe one day they could. Once all of this was behind them. He had always been a soldier. He didn't know anything else. Life was Xuria. Now it was becoming clear that there was so much more than Xuria and Analicia. Lenala leaned back on him as they flew. She liked the vibe he was giving off. He felt happy and peaceful. The same way she felt every time she and Farka flew together. They flew around to the back side of the castle and landed on the roof right by Lenala's room. A perfect landing, almost completely silent.

Now, all she had to do was keep Farka hidden until the concoction was made and she talked to the queen. Of course, they would have to update Quade. He would be eager to know what had become of the trip to the Dealer.

Daylight came too quickly. Lenala barely had time to shower and get ready. Today was going to be rough going with no sleep whatsoever. She moved Farka into the bathroom to sleep. There was no telling whom she could trust right now. She could not let anyone see her.

The day moved slowly and Tion was stationed near the queen all day. Lenala prayed to Draygon that the queen would not call on her for any chats or special requests. She was exhausted emotionally and physically. Every now and then, she would press in and make sure Farka was ok. Farka was fine. She had been resting all day.

Lenala found herself staring at Tion throughout the day, fantasizing about how she would love to attack him and make him pay for what he did to Farka. For selling her off as a drug Dragon. She only knew of DB farms from what the men had told her. They allegedly existed on some of the remote planets in the galaxy. Those poor Dragons were said to be bred into captivity for their blood supply. She kept wondering how he kept himself so composed at all times. Most DB users she knew of were on the streets begging for money. Not Tion—he acted perfectly normal aside from his dark demeanor. He worked every day, he seemed appropriate, he trained hard, and he was in impeccable shape. He was one of the top soldiers. How was he an addict? There was so much about DB she did not know. This was a whole new world to her.

Lenala's anger grew with each passing moment. Every now and then, she reached down and placed her hand on the hilt of Escitalo, feeling the reassuring pulse of the fang grip. The grip came alive in her hand, pulsing with power and giving her a sense of calm and strength. Semian was on guard nearby and she had caught him giving Tion a death stare several times.

He had already updated Quade, who despite being surprised, believed them because this was the only thing that made any sense. Even Quade was watching Tion's every move. He had wanted Lenala to report this to the queen immediately, not knowing that they were waiting intentionally so they could make the poison. She made up an excuse about needing to be sure Farka was ok before she went to her. He bought it. But not without some persuasion. He was a man who wanted things done right away. He was used to having things done his way. This was why he was the leader. He was persuasive but with good intention and fair reasoning.

The day continued to drag until finally, the dinner bells rang. Relief ran through Lenala.

After a quick check on Farka, Lenala was at the table. She hardly had an appetite. Neither did Quade or Semian. In fact, neither did Tion.

Crand and Drac made their usual small talk and jokes. Enhan and Doran chatted and occasionally asked Quade a few questions. Lenala had been quieter since Farka had been gone, and now she realized Tion knew exactly why all along. Her face felt hot as she balled her fists under the table staring at her plate. It was so hard to stick to the plan they had. She wanted more than anything to call him out. She was angry and exhausted. She relaxed her hand and placed it on Escitalo. One deep breath and she was reminded of what she had to do. Once again, she needed to play a part and stick to the plan: After dinner, they would meet in her room with the herbs and sneak into the kitchen. They were on duty until the night guards came on. They only had a limited amount of time and would have to find the right moment to sneak away. Lenala asked Quade to place them on general guard duties that evening; those duties included patrolling the kitchen. He obliged, knowing how tired they were from the night before.

Finally, the time had come. The kitchen was silent; the cooks were already gone for the night. It was a big area with several stoves and fire pits, some of which were still hot from dinner. This was to their advantage as the coals in the fire pits would continue to burn for hours after they closed up.

Lenala and Semian needed a large pot to boil the herbs in. That would take about an hour. Lenala got the herbs ready and soon the poison was brewing on a fire pit in the back of the kitchen. They knew that the longer they let it sit, the more potent it would become. They had to be careful not to get caught. Everything was in place. Now, they just had to wait.

THIRTY-THREE

Morning had once again come too fast.

Farka was wide awake and was doing much better. She was back in her usual spirits. The harvest had gone well. They ended up with two large jars full, which was more than they expected. Now that they had it, they would have to request a leave of absence to carry out their mission. But first, Lenala needed to break the news about Tion to the queen. She wasn't sure how she would take the fact that her soldier had stolen a Dragon and was addicted to Dragon's Blood. She and Semian had discussed all of the possibilities until they were sure they'd thought of every single angle. Lenala planned to request a meeting with the queen before breakfast. She had rehearsed over and over what she was going to say. She had also decided that she would take Farka with her to the meeting. She could use some moral support. "Ok, Farka, let's go. It's now or never."

Tingles ran up her spine as they approached the queen's quarters. She hoped the queen would believe her and grant her permission to have time off, but she was fully prepared for whatever might happen.

When she arrived, she was met by one of the night guards. "I'm here to see Queen Halice." She prayed that the queen could see her now and she wouldn't have to wait. He disappeared for a few minutes and then returned and ushered her in. As they neared the lounge area to wait, Farka began to sniff the air and take small, antsy steps. "What is it, girl?" Lenala tried to calm her down with soothing vibes, but Farka was not relaxing. Her ears were perked up high and she was hyper-alert. Lenala felt a surge of anger rising inside her. The anger was not her own; it was Farka's. "Be calm, girl. We are getting your revenge soon enough."

As they rounded the corner into the lounge, Queen Halice was already seated. There were two maids in the back of the room and the queen was talking to none other than Tion. Lenala's heart dropped as adrenaline pierced her veins. The queen and Tion both turned their attention to Lenala and Farka as the door closed behind them. As soon as Tion laid eyes on her and Farka, he froze. His face became pale and his eyes widened.

"Lenala," the queen called out as she saw her enter the room with Farka. "Hello, Farka," she greeted with a smile. But her expression quickly turned to horror as Farka lowered her head and began to growl. Lenala spun to see Farka taking deep breaths and stomping, her wings spreading wide as she began to transform.

Lenala watched in shock as Farka grew at least four feet taller, shaking her head and neck from side to side. Her eyes turned red and a fierce fire burned inside her. The amount of rage emanating from Farka was frightening. Lenala had never seen or felt her so angry.

Before she could react, Farka started running at full speed toward Tion. Screams echoed through the room as Farka threw her head down and started spitting fireballs directly at the two maids. The flames hit them, completely incinerating them on the spot. Tion was momentarily paralyzed with fear before quickly stepping back to avoid being hit by the fireballs.

But he was too slow. She reached him in a matter of seconds and towered over him. Her gaze was fierce and fixed on him. He was trembling all over. He instinctively dropped to his knees and started begging Farka. "I'm sorry, Farka. I'm so sorry for what I did to you. Please spare my life, I need help, please. I'll do anything." Her red eyes were focused solely on him, her ears were back, and her wings were spread wide. She stomped and snarled in Tion's face. His apology only seemed to anger her more. Tears streamed down his cheeks. He looked so vulnerable and weak. This man who was a soldier and one of the toughest men she'd ever met was on his knees, crying and begging for his life. Lenala felt yet another moment of pity for him. She knew that Farka was not herself, but was consumed by her rage and anger. In a split-second decision, Lenala tried to plead with Farka internally, hoping to reach her and give Tion a chance.

"Farka, please listen to me," Lenala thought urgently. *"Tion is not himself. He's been affected by the Dragon's Blood. He needs help, not punishment."*

Lenala could feel her hesitating for a moment. It was enough of an opening for Lenala to try again.

"Farka, please, I know you're angry, but we can help Tion, together."

Farka began to calm down. Her breathing became steady. Lenala breathed a sigh of relief. Farka took two steps backward and lowered her head, signaling that there would be no mercy from her. She took a deep breath and let out a rain of fire, igniting Tion from head to toe. He screamed out in agony as flames engulfed him. Farka showed no remorse as she continued to unleash fire upon him until he was nothing but ashes.

Lenala watched in horror as Tion was consumed by the flames. She knew that Farka's decision was final and that there was nothing she could do to stop it. Dragons had little patience for those who crossed them, and they could be ruthless when it came to protecting their own.

Farka let out a few grunts, then fixed her gaze on Lenala for a long, silent moment. They stood there, eyes locked.

Farka gave Lenala a nod. Lenala nodded back. It was a mutual understanding that Farka had her own mind and that this was a personal matter.

She shook her body a few times, bringing it back down to her normal size, then she turned and went to the corner of the room and lay down as if nothing had happened.

Lenala felt a sense of sadness and regret that Tion had reached such a tragic end, but also a sense of relief that he could no longer cause harm to anyone.

Suddenly, the guard who let Lenala in came bursting through the doors. He had heard the commotion and he ran to the queen. "Are you ok, my Queen?" His expression was grim as he looked around the room. There were small piles of ashes and the smell of smoke was heavy in the air. "What happened in here?" he stammered.

"I am fine. Farka got spooked and burned up my couch," she lied.

His eyes got wide as he looked at the Dragon. "My Queen..." He started to reach for her. His hands were trembling. "Let me take you to safety."

"I am perfectly safe." She waved her hand at him, shooing him away. "Farka is harmless and we can replace the couch. Now leave me. I'll be ready for my breakfast shortly."

As soon as he left, Lenala turned her attention to the queen. *How am I going to explain this?* She and Semian had rehearsed every possible scenario. *Except this.*

The queen sat down. With the guard gone, she could let her emotions go. She began to shake and tears streamed down her face.

"What just happened?" she asked. "Why did Farka kill them? What did they do?" she started in her usual fashion of asking questions without waiting for an answer. "What did Tion mean when he was begging for his life?" This time, she turned her tear-stained face to Lenala. *Time to answer.*

Lenala sensed the queen's sorrow and detachment as she proceeded to explain Farka's disappearance, the clues they had uncovered over the past weeks, and their encounter with the Dealer. Despite the gravity of the situation, the queen's expression remained unchanged as she sat silently, absorbing Lenala's words.

After a few moments of tense silence, the queen finally spoke, her voice barely above a whisper.

"Had he not admitted to some wrongdoing right before

she killed him, I would not believe you, Lenala," she said solemnly. "Tion was one of my most trusted men and the maids, they must have been his accomplices," she rambled.

That's true—the maids must have been in on it or else Farka would have spared them, Lenala realized.

"I am so sorry for what he did. He went way too far." She looked over at Farka. A newfound form of respect and fear engulfed her.

"She must have been terrified, in that dark place, with those awful strangers." She trailed off as she stared at Farka. "Is this what you came to see me about?" she asked Lenala.

"Yes, Your Highness. I just found her and I kept her hidden until I could talk to you. I never would have imagined she would react like this upon seeing Tion."

"Well, how would you have known that Tion was even here with me?" She paused briefly. "But why didn't you bring this to my attention sooner?" she asked, skepticism rising in her voice. Lenala was prepared for this question. They had rehearsed it.

"I could not risk anyone overhearing us. I mean, even the maids were in on it." That part was a surprise, but it made sense. Someone had to have been helping Tion. There was too much involved for one person to pull that off.

"Well, did you suspect *me*?" the queen asked, her eyes locked on Lenala's. Anyone else would have been made nervous by this question—she was directly asking Lenala if she trusted her. She had rehearsed this answer, too. The truth was that even with her gift, Lenala didn't know if she could trust the queen, and she was not afraid to speak the truth. Another trait she got from her father.

"I could not rule anyone out," she said, returning her gaze. She knew the risk she was taking by being honest. This was a calculated risk she and Semian decided they were willing to take. They knew the queen was not someone they should try to pull anything over on, and lying to her would be far worse than telling the truth.

A small pang of regret ran through her as the queen silently looked at her.

She was supposed to be playing a part and just as soon as the regret came, it went away. No one messed with Farka. Plan or no plan. This was a dealbreaker and she was prepared to be dismissed if that was the queen's wish.

The queen took a deep, ragged breath and let it out rapidly. She looked around the room, then back at Lenala. Her eyes were dull and her lips pressed tightly together. Tion was someone she would never be able to replace. He had been a good soldier and even something of a friend to her. She believed Lenala about what he had done. He went too far and paid dearly. They sat in silence a little while longer as the queen collected her thoughts.

"As much as it hurts my pride that you did not rule me out immediately, I do understand your reasoning, and the fact that this was happening right under my nose shows me you had the correct thought process," she said in a low voice. There was a different tone to her words. Sadness echoed in everything she said.

"It's hard to know whom to trust these days. To think that Tion would steal from you and have the maids helping him baffles me. It's very disappointing." She lowered her head as she wiped tears from her eyes. She took a deep breath.

"Do you think anyone else was involved? Will Farka be

taking out her revenge on anyone else?" she asked hesitantly.

Relief washed over Lenala. *She believes me.*

"My Queen, I am also disappointed. Tion was a great soldier who got stuck in a bad situation. But I'm sure he was the one who planned everything, including instructing the maids to steal Farka's blood. I believe that has been happening for a long time."

Lenala reminded her of the cut.

"Oh yes, the cut," the queen exclaimed, raising an eyebrow.

"How did I not see it?"

"No one did."

"Lenala, I am so sorry for what you have been through."

The queen slowly rose to her feet and approached Lenala. Without a word, she opened her arms and embraced Lenala.

After a brief moment of silence, the queen pulled away and spoke solemnly. "I need some time to think about what I am going to tell everyone," she said, waving her hand dismissively as she walked away from Lenala and Farka.

Lenala escorted Farka to her room, and despite the tragic morning, she knew she had to act like everything was normal during breakfast. Tion's absence at the breakfast table would be noticed, but she had to play it cool and act as if nothing had happened. She would tell Semian and Quade about the situation as soon as she could, but she needed to wait for the right opportunity. "Stay here for a while, Farka. I need to take care of a few things, but I'll be back soon." Farka nodded in understanding, and Lenala left the room, closing the door behind her.

As she made her way to the breakfast hall, she thought about how Farka had reacted. She knew it was in rage and with revenge, but it was scary and Lenala couldn't control her. Or maybe she could have, but she was just too surprised to react strongly enough. *I never thought Farka would kill someone who wasn't directly threatening me.*

Farka made it clear to Lenala that she knew what was best for her and that she would do whatever she deemed necessary. As a Dragon that had suffered at Tion's hands, she had the right to decide who deserved mercy and who didn't. Lenala couldn't judge her or dictate whether she was allowed to seek revenge.

Farka was a full-grown Dragon with her own mind and autonomy, and she had never acted irrationally in the past. Lenala resolved to give her the benefit of the doubt and trust her.

Farka had fully stepped into her role as a Dragon. They were passionate creatures, fiercely loyal to those they loved and willing to do anything for them. But if you crossed them, there would be consequences. You didn't vex a Dragon, and Farka had made it clear that Tion had passed a line that couldn't be forgiven.

THIRTY-FOUR

He tried his hardest to get her to breathe. He didn't want her to die. At least not like this. He wanted to be the one to kill her, and she took that from him. He gazed down at her lifeless body, and the same cold and bitter feeling he had felt when Trayana's name was called flooded over him. The sensation of betrayal, fury, and powerlessness boiled inside him, threatening to consume him whole. He was never meant to be defeated again, always the one calling the shots, and yet now he found himself losing. Both of them had cheated him with death. As he sat there, he looked at her. The smile on her face was pure. It was a smile of relief and peace. Resentment began to fill him. Not only had she duped him but she had escaped Xuria. Something he had always longed to do. She was gone, Trayana was gone, and Lenala was gone. He was alone. Defeat consumed him as he sat there in the dimly lit room. The overwhelming flood of emotions that he felt only fueled his hatred and despair. He yearned to erase it all from his mind. As he stood by the dresser, he held the small bottle tightly, telling himself to take just one drop. With trembling hands, he carefully placed the drop in his mouth and shook his head, desperate to clear his thoughts. He stared at himself in the mirror as he felt the blood taking effect, soothing every ache and pain in his body. His mind became sharp and focused, free of any lingering doubts or fears. The emotions that had once consumed him were now gone.

He looked back at Kineah's body, knowing that he had to dispose of it before anyone discovered what had happened. After careful consideration, he decided that the safest course of action was to place her in her room that night and let the maids discover her. DB was difficult to trace, and he knew that they would never suspect murder or suicide. They were too ignorant to see through the deception.

The hours dragged on, and he spent the entire day in his room, shooing away the maids and refusing to eat anything. He kept Kineah's body wrapped up and hidden in one of his robes as he waited anxiously for nightfall to arrive so he could dispose of the evidence.

He waited until it was well past everyone's bedtime to sneak her back into her room. As he laid her in her bed, she looked so innocent. A brief moment of softness passed over him. He leaned down and gave her one kiss on the forehead. *"Such a waste. You were a good one,"* he whispered as he left her room for the last time.

Over the next few weeks, with nobody to take his rage out on, his blood intake almost doubled. He considered taking on a new girl but he knew things were too volatile right now. The queen even questioned him about Kineah's death. She was still suspicious of him and had been more involved in the happenings at the castle lately. She was too nosey and always meddling in his business, and she was not happy with the recent stir in the Castle of Nahkei. Especially since her younger daughter, Princess Anala had joined the castle.

Time continued to pass. There he was living the same charade, and more miserable than ever. He felt like he was living in a fog. Nobody even noticed that anything was wrong with him. Night after night, he would sit in his room staring into the fire. His vices were not strong enough to control his anger anymore. He began fighting back and forth with his thoughts. It was as if there were multiple voices talking inside his head at once. Many nights, he would pace around his room and argue with those voices for hours.

The voices never truly left him alone. They would only get louder and clearer as the night went on. When he lay down to sleep, it was the worst. He couldn't shut them up. This caused many sleepless nights.

The voices fought about all kinds of things but one name always came up. Lenala.

They told him this was mostly her doing. Trayana and Kineah were both dead but she was alive, and living her life as if nothing ever happened. He stewed on this constantly. *She gets to be free while I sit here and suffer?* He grew to hate her more and more.

If only he could find her and make her pay for what she had cost him. He still had his power, but he had lost his self-respect, and more importantly, he'd lost control over his thoughts. He was haunted by his past and present. The last nine months had been a blur of his life spiraling out of his control.

Brantog was finally out of drugs, and the withdrawal symptoms were becoming unbearable. His body ached, he needed sleep, and his mind felt like it was suffocating. He had sent for a Murke to bring him more, but they were very late. They should have arrived two days ago, and he was growing desperate.

Finally, one morning before breakfast, there was a knock on his door. Brantog jumped up to answer it, hoping it was the Murke he had been waiting for. To his relief, it was him, disguised as a royal messenger. "You are late," Brantog hissed at him as he stepped to the side, giving him room to enter.

"Your Grace," he said hesitantly. His cautious demeanor irritated Brantog even more. "I apologize for the delay, but the supply has been almost cut off." He maintained his distance.

Brantog narrowed his eyes. "Really? Almost cut off in what manner?"

"All of the unrest with Princess Anala has caused the king to tighten the borders. We are having trouble getting in and out."

"Trouble with the princess?" Brantog had heard nothing of it.

"Yes, but it's not anything anyone knows about.'' Of course, the Murkes knew. They had spies almost everywhere and for the right price and political pull, anyone could get information.

Brantog decided to take the bait. "And what do you want in exchange for this knowledge?" he asked. His head was throbbing and all he wanted was the blood, but he knew this was important information he needed to know. Especially if it could affect his supply. The Murke wanted money. They always wanted money.

Brantog had plenty of that. He reached into his bag and placed two gold coins on the table. "Sit down."

"There were two bodies of royal guards found recently just outside the borders. They appear to have been dead for several months."

Murders? Brantog thought. "And?"

"Well, Your Grace, Princess Anala was also spotted near the border recently with the prince of Piatees."

Brantog's eyebrows shot up. He knew the king and knew how angry he must be.

"It gets worse. But that will cost you more." He paused, looking at Brantog expectantly.

"Done," Brantog said, sliding two more coins over. "Just get to the point."

"The king is furious. He believes Anala and the prince had something to do with the deaths and has placed her under house arrest." Brantog knew not to pry, so he just let the Murke talk until he wanted more money. "The prince escaped and went back to Piatees. So we assume.'' He stopped talking and looked up at Brantog. Two more coins hit the table.

"Go on, go on," Brantog said impatiently.

"He has ordered a hit on Piatees. He is sending a group of men over there to kill the prince and anyone who gets in their way. He has gone mad. Do you know what the Dragons will do if they find this out?"

Realization hit Brantog. *It's not if they find out, it's when.*

"And there's one more thing."

Brantog put down two more coins. The Murke fixed his

gaze on him but didn't speak. "Oh, really?" Brantog spewed. He sighed and slid one more coin over. Silence. "Don't toy with me, Murke," he said as he slammed his fist down and leaned close to his face.

The Murke jumped. "Ok, ok," he said, clearly afraid of Brantog's sudden rage.

"It's the queen." He hesitated as he spoke. "She knows everything and is threatening to go to the Dragons with some incriminating details about you if the king goes through with the attack on Piatees. That is all I know, Your Grace."

All of this information had Brantog's head swirling. *These damned princesses are ruining everything*. He put the blood away. He knew he needed to think clearly right now and save his supply. He knew the king was arrogant enough to go through with the attack no matter what the queen threatened. *As sneaky as he thinks he can be, the Dragons will find out eventually. If the queen goes to the Dragons and sells us out, they will kill us both for sure.*

He thought about it for a while. "The only other option would be for the king to kill me," he thought out loud. The Murke gave him a knowing nod. "With me out of the way, the queen has no leverage, and King Byreon can do as he pleases."

The more he thought about it, the more certain he was that this was what was going to happen. "I have to leave Xuria," he said suddenly with certainty. "Can you get me out of here?"

The Murke looked taken aback. "Your Grace, with everything that is going on, this would be suicide."

Bastard! "I didn't ask for your opinion. Now, name your price," he barked. *I'm a dead man anyway,* he thought.

The Murke thought about it for a moment. "Where will you go?"

"That's none of your concern," he snapped back. He had no idea where he was going, but he was going to search high and low until he found Lenala. Then it occurred to him. "Do you know where the other princess is?"

"Princess Lenala? No, but if you give me time, I can try to find her."

"I don't have time, now do I?" he said.

"Your Grace, I have many connections. I will search and when I find her, I will find you, and we will go from there."

"What will it take, Murke?

After a moment of silence, the Murke finally spoke up. "All right," he said, his voice gruff. "We can sort out a deal. But let me warn you, it's going to cost you."

Brantog sighed. He knew he had limited options. "I understand," he replied. "I'm willing to pay whatever it takes. I just need to secure an exit from this planet and find Lenala."

After some intense negotiation, they settled on a deal that Brantog knew was more than he should have paid. However, it was the only way. The Murke agreed to provide him with an exit from the planet, a horse for transportation, a large supply of food, and the promise of Lenala's location once they found it.

"Deal," Brantog said firmly.

They made a plan to meet under the cover of darkness. This would allow Brantog enough time to pack his belongings and make his way to the designated meeting point.

~

He packed several of his weapons, money, clothes, his darts, and his DB. The only things he really cared about. He got to the meeting point quickly and waited.

The Murke arrived punctually, cleverly disguised as a humble vegetable peddler. He arrived with all the necessary supplies, including the horse he promised.

To avoid detection, Brantog was instructed to conceal himself in the bottom of a small carriage that was then loaded with a few baskets of vegetables. This would enable them to travel to the edge of the mountains unnoticed, while also providing the Murke with a means to return to the city, undisturbed and unnoticed.

As they sneaked away toward the mountains, his mind flashed back to his younger years when he had tried this and failed. If only he had known then what he knew now. He didn't look back even once. He would not miss this prison.

THIRTY-FIVE

Lenala still had not found the right opportunity to ask the queen for personal leave time to go home. Her fabricated excuse was going to be that her mother was ill, but it would have to wait. All of the chaos was throwing a big wrench into their plans, once again. She would have to wait for the right moment, once this all settled down. *Damn, another setback. We can't keep buying time.*

The chances of Anala being in real danger increased as each day passed. They needed to move quickly.

Breakfast was quiet and Tion's chair was eerily empty. Lenala felt sad, angry, and relieved all at the same time. Semian kept eyeing her. She could tell he knew something was up and he was anxious to know about the meeting.

The men didn't seem bothered by Tion's absence, but they noticed.

As they were eating, there was a sudden shuffle in the chairs. Lenala looked up, and her stomach dropped as she saw Queen Halice approaching. They all stood as she entered the room.

"Please, as you were," she said quietly. "I have very heavy news for you and there is no way to put it lightly.

"Tion was found dead in his room this morning."

A rumble of sighs and murmurs went through the room.

"Dead? Do we know what happened?" Enhan asked as he stood up.

The queen sighed. "We do not know what happened yet, but we are looking into it. What I can tell you as of right now, is that it looks as though he died of natural causes." She didn't look at Lenala.

"Natural causes?" Crand chimed in. "He was young and healthy. How could he just die?"

A few of the other men agreed. "How do we know someone didn't kill him?" Doran offered. "We need to search the castle for any signs. We need to search everyone," he said. His face reddened.

Lenala froze. She and Semian each had a jar of the lethal concoction in their rooms. If that was found, they would have a problem. The queen would have to tell the truth and cover for them, but having poison would be suspicious no matter how they looked at it.

"Enhan, Crand, sit down," the queen barked. They sat immediately. "My investigation is being conducted by professionals, and is headed up by me. He was young and healthy, but the examiner said his heart may have been weak," she explained. She was good; the men were buying it.

"We will get to the bottom of this but until we do, we will all be mourning the loss of our fellow soldier. I am going to spend the day in my room. Lenala, I need you to help me with arrangements for his burial ceremony."

"Yes, Your Highness," she said.

Lenala felt Semian's and Quade's eyes burning on her. They wanted an explanation fast. "Come to my quarters this afternoon." Lenala bowed in response.

Semian and Quade were both waiting for Lenala outside her room.

Quade spoke first. "Lenala, what happened? Did you kill him?"

"What?" she asked, somewhat surprised that he would assume that. "Of course not," she said as she ushered them into her room, where she recounted the whole story.

Both of the men looked astonished. Quade was speechless. He looked over at Farka with a look of awe and fear. Farka was licking her tail like nothing had happened, seemingly oblivious to them.

Lenala, however, knew she was upset, that she had been scared after she reacted with so much rage. Farka was always a sensitive beast but now, she was proving to be a true Hite.

"So, the queen is covering it up?" Semian asked curtly.

"Well, we can't have everyone knowing he was an addict and a thief." Quade's reply was just as short.

"But he *was* an addict and a thief." Semian's eyes burned with intensity as he spoke. "To make matters worse, he put us all at risk and could have killed Farka. He does not deserve the respect of an honorable funeral. How can you protect him? He deserved what he got."

"Guys," Lenala interjected. "This is for the sake of the queen, and for the sake of saving face. We know what he was, but we don't need to rub it in to the men. It's over," she said.

Semian growled, "I refuse to attend his hypocritical burial. It's ridiculous."

Quade nodded in understanding. "I know it's not going to be easy, but Lenala is right. He was one of the queen's most trusted men, despite what he did. He doesn't deserve to be praised, but we should try to remember the good in him."

Semian scoffed, "Good in him? The guy was a complete ass."

The rest of the group nodded in agreement.

"But," Semian continued after a moment, "I suppose he was good to the men and a reliable soldier. That's the only positive thing about him." He fell silent for a moment before his expression turned dark. "I think he deserved to burn," he said, directing his glare at Farka.

Farka met his gaze, sensing the anger behind his words, and their eyes locked in understanding. Semian's reassurance gave her a sense of pride and validation. Tion had caused both Farka and Lenala immense pain and suffering, and he deserved to pay for his crimes.

It was clear that Farka wanted to be strong but was afraid of causing harm to innocent people. Semian offered her a silent nudge of confidence, letting her know that she was capable of making the right choices. He understood that every soldier struggled with this after the first few kills, and Farka was no different. He reassured her that she had done the right thing.

Quade and Lenala stood there and watched the silent

exchange between Farka and Semian. The air seemed to hum with an unspoken understanding.

Plans had been made for Tion's funeral. Lenala really didn't do much, but the queen wanted her input on every little detail. The workers of the castle were the ones doing most of the work. Planning a military funeral was a big deal in Analicia.

It was going to be a big to-do. She was dreading it.

She still could not find the right time to ask to leave and she was getting anxious. The timing just never felt right. She and Semian would have to wait until after the funeral—four additional days added to their wait time. It had been over a year—what was four more days? She desperately tried not to think of all of the reasons she should leave now.

Once the funeral was over, she would go to the queen. No matter what, they were leaving. One more day.

It was finally her day off and she decided to go to the city. She wanted to be alone and needed some fresh air away from the castle. She also wanted to pick up some supplies for their journey.

As she walked through the streets, she decided it was time to fully focus on the task ahead of them. The time had come. Everything she had prepared for was going to be coming to fruition. She took a moment and thought about how far she had come. Not without trouble, though. There had been many sleepless nights, intense training, heartaches, and disappointments. However, the good that had come from her exile far outweighed the bad. There was happiness, thrill, love, and excitement. She had found a person in herself that she never knew existed. She felt like she finally belonged and loved what she was doing. Even Farka had blossomed into an independent, incredible Dragon.

Lenala stopped at a river along the way and sat on the edge. She kicked off her shoes. The cold water stung her feet but felt refreshing. She sat there for a while soaking in the light of Haruelio and letting her mind be free from stress. Suddenly, she felt a familiar wave of unease. The feeling that she was being followed. She looked around but didn't see anything out of the ordinary. The last time she felt this way, she thought she was being paranoid, but she really was being followed by Murkes. Then, she was being followed by Semian. Her instincts had been on point.

Maybe someone had seen them sneaking around the city a few nights ago. Maybe they suspected that she was involved with the shop blowing up? She quickly put her shoes on and got up. She slipped her hand under her bag and grabbed hold of Escitalo. Just in case. The sword vibrated slightly, making a small buzz in her hand, ready for whatever may come next.

Just then, a woman appeared down the road, emerging from behind a nearby building. She was walking directly toward her with purpose. Despite the distance between them, Lenala could feel the intensity of the woman's gaze fixed upon her.

As she drew closer, Lenala could see that the woman was strikingly beautiful, with flowing blonde hair and fair skin. She was tall and statuesque, with bright blue eyes that seemed to pierce right through her. She wasn't from Analicia—Lenala had never seen anyone like her before.

Lenala couldn't look away from the woman; she was mesmerized by her striking features and confident stride.

She continued closing the ground between them.

Lenala's guard was up. Her hand was still on her sword hidden beneath her coat. She was ready to draw it at any moment. She squeezed the grip. The woman was almost within striking distance. Her heart was pounding. Escitalo was pulsing. She stepped into a fighter's stance and started drawing her sword.

The woman stopped abruptly. "Lenala?" she asked.

"Who is asking?" Lenala replied defensively.

"I've been searching for you for a while and waiting for the opportunity to get you while you are alone." Lenala was speechless. She lowered her sword slightly. "I have a message for you." Lenala still said nothing.

"It's from Anala, and it must be opened immediately and in private." As she continued to speak, it became clear to Lenala that this woman was a Murke. She was disguising herself as a human to deliver the message. Her eyes were different—they were cold and she didn't blink. It was subtle but Lenala could see it.

"A message from Anala?"

"Yes, please. It is urgent."

Lenala quickly sheathed her sword. Her heart was racing. The Murke reached into her pocket and handed Lenala a small item wrapped in brown paper.

"Go and open it immediately. Don't let anyone see it or your cover will be blown."

Before Lenala could say anything more, the Murke spun and moved away as quickly as she had come. "Thank you," Lenala managed to sputter after her as she faded into the distance.

A letter from Anala? Everything in her wanted to rip open the letter right there, but the Murke's words hung over her. "Your cover will be blown." She had worked too hard to blow it now. She needed to get back to the castle immediately.

She tucked the letter away and hurried back, forgetting about the supplies. As soon as she made it to her room, she ripped it open. Adrenaline and fear were surging through her.

Farka jumped up when she felt Lenala's emotions, and she ran over to her. She sniffed the letter and let out a few grunts. "It's from Anala," Lenala said as she sat and read it aloud.

My dear Lenala,

May Draygon speed the Murkes in finding you. Father found out about the Pitian prince and he went mad. He took a small group of the royal guards out of Xuria and into Piatees. He's captured both the prince and his sister.

The Dragons don't know. Yet.

He's burned and destroyed Piatees and has killed many of their people. He put me, the prince, and the princess in jail. I'm going to be tried in front of the high council on the next high moon. He'll either exile me or condemn me to death, and I fear the worst for the prince and princess. I can't let Father harm them.

We are making plans to escape before the trial, but I fear this letter won't make it to you in time. Meet me at Danix Point as soon as you can. If we're able to escape, we'll wait for you there. If not, go home and tell the Dragons everything.

More than a year has passed

since you left and much has changed. We desperately need your help.

May Draygon be with you,
Your sister,
Anala

Dear Reader,

Thank you for choosing to read Xuria. I hope you enjoyed the journey as much as I enjoyed writing it. Your feedback is incredibly valuable and allows independent authors like me to continue sharing our stories. If you enjoyed this book, please consider leaving a review on Amazon or your chosen platform.

Thank you for your time and support, and I look forward to your thoughts.

Erica Ebanks

About the Author

Erica Ebanks is a Florida-based writer with a passion for storytelling. She has created imaginative worlds and compelling characters that transport readers into the realms of fantasy.

In addition to her writing pursuits, Erica is a traveling respiratory therapist, working in and exploring different cities alongside her husband. She also enjoys traveling abroad. Her experiences in different places bring a variety of sights, sounds, and cultures that fuel her creativity. From a busy metropolis to the peaceful wilderness, she finds inspiration everywhere.

When she's not working or writing, Erica can be found practicing Brazilian Jiu Jitsu, a martial art that she is deeply passionate about, having achieved her black belt. Her commitment to the discipline mirrors her determination and dedication in all aspects of her life, including writing.

Her upcoming book promises to enchant and delight fantasy enthusiasts, offering an escape into a world where suspense and adventure await at every turn.